MYSTERIOUS
FRAGRANCE *of the*
YELLOW MOUNTAINS

MYSTERIOUS
FRAGRANCE *of the*
YELLOW MOUNTAINS

YASUKO THANH

HAMISH HAMILTON
an imprint of Penguin Canada Books Inc., a Penguin Random House Company

Published by the Penguin Group
Penguin Canada Books Inc., 320 Front Street West, Suite 1400, Toronto, Ontario M5V 3B6, Canada

Penguin Group (USA) LLC, 375 Hudson Street, New York, New York 10014, U.S.A.
Penguin Books Ltd, 80 Strand, London WC2R 0RL, England
Penguin Ireland, 25 St Stephen's Green, Dublin 2, Ireland (a division of Penguin Books Ltd)
Penguin Group (Australia), 707 Collins Street, Melbourne, Victoria 3008, Australia
(a division of Pearson Australia Group Pty Ltd)
Penguin Books India Pvt Ltd, 11 Community Centre, Panchsheel Park, New Delhi – 110 017, India
Penguin Group (NZ), 67 Apollo Drive, Rosedale, Auckland 0632, New Zealand
(a division of Pearson New Zealand Ltd)
Penguin Books (South Africa) (Pty) Ltd, 24 Sturdee Avenue, Rosebank,
Johannesburg 2196, South Africa
Penguin Books Ltd, Registered Offices: 80 Strand, London WC2R 0RL, England

First published 2016

1 2 3 4 5 6 7 8 9 10 (RRD)

BRITISH COLUMBIA
ARTS COUNCIL

Canada Council   Conseil des arts
for the Arts   du Canada

Manufactured in the U.S.A.

LIBRARY AND ARCHIVES CANADA CATALOGUING IN PUBLICATION

Thanh, Yasuko, author
Mysterious fragrance of the yellow mountains / Yasuko Thanh.

ISBN 978-0-670-06878-4 (paperback)
I. Title.

PS8639.H375M97 2016   C813'.6   C2015-905587-3

eBook ISBN 978-0-14-319327-2

www.penguinrandomhouse.ca

For Hank,

Plunging streams —one after another

MYSTERIOUS
FRAGRANCE
of the
YELLOW
MOUNTAINS

PROLOGUE

If you fail to bury a body, if the body dies away from home, if it dies unloved while hurrying from a coal mine shaft, or without its head, in the middle of a field, lonely, if it dies in the street, lost, if it dies a violent death, if it dies with a bamboo pole on its neck, the shoulder callused from heavy work without the proper rituals of mourning, if it dies alone, it will become a wandering ghost.

In 1908 the French rule Cochin China. The pro-independence movement is scattered and unorganized. In the south, an army trains, not to fight, but to turn invisible, the general working on a potion that will make his army vanish before the eyes of the French.

In a hundred years, one will be able to board a plane to Ho Chi Minh City and pay a woman with small feet and waist-length hair a few dong for a body massage, to be rendered and received naked in a room that smells of coconut oil.

Today only a small number of English and German merchants discuss the politics of Italian missionaries with French Navy officers while they dine in restaurants with waiters who must adhere to curfews and by colonial-era law carry lanterns to identify themselves at night when they go out.

The French expel Vietnamese nationalists to South American jungle camps or chop off their heads, leaving them on stakes at the marketplace.

The country, some say, is shaped like a dragon. In the north, near the Gulf of Tonkin, one spies a bay full of pirates and fishermen's houses clinging to the shore. Knee-deep in water, women work in the fenced-off plot of a rice paddy. On the other side of the hill, a Tonkinese coal mine and a small cattle farm shelter a group of houses where pottery makers and brick makers live.

The dragon's slender waist is home to the Chams, an ancient tribe. The villagers wear caps decorated with polished pebbles, sing songs, and hunt rhinoceros with sticks made of sharpened bamboo. A man smokes marijuana from a pipe and its perfume spires into the giant kapok trees. A child tires himself scurrying through the underbrush all day and goes to sleep on a woven, movable floor that can be elevated when the river water of the Central Highlands rises.

The Chams share their river with the Moys, a tribe descended from Hindu kings. They wind in procession through the fire trees, arrows in bags slung across their backs. The women stroll with squares of fabric that barely cover their breasts, and both women and men pierce their ears. Their toes are spread wide from years of walking barefoot.

So legend has it, both tribes are such good hunters, they can shoot a bull so not a single drop of blood is spilled.

In the south, in the Mekong Delta, water buffaloes pull wooden harrows to plow seedbeds. Lotus flowers sprout from mud flats. Fish ponds flank roads busy with farmers, lazy with bamboo.

In Saigon, Vietnamese women work cramped shops lit by red lanterns. In theatres men dressed as women play the parts of women so well it's impossible to tell them apart. Gigantic barracks built by Chinese labourers sidle next to French-built houses of several storeys with encircling verandas. A closed carriage with two horses rides beside an open carriage with one horse. There is a pagoda, a covered market; on the banks of the river thousands of boats bob up and down.

Along the Saigon River, arrack palms preside over the large open spaces between houses on the shore. The roofs of wooden houses are woven from palm leaves, and wickerwork walls divide the rooms within, affording little privacy, since they do not reach all the way to the ceiling and, moreover, are thin and let through every sort of sound. (A few of the houses built by Chinese immigrants a hundred years ago are made of stone with red tile roofs, and these afford slightly more privacy.)

And now we arrive at the villa of Dr. Nguyen Georges-Minh. His neighbours' houses rest on the far banks of the Saigon River, where fog sweeps the waters the way a bridal veil might sweep a lover's face. One day, Georges-Minh, too, will get married.

For now, Georges-Minh lives alone in a mansion in the Thao Dien area. Neoclassical in design, modern in every aspect, built by the French fifty years ago (although his toilet is just a hole cut out of a wooden plank, over the river, and open to the sky—fish charge the pilings when they hear his footsteps on the jetty, but no mind).

In addition to working in his home office in one wing of the villa, and making his own pharmaceuticals in another, Dr. Nguyen Georges-Minh spends a few hours each week at Clinique de la Dhuys near the floating city, treating the growing number of prostitutes for political reasons. To him they are a result of colonialism: poverty and class oppression, and the sexual decadence of the wealthy and powerful.

Furthermore, to him, any Vietnamese person who would collaborate with the French is simply a political prostitute. They deserve no pity, in contrast to the girls, boys, men, and women whom he sees at the clinic, dying, who have no option but to sell their favours, who have an unquenchable yearning for imported French goods that lie beyond their means: vestments, sweets, food, medicine, perfume, cosmetics, betting on horse races, tennis racquets, bicycles, wanting to paddle-boat, wishing to attend a cocktail party. Clinique de la Dhuys is funded by the Ministry of Health of France.

Georges-Minh's neighbour, the manager of the Banque de l'Indo-chine, who is from Paris but no devil, and who has this way of wiping his son's mouth with the hem of his shirt with a tenderness that Georges-Minh finds touching, on many nights plays racquetball with Georges, and last week offered Georges-Minh some trout heads from his recent fishing trip. Sometimes Georges-Minh considers speaking to him of these things, but always closes his mouth again.

Georges-Minh has a medical degree from the Lycée Condorcet, Paul Verlaine's university. What he owes to the French, and how they've fucked up his country, together carve rifts in his psyche, and he is slowly going mad.

PART I

——————————

Poison

1

Killing a man is easy. Life is fragile, for one. And the world is poisonous, for two. How poisonous? Cobras, mushrooms, stonefish, apple seeds. Consider the datura plant. *Datura stramonium.* White flowers the shape of a trumpet and the size of a human heart. The seeds, crushed with a mortar and pestle, are easily processed. Thieves and prostitutes favour its killing properties. Georges-Minh has seen the results in his practice and he has such a flower blooming in his courtyard.

Five men plotted in a circle. Five men, none of them yet thirty. Five men, cross-legged on Georges-Minh's bed, which took up half the room, no mattress in the Chinese style, carved from the rarest red wood, Georges-Minh's command centre, where he ate, slept, played cards, and officiated the meetings he held at his house twice a month.

"Mysterious Scent of the Mountains," said Khieu, who owned an inn with his wife and spent his spare time painting poetry onto the inside of rice-paper sun hats. *Had it not been for winter, / the falling snow / might have been cherry blossoms.* One day he would close the inn and just sell the hats whose words could be read only when they were raised to the rays of the sun.

His suit was the same type of linen as Georges-Minh's except that Georges-Minh's was ironed. His knees sloped, and the collar of his white shirt, where it met the dark line of his stubble, was wrinkled like the rings of a pineapple tree. Smaller than Georges-Minh's, his thin mouth appeared somewhat lecherous. His powdered hair smelled like jasmine.

He sat to Georges-Minh's right, so close their knees touched. Georges-Minh stared at his best friend's thick betel-nut-coloured hands rolling a cigarette as he shielded the tobacco from the wind of a small oscillating fan, wondering why he hadn't spoken of his wife in so many months.

"No, no, no. I still like Fighting Dragon," said Trinh Van Phuc, the musician of the group, in an accent that sounded like he was chopping vegetables. Rumour was he'd been married, though he never talked about his wife.

"Or, like I said before," Khieu said, staring straight at Georges-Minh, "we can make a poison." He looked at the back of his hand, examined his nails.

Georges-Minh's cheeks grew hot. "How's your brood, Khieu?" Georges-Minh asked nervously, trying to change the subject.

"Don't know." Khieu lowered his gaze, picked up his hand of cards.

"Mysterious Scent of the ... *whatever* is too ... too ..." Phuc waved his teacup, trying to catch the right word.

"Don't know?"

"Haven't seen Mai in months," Khieu said sheepishly.

"Perfume sounds like something from a song," Phuc said. "We're a revolutionary group—not *minstrels*."

"Perfumes are transcendent," the third man, a horticultural-ist, said. The fellows called him Bao, though at his shop he responded with equal ease to Bao or Victor or Mr. Le.

"Not even the kids?" Georges-Minh said. Mostly they kept their private affairs private. Still, the revelation shocked him because Khieu had been married to his wife, Mai, for seven years; they had three children together.

"These things happen," Phuc said and shrugged.

How did they happen? Like a storm that washed your memory of a family the way a rain washed a road in a sudden burst? Or did they happen the way a thief with a bludgeon attacked a family, leaving death in his wake? He imagined Mai running the inn alone, looked down at his cards as if it was his hand that troubled him.

"How many soldiers can there be?"

"Thirty or forty?"

"I heard fifty," said Khieu.

"You're both wrong. The exact number is eighty."

"Do you know nothing? They number over two hundred!"

"We will drive out the French bandits."

"We will restore Vietnam."

"We will create a democratic republic."

"No, a monarchy."

Their hearts were in the right places, these members of the MFYM, Mysterious Fragrance of the Yellow Mountains, who didn't yet have a name, perhaps because most of their meetings were spent drinking and playing cards. They discussed lofty ideals. Drank. Outlined what a free and democratic Vietnam would look like. Drank. Compared international political systems. Drank. Cited historical precedents. Cursed the French.

Each man held some playing cards and a glass of mulberry wine. They were teacups, not wine glasses, and none of them matched, but Georges-Minh wanted people to believe he didn't care about such trifling details. He could have afforded matching wine glasses, but only shallow men cared about such worldly things.

"If we can't agree, let's move on," suggested Bao, who raised moonflowers and other exotic flora for an exclusive clientele.

Le Bao Victor's father was the junior minister of the Annamese cabinet of Cochin China. As a child Bao had travelled with his father to the Dutch East Indies and France, when his father had still thought he might follow in his footsteps and enter the cabinet himself. But the junior minister's power was in name alone. Had the family any jurisdiction at all, perhaps only the alleys knew it. The jackfruit trees. The sewers and opium dens. Delinquents with slingshots. Women at the market. Shoeshine boys.

The Les flaunted their material wealth as if in spite. Tennis lessons for the children. Rowing. Elocution. Music appreciation.

Bao's wife, Mimi, married him not because she wanted a better life. Not only because. But if she'd known a few rooms next to a flower shop awaited her? He turned his back on politics two years after their marriage. Began wearing a bicycle chain for a belt. Fell in love with orchids, chrysanthemums, bellflowers, hibiscus. After reuniting with his elementary-school mates Georges-Minh and Khieu in a bar.

"Let's talk about what we're actually here for," Bao said, "as our esteemed colleague Khieu suggested when he brought up a rather interesting idea. Why don't we talk about that?"

Khieu and Georges-Minh had been best friends since grade school, when they'd run loose around Saigon's back alleys, climbing trees and scaring cats.

Khieu, whose family lived in one of the many shacks built over the river, hated the sellout, the collaboration of his family with the enemy that included his Christian name, Henri, but he stopped short of hating the urchins who called to him across the alleyways of Cholon—"Hon-riii, Hon-riii, give us a tien, give us your school tie"—who worshipped anything French, giving themselves French nicknames for fun.

"Chosen well, a good name helps define a group's beliefs, bestows desired traits," Georges-Minh said, because Khieu was the kind of person who as a child had given away his pencils and schoolbooks to those same urchins, and now sat with a cracked teacup of wine in his hand goading him. Even as a child Khieu had cared about things. Georges-Minh couldn't have cared less. Georges-Minh was too busy lusting after a new mechanical boat or model train. Khieu, who'd had nothing, had ideals, and hadn't even wanted his French name. Georges-Minh shrugged. "Look at all the fuss and divination that goes into choosing a child's name." He would go to as much trouble when he named his son. When he had a son. When he found a woman. When he got married. Which he would. Any day now.

"Not a *monarchy*, a republic," Khieu said. "Haven't you read Rousseau?"

"They should die like dogs."

"They should die like a snake under a rickshaw driver's wheels."

"They should die a bad death. Not a 'death in the house and home' but a 'death in the street.'"

"They should die like an iguana in the mouth of a hungry dog, swelling at head and tail until they burst under the pressure of his powerful jaws."

"Poison the lieutenant colonel of the garrison with *gan cong mak coc*, liver of a peacock, bile of a frog."

"No. People should use a beautiful woman to kill a king."

"Yes, love them to death."

"You're suggesting a strategy?"

"Poison doesn't always kill. Did you hear about the guy who was dying? Of cancer. So he took liver and bile and the poison started to cure his cancer."

"Actually?"

"Actually."

"They can die like a lover in the arms of a woman," Khieu said. "I don't care. So long as they die."

Making a poison strong enough to kill a man is easy. Remove the seeds from the stamen. Crush with a mortar and pestle until the dry seeds stop crackling. The powder is now so fine as to be invisible and weightless. Season chicken, shrimp, or buffalo with the dust. Steeped in fish sauce, the poison is tasteless.

Because he was a little drunk, Georges-Minh fell against Khieu. He righted himself and dabbed with his thumb at the spilled wine on the wooden bed slat. "I don't mind talking about the group name some more. A thing becomes its name and vice versa. Can you imagine a militant group with the word 'bananas' in its moniker?"

"Bananas is definitely out."

"I second."

"Third."

"Obviously."

"This is absurd."

"What was that name you said? Mysterious perfume ..."

"Mysterious smell."

"Fragrance."

"No, it was mysterious scent, but I like perfume better."

"Me too."

"Perfume then," said Chang. Chang was an ethnic Chinese, born in Cholon, a court translator and lover of books. "But mysterious is the important part, because it's how we must remain. Elusive. Who said elusive? As in impossible to catch. By soldiers, police, any and all enemies."

"Well, perfumes are important, too," said Bao, who would have said such a thing. "And sweet, right, because *that's* what we want to be. But the *transcendence*. That's the part that's important. When something becomes a perfume it transcends its lot as a fragrance to become something else. See?"

"Maybe you're not that much of a blockhead," said Chang, the translator with the thick and beautiful lips. "Sweet as a flower that rises in the spring. In the spring there's hope. Especially in the north."

"Where at present," said Georges-Minh, striking a serious face, "the news is one in three women are now prostitutes because of the regime. Did you know they're starving in Tonkin? Picking individual grains of fallen rice from between stones with their fingers. Eating farm animals dead of disease."

The men sympathized with silent nods.

"Invisible as a fragrance," Chang continued. "Invisible as hope, invisible as a guerrilla fighter. Mountains, of course, are a symbol of strength. Where were we then, mountains?"

"Don't forget, prayers are invisible, too," Phuc said, chain-smoking. *The rich ate, the poor smoked.*

"True," said Georges-Minh.

"Like the fart I just let out?" Phuc said.

"God, Phuc. Will you ever grow up?" Bao said.

Khieu took a sip of his wine, then drained the cup, avoiding the chip on the rim. After lighting a cigarette he said, "If we're not going to move on to the poison until after we choose a name then I say let's add 'yellow'—Mysterious Perfume of the Yellow Mountains. Makes us sound more poetic."

Was Khieu playing it straight with the group? Yellow? Georges-Minh couldn't tell much about the man these days. Khieu had always dreamed of travelling to distant places, Africa, Borneo, and Antarctica, and carried maps with him wherever he went. Then one day he'd thrown them in the river. He had recently started growing his hair long again, like some of the Hindu holy men in the marketplace. He had discarded his topknot and traditional turban in favour of clipped hair long ago, but now he no longer kept it sleek, no longer washed it. He wore his hair unkempt and ran around the marketplace pushing a broom or borrowing rickshaws that didn't belong to him. This, in itself, wasn't completely new. But he'd changed since the hauling of those French contraptions of horror into the square, the guillotines.

Georges-Minh hated the French—he could say those words. But could he write someone's name in poison? Georges-Minh didn't know if he could kill a man. Maybe one man. But could he poison a whole garrison? *Poison.* Khieu's earlier words hung in the air along with his cigarette smoke, waiting for Georges-Minh's response.

The truth was, ever since that day as a schoolboy, when Khieu with his one green eye that emphasized his craziness had stood nearly naked in the marketplace in Cholon, Georges-Minh had admired him because he was everything Georges-Minh was incapable of being by nature, lacking the inner rigour. Or thought he had admired him because at least he stood for something. A few years later, as a teenager, when Khieu stole a driver's rickshaw one afternoon and pretended he was a coolie, returning the rickshaw and all his earnings to the rightful owner that evening, Georges-Minh had wanted to be him. Khieu, who had a neck as solid as an ironwood tree, was strong. Even now, as an adult, when he returned to Cholon and swept the streets with a broom or collected garbage with his hands, barefoot as a peasant—for the love of work or to prove a political point, Georges-Minh wasn't exactly sure—everyone knew him by name. Now Khieu was looking at him and Georges-Minh could feel whatever small admiration he'd built up for himself in Khieu's eyes over the years slipping away by degrees like a small village down a water-logged hillside during the monsoon rains. Khieu, looking again with that provocation in his eyes Georges-Minh decided was his friend's way of mocking him, for being weaker than him, teasing him for his reluctance to get involved. Provoking him into being more than the wimp he always was. Taking a stand.

Khieu still enjoyed mathematics, detective novels, astronomy, searching with his telescope for alien life in the skies, but another part of him had evolved into something Georges-Minh no longer recognized after hearing men screech nationalist slogans, watching the blade fall, heads tumbling into baskets. The heads were collected and mounted onto spikes as warnings to others. Punishments were distributed to Vietnamese who tried to remove the heads too soon. Even as he sat there now, with Khieu waiting for his response—would he or would he not make a poison to kill the soldiers stationed at the French garrison of Saigon?—he knew he was disappointing his friend. And his country by extension.

He was the natural choice. The doctor of the group. Private doctor to the lieutenant colonel of the garrison.

Georges-Minh looked out the window. Subterfuge. An irrational ploy. Smile and no one will bother you. Look away and what you don't want to see turns invisible. Gazing at the river that flowed out back. Now the shade of a ball bearing. Now the shade of dirty cotton. Now the shade of belly button lint. He could pretend the river was something fleeting. A minnow, a swordfish, a dragon. Then the dreaded thing happened. It must. It had to.

"Yes, of course. He could make the poison."

"Naturally, he's a doctor," Bao said, scratching his eyes. His lids were swollen again. Last night, he'd gotten drunk and sat with the cuttings, singing to them. "March to victory, sway, sway." Using the wine bottle as a door knocker, he'd tried to wake Mimi. She, angry as usual, had refused to join him in the room where he nurtured the rooted plants, encouraging them to grow.

Who knew this was something he'd be good at? If sore eyes was the price? He stumbled to each pot, ensured the proper mix of soil versus food. His own blend of which he was proud. Sang to them, while Mimi hollered he would wake the dead.

"What do you say?" Phuc said.

"Georges-Minh?"

"Aren't you listening?" Phuc said.

"He's drunk."

"Could you or couldn't you?"

"Daydreaming."

"No, I was paying attention. Poison."

"Well?"

"There are many ways to poison a man."

Georges-Minh stared into Khieu's one green eye. Mulberry wine made all the fish in the near dark leap out of the river and hover over the water. They spun and danced and galloped through the air, a synchronized ripple, the way the water puppets shimmer and perform boisterous art over Saigon River currents.

Georges-Minh heard a knocking before bed. At night the street may be filled with wandering spirits, common marauders looking for what they could steal—a bicycle, a garden rake. When Georges-Minh had kept chickens and pups for a short time, he'd woken up one morning to find all his pullets removed from the henhouse and his puppies placed inside. The pullets were running loose all over the yard—the ones who hadn't been picked off by foxes. The door to the henhouse had been locked (he still had the key), so it couldn't have been neighbourhood kids. It was the ghosts, for the third or fourth time; they liked the Thao Dien neighbourhood, and why not? They rambled around in packs, like hoboes, carrying off what they could find, then abandoning it along the way. Since the northern famine decades ago, which caused the migration of peasants and a million dead by the side of the road, too many men and women had gone without good deaths in their homes. How could a soul go to heaven without the proper send-off: the ritual words, the money burned, offerings of clothing and shoes? Even the government admitted the problem was getting out of hand. Add more recent deaths and ghosts were popping up everywhere; once five or six ghosts startled Georges-Minh by rising from the ground at a crossroads and nearly crashing his car. Georges-Minh locked his shutters at night because the cockiest ghosts would crawl across his rear garden and come into his house through his kitchen.

The worst scare he'd ever had was accosting a confused prisoner with a mutilated body and a flicking tongue one night when he'd been too drunk to shut up the house properly. The spirit, similar in appearance to Mau Ma, the seductive Water Spirit who sometimes appeared as a woman, with bare chest and long hair, and summoned people to their deaths, was licking the mangoes Georges-Minh had lined up on the counter for breakfast. A girl Georges-Minh had known in school had seen this spirit and lived in the care of her mother to this day, catatonic as the afternoon she'd beheld her at the lake.

Georges-Minh wanted nothing to do with ghosts. Spirits. Necromancers. Geomancers. Pyromancers. Palmists. Astrologers. The mythology of people who believed their Monkey God had been shit from the bowels of a rock. Whose emperors ate immortal peaches. Who made clay dolls and channelled into them the souls of the dead.

The French had stirred his mind like a great hand stirs the clouds, infused it with strange notions, and Georges-Minh's clarity became the occupation of Western medicine. Embracing all that was European meant denying his father's Purple Emperor Fortune book, his spirit lens, shameful keepsakes, now dusty on his office shelf.

The knock persisted.

Georges-Minh opened the door a crack to find a dishevelled man with a goat tethered to his arm.

"I can't remember a thing and I don't know how I got here," the man said. "You're a doctor, right? I read your sign."

He looked so pathetic that Georges-Minh led him to his home office even though he was already wearing his pyjamas.

Georges-Minh sat him down on the examination table and got him to remove his shirt. "Have you been smoking opium?"

"I don't know. I feel like my head's going to break open and a thousand ants are going to come spilling out."

The man's eyes were clear, not red. His skin, however, was covered with fine black marks as from a pepper shaker. Georges-Minh conducted a quick exam of his nose and throat before asking the man to lie down.

Georges-Minh wiped his own forehead with his forearm. Whether it was the heat of his office or a contagious illness the man had brought into his house, Georges-Minh didn't know. He thought he felt a little queasy but maybe the earlier conversation about poisons had given him a nervous stomach. Maybe he'd merely had too many glasses of mulberry wine. His head spun.

The man, lying on the examination table, clenched Georges-Minh's hand. "I itch, I want to tear off my skin. What's inside wants out. I'm burning inside."

"Like indigestion?"

His eyes were panicked. "I have a monster inside me."

In old-fashioned spirit possessions, a priest beat the patient with a mulberry stick. If that didn't remove the spirit, the priest put a spell on the spirit, to divine what it needed. If the spirit was lonely, the priest provided friends, however many, made of papier mâché, built on bamboo frames. Hungry, the best food would be provided. While still under the spell, the spirit would be forced to sign a piece of paper. In this manner, the spirit was contractually obligated, having had its needs met, to exit the body.

The patient sat up. "Don't you see?" Yanked the hand he held toward him. "Or do you see?"

"I'm going to have to ask you to let go." Georges-Minh pried the man's fingers off him.

"I see a monster inside you."

"Calm down, please."

"If you try to push them down and bury them they'll only get angry and crawl back out. These monsters are like hungry ghosts that way: the country is full of them. Invisible monsters living inside people, only the people don't know it, or they do and try to ignore it. They come out most easily when you're sleeping, or when you forget yourself for a moment. That's why drinking is so dangerous. Don't you see? Conquerors want you to do that. Drink. Do opium."

"Let me give you a sedative."

The man kept fighting him. His fever, whatever illness was causing it, made his delirium peak to the point where Georges-Minh was beginning to feel truly afraid.

"No sedative!" the man shouted. "Listen to me. The Chinese wanted a nation of addicts. How much of yourself can you hide before you no longer recognize your reflection? It's in the opium. I'm trying to tell you. Warn you. They're coming for you too. The monster's already inside you. It's happening now. The country will die in its sleep. Lulled by false promises."

"Everything will be fine, I promise."

"You tell yourself lies, covered by more lies, and then more lies till you forget what part is the truth. That's how the oppressor has always taken over the oppressed. They put the country to sleep. Please don't put me to sleep."

When the man was safely asleep Georges-Minh sighed deeply, then he sat in his chair and looked at himself in the mirror.

The man had mentioned opium. He shook his head. How could he know?

He would contact Infectious Disease Control in the morning and they would chat about the usual things, lack of resources, lack of infrastructure, lack of hygiene among the peasants and working class.

It was the third man he'd seen in as many days like him, and all three had yet to regain their memory. As with the others, he wondered if it might be some kind of new rice paddy fever.

He was filled with a deep sense of unease.

2

Mai sat on what she still called the porch because Khieu had called it that, although it was really just a flat lonely weathered landing with stairs leading up to it that had grown rotten and pockmarked in Khieu's absence. He didn't know about the baby. Nor the blackness of her nights. The clawing brightness of her days.

"Let him go already," Thu, her maid, said. "What are you waiting for? Permission? Absolution?"

But Mai couldn't. Because her baby, Cong, was dying by degrees and he was the last thing Khieu had bestowed her. The last time Khieu had come in the night had been over a year ago. Now his baby was expiring with all the drama and tragedy of the theatre, or so it seemed to Mai, for when his fever broke, he'd play with his toes as if he hadn't been sick at all; an episode could last for hours, or days, and Mai would sit at the edge of his rush mat on the floor, afraid to breathe, thinking perhaps, yes, this time surely he'd stay well. But then his eyes would close and he'd tumble into another sleep from which no one could rouse him.

Her father had once taken her to a Chinese opera when she was a girl. She remembered the seats and how large they were in comparison to the size of her bottom, the noise of the audience, her excitement at having her father all to herself, a handsome man she believed made people's heads turn because of how intelligently he spoke and his suit's shine. When characters died on stage, unlike in life they were reborn: first they went down, clutching at their throats, screeching like stabbed pheasants, only to rise in health and stroll around. It happened again and again, death in slow motion; they sang, slapping their chests, then dropped to their knees, then rose, then fell, then rose, then died, dying and rising. Cong, too, ailed and recovered, ailed and recovered. The baby's fever spots clouded him in purple and red, as when one takes a brush and flicks it toward waiting rice paper. Mai prayed and wailed during her own year of small deaths and adjustments. Running the Paper Flower Inn, just her and Thu and Crazy Auntie Number Three. Not to mention her row of children, their waiting mouths.

After six years she'd grown used to Khieu's comings and goings, as used to it as someone could, but this last time he left after getting her pregnant, and he hadn't returned, except while she slept to collect the money she kept hidden under the vase in the front room. Sadly she felt no anger. Her hammering heart reminded her only that she was alive, knowing he'd been in the house; this was enough. Who was his latest mistress? "The Portuguese," she had heard. He was painting hats and she sold them in the brothel where she worked.

Mai stayed home for fear of running into them. She didn't know what she'd do and the fear took on a life of its own.

She and her children lived in a converted laundry room on the main floor of the inn, squished together like fish in a net, close enough to feel each other's heat, one of the many costs of marrying young.

If a tally forced its hand, could she break it?

Now on the porch that wasn't a porch, the baby suc_._ her breast, drawing a thread of milk, this habit of afternoons. Because he no longer ate, not really. This comfort for both of them, looking at the sky, the occlusion of clouds, the air at four o'clock, at five, at six, waiting for night, the comfort of sleep and oblivion. What else was there?

She tried not to hear the beating of her blood. Flexed her hand, her arm, what else was there? The boy's heat. A thousand-year-egg pot decorated with dragons. A bougainvillea bush. It had blossomed for the second time this year and into the greenery hummingbirds came now and then in arrows of red. From a little after four o'clock until well into the dusk of the sweet, hungry monsoon autumn she and her baby son sat on the porch and the storm clouds greyed on that side of the inn, which had begun to show signs of decay just like the porch.

On went the buzz of hummingbirds. Her second-youngest, Trang, ran by spinning fistfuls of lemongrass in the manner of a propeller. For the last year she, Thu, and Crazy Auntie Number Three had constructed their survival, sculpting a war of defiance against her husband's truancy. Survival in his desertion meant winning—never forget life was a contest from which only the most cunning would emerge. Her survival was an armour for the day she saw Khieu again, for one day it would happen, and she didn't want to crack. If she cracked, all her pieces would fall out. Something terrible might be let loose. Like a vicious animal escaping from its cage.

Mai's own mother had wept behind a closed door. Because of her husband. In spite of his drinking and womanizing, Mai's mother continued to set a place for Mai's father at the head of the dinner table. Mai, a child, easily distracted by the lustre of her father's gold tooth, the sheen of his hair oil, and intoxicated by the scent of the cologne he wore only when he went out to meet his mistress, could be forgiven for listening when her father argued that love was a gift. And that to love just one thing, or one thing at a time, was selfish and minimized the worth of the thing loved. She saw his point, partly.

Mai's mother saw herself charged with promoting established traditions no matter the personal price. "Traditions are the skin in which we are born."

"The ox stands its ground."

"There is a right way of behaving which is not pride or stubbornness. One should never bow or meet the world halfway," she said, unable to see, or simply refusing to see, her own complicity in the matter. She would not distort her shape to move more easily through obstacles. She was too stubborn to move, rather pretending the floodwaters weren't rising all around her. She refused to acknowledge that bowing and meeting the world halfway was exactly what she was doing in allowing her husband to carry on with his mistress and letting "tradition" take its course.

Her mother, who had respected her husband and raised her children, on the day of her death, sang an old lullaby. "Sleep, ghost, sleep. Come afternoon, I stand in the backyard, looking toward my mother's land." And, rather than murder her husband, swallowed the pills and killed herself instead. The vengeful ghost she became begged worship.

Mai didn't blame her father for the suicide, nor for the haunting, nor for sisters who slunk to the ghost in fear, wilting in its presence, seeking its advice on everything from homework to hairstyles to boys. But she couldn't stand the sight of a man who prostrated himself below a shaking altar to beg her forgiveness, who pulled out his own gold tooth for more snake liquor, who drank in a yellow undershirt. Not when his cologne had once made her giddy.

Now he talked to a ghost for company—when he wasn't running from it in fear. She'd once begged her father to take her to the opera. In her seven-year-old heart she was his only princess. His mistress had laughed and said to bring her along.

Ten more years Mai lived in that house. Her father continued to destroy himself, drinking and losing the rest of his teeth, pawning his suits, and she watched.

If she did not have the courage to face a father who had let himself slide into pitifulness and tell him so, how could she defeat a ghost? Caught between the straitjacket of the past and the open horizons of a modern future, Mai agreed to marry Khieu, the owner of a local inn who had asked for her hand, though rumour had it he was a philanderer and simply needed a maid.

Last week Thu had found the baby Cong with his fist in his mouth, eyes open, as if he'd seen something during the night hideous enough to make him ram his own scream down his throat. Ideas escaped her. What evil hunted Mai now? She engineered her luck: Snuck through doors backward. Never swept on auspicious days. Stayed put on inauspicious ones.

Though not wanting to become her mother, she hadn't travelled far from superstition after all. Donated what she could to the ritual specialists who called to the wandering souls. The *cau chu* experts travelled the country living off donations, especially from people who were being haunted by particular ghosts, those who'd died sudden violent deaths, or who'd died without anyone knowing and far from home. Mai never stopped hoping that one day her mother's ghost would join them, would be lured by the *cau chu*'s offerings of fruit nectar and rice porridge. She could only hope as she watched them parade through the market. "Why are you standing in the middle of this empty tennis court? Are you afraid? The call of the rooster in the morning frightens you, doesn't it? Come to us, those whose burdens are heavy, who've died without heads, who've died at sea, who've died without coffins, who've died so lonely," a ragtag procession of the undead behind them.

Sometimes the ghosts would follow for a while but then turn their backs laughing, having made fools of the *cau chu* experts after pretending to eat their porridge and fruit nectar, only to return to stealing and marauding for another day. But the ritualists always persuaded one or two to receive their offerings and stop wandering, and Mai kept wishing that one day her mother would be among them.

Her oldest boy, Vinh, had waves of hair that lapped the middle of his back. Thu explained to her that cutting one's hair was a political message everyone from peasants to intellectuals could send to resist the French. "The hair," Mai shot back, "has the soul in it." Mai refused to cut her sons' locks; she felt the danger of it in her gut. But despite her designs, Cong got sicker.

Crazy Auntie Number Three held a slice of bean cake between her fingers, the kind of cake Mai had loved since she was a child. Already they were eating the leftovers of guests, combining what remained of their dishes into stir-fries, mixing pancakes with pork, eggs with fish, rat with turnips, anything and everything, it didn't matter, Food was Good Food, Mai told her children.

"Is your toe healing well, Auntie Number Three?" Mai asked.

Crazy Auntie Number Three wiggled the culprit ingrown nail. Blackflies lifted and hovered before trying to settle again on the open wound. "Thank you, dear, for asking and yes."

"Something bad's come," Mai said. "And now it's in the house." As if on cue wind rustled the blinds. "*She's* here," Mai said. "I can smell her."

Storm clouds pulsed. Shadows drifted over the crumbling inn, and moist droplets, which Mai thought of as tears of the gods, began to fall.

"Have you smelled the reek of rotten potatoes lately?"

"Relax, niece," Crazy Auntie ordered.

The clouds had clutched their anger too long and Mai heard the raindrops pummelling the roof above them, washing the chipped porch boards outside, too, landing also wherever her husband Khieu was. Maybe she had angered the gods somehow.

"I'm trying to appease the gods, what else can I do about it?" Mai said. "The time has come to square things."

"Have you burned incense?"

"Yes."

"Offered prayers?"

"Of course," Mai answered. Naturally she'd tried these things.

"Buy some dog," Crazy Auntie said.

Mai sent Thu to the market in the storm and Thu, as diligently as she did everything else, came home with a mutt the size of a watermelon. She tied its throat, cut it from ear to ear, and bled it. She boiled off its fur, then grilled it on an open fire under the porch that wasn't really a porch but which Mai called a porch because Khieu had called it that.

Mai, who didn't want to get her hands dirty, watched from a window and her mouth watered.

Hoping for luck, they ate bites seasoned with lemongrass and garlic.

Sometimes Cong's healthy spells lasted for hours, and Mai dared think perhaps he was recovering. Then, from one moment to the next, he'd fall into a stupor, catatonic as a doll, his skin lustreless as old silk.

One day the ghost knocked the cleaver out of Thu's hand as she chopped off a chicken's head for lunch. Another time she threw Mai's comb into the mud of the koi pond. Then her mosquito net was soiled with pig's manure. As during Mai's childhood, when her mother's ghost had roared through the house smashing things, the inn's altar was buffeted while Mai tried to light the incense.

Yasuko Thanh

Mai offered Cong her nipple, a vain hope. Even when he managed to coax milk from her puckered breast, minutes later he would vomit and collapse into another bottomless slumber. Heartsick, Mai retreated to her bed.

Was she being recruited? Spirits summoned the dying as mediums because from the edge, they could better see.

Hadn't she always had a sixth sense? A sign, this, as were her dreams about flying, her mother had said. She'd always known she was special. So had her mother. And her father, even drunk, had made her believe it.

If a ghost entered her body, what would she do? An erotic quiver shot downward from her head. She played with her hair, remembering how when she was a child it had once tangled itself into knots. Another sign.

What a terrible time her mother had had combing them out—to cut them free brought bad luck.

Women mediums left pigs' heads as offerings and danced. Women, to tempt the spirits, danced with sexual movements to channel their power. And the spirits mounted them, and possessed them. They were wanton, and charged a great deal to be possessed, to be mounted, to consort with spirits and be enabled to answer questions of all sorts, such as where someone's son, lost in battle or at sea, might be found. The exact location of his corpse.

Some mediums were merely looking for an excuse to dance in the Western way, only saying they'd been possessed. They writhed with the spirit and gave advice and charged money. Some people, like Thu, accused all soothsayers of charlatanism. Destroying morals. Copying French bawdy-house acts.

A soothsayer had once told Mai's friend not to leave her husband, a cheater. A pyromancer advised the same friend to leave him. Some people simply waited for the answer they wanted to hear and visited medium after medium until they received it.

24

Mai saw no reason one had to lie on coals or skewer one's nipple with a blade to summon a spirit—as men did, and had done for hundreds of years—when Western dance moves would do just as well.

A woman's touch had more finesse.

Not all female mediums were charlatans.

Mai could be a good one. She knew it.

At the very least, she'd pick a good one when it came time to consult one about her dying son.

3

The morning glories had been varnished to the inner sole of Thu's shoe to protect the paint and keep the flower from fading under the sweat and grime of her heels. A present from Birago, her Senegalese soldier. She liked to say "Se-ne-ga-lese" as her feet clapped down the hall.

Birago was a skirmisher. A "tirailleur sénégalais," an artillery-man conscripted from Africa to man an 80 mm field howitzer under the command of a Lieutenant Colonel Janvier. Officially he was a tirailleur, second class, but Lieutenant Colonel Janvier, who had taken an exaggerated shine to him, affectionately called him "*gabier*" when no one was around. The word meant "sailor," but also referred to a small bird that lived high in the treetops known for its sweet singing voice.

She timed the words to the drumbeat of her feet as they scratched the floor, driving Mai crazy. No whispered steps as she clomped and stomped. No echo into nothing, not her. Clonk and pace, delivering a bowl of shaved coconut with ice, these long days between visits from her Senegalese, her

African, with scars on his cheeks like a second pair of eyes.

"Thu, are you wearing those shoes again?"

Thu refused to temper the racket because Mai refused to get out of bed this morning. Where Thu came from a person got up when they got kicked. Those who didn't died.

Teak frame holding her up like some kind of queen. Milk skin and melon lips.

"Stop looking at me like that," Mai said. "It's not like I mean to be sick."

"Like what?"

Last week Thu had seen a serpent eagle at the market on its side. Its head was cocked at a strange angle, maybe it had fallen from one of the vendor's crates, and it lay with one wing splayed like a fan. When the feral cats began to play with it and batter it to pieces the bird looked at Thu unable to save itself and it was still alive as they began to eat it, starting with its crested breast feathers. Thu had crouched on an overturned basket and watched with her chin in her hand, disgusted. Only the foolish counted on rescue.

Instead of finishing the coconut Thu gave her, Mai put it on the nightstand. "Sit with me, please." She patted the bed.

Thu sat in the rocker.

Mai shared this room, this laundry, which in better days, more prosperous days before Khieu had left, one could never have imagined serving as a bedroom, with her four children. They slept on rush mats on the floor, a window overlooking the river, Mai's the only well-woven mat that had a teak frame. The river flowed in front of the inn, moving, yet not moving, for as it travelled from the mountain highlands to the central plateaus to the lowland deltas, the river god was the most clever of all, managing to be adventuresome yet belonging to no one. Everywhere at once, yet staying rooted to the land at the same time.

Thu eyed the room with envy: bigger than the closet she shared with Crazy Auntie Number Three. Mai still had a few nice things left, more than Thu: a flask, a letter opener, a feather with blood dried in the tip of the hollow quill, a perfume decanter, a silver picture frame, a tortoiseshell hair comb, a green silk *ao dai* with lilies embroidered from the hem to the neck, all on a wooden shelf.

As things mildewed, rotted, were neglected, what was nice, what was clean, what rats hadn't gnawed, what cockroaches hadn't chewed, what dirt hadn't soiled went into the guest rooms. What was spoiled, what needed mending, what could do for family use but couldn't be shown, what wasn't usable but could be gotten by on, what was last season's, what had a hole, what whistled, what leaked, what was loose, what cinched, what pinched, what made one cramp, ache, what had fleas, what was unsafe, unfit for human consumption, these things became Thu's and Crazy Auntie's and Mai's.

What was left behind by the guests, a bottle of shampoo, an old pair of stockings that could be laundered, a box of chocolates with a few left, a long cigarette butt, half a bottle of wine, these things were greedily savoured by Thu and Crazy Auntie.

Thu figured Khieu had married too young, and the shock of having three children in quick succession had pushed him over a cliff. A painter. Ha! On street corners, selling hats. So, he saw himself the leader of some sort of hat-selling empire and by the wayside fell his family, moving into smaller corners of the inn. Who did he think he was preaching to? Just an excuse to get out of the house.

At first Thu shared the riches she found. But poverty had made them greedy and Thu had a bottle of Mairie de Chasselay perfume in her room that she thought no one knew about.

Crazy Auntie had adopted Thu—she'd raised six street kids as her own—when Thu was thirteen years old. Thu's own mother had lost her mind in the market one day and lined as many men up as could pay her and with her children to one side had done business until the police came. Thu barely remembered her. She felt she'd been on her own forever by the time Crazy Auntie found her "like an alley cat" one day.

To maximize their earnings by freeing up as many rentable rooms as possible and minimizing wear and tear by allowing the children free rein in only a small fraction of their own house, Mai lived in the laundry and Thu and Crazy Auntie lived in what had once been a large walk-in closet on the top floor. Barely enough room for two beds and hardly enough space to turn around.

Thu caressed the blessed find, the perfume bottle. Inhaling the sweet fragrance, raising the glass stopper to her nose— inhaling—slowly—Mother asleep—as close to her nose as she dared not because she feared Mai's yelling, her slaps or silent treatments or looks of hurt for at the start they'd been friends— but simply because a secret was made more powerful by the swirling currents that danger kept hidden in its depths.

Thu rocked in the chair by the bed. The rockers squeaked. Absent-mindedly, she lifted the bowl of shaved coconut with ice from the bedside table and began eating.

"Yesterday," Mai said, "I was having a bath and some man was banging on the door."

"Huh?"

"Are you listening? He was rapping on the door insisting on his tea. I can't do this alone. Where were you? I had to get out of the bath, dripping wet. Make him tea!"

"I was with your kids!"

"I had to make him tea. I was dripping wet! He kept saying, The inn promises tea. I was in the bath saying, But I'm in the bath—can't you make your own tea? The kitchen is right there. He says, But your advertising promises tea. I think this is a case for the magistrate. If you are going to advertise tea, then you must make me tea. He was leaning against the door, I could hear him breathing. I was *trapped* in that bathroom, I was *naked*."

"Don't be so dramatic."

"For forty-five minutes this went on."

"Well, why didn't you just get up and make him tea?"

"I did. But I was scared to get out of the water."

"To make him tea. Now you *are* being melodramatic."

"I was scared that he was going to *rape* me."

"So did you make him tea?"

"Yes. With cookies."

In former times they would have laughed.

"I can't be everywhere at once," Thu said. "Auntie's been in her bed for a month. Since Cong got sick, you're in your room with him half the time, too. The other day Trang grabbed a wallet. A guest left her purse on the floor. I made a joke. I said, 'Did you get the money?' She didn't laugh." Thu shook her head. "The boy's only three. I handed her the wallet back. Some people, no sense of humour. My point is." Thu waved her hand, then brought it to her forehead and rubbed the creases. She sighed.

"You're more than a maid to me, you know that, don't you?"

"Don't give me that." Though it might have relieved Mai's conscience to call her sister, Thu knew better. Raised as an "adopted" cousin, Thu would never be considered a real relative.

The room filled with silence.

"You know, Birago is your inferior. Not good enough for you," Mai said.

When Birago visited the inn, Mai's eyes walked all the way up his fingers to his face then slid back down his biceps to his feet to the floor. She disguised her flirting now. Protected herself from feelings of guilt as some sort of racial animosity; for all her educated talk about freedom for the people, imitating her flown-the-coop husband, she was no better than the rich who kowtowed to anyone in power.

As if reading her mind, Mai said, "I'm not talking about his race."

"What, then?"

"I love you like a sister."

Thu snorted. "As if."

"What?" Even in the throes of her supposed illness Mai managed to prop herself up on her elbow.

"I can't be all yours. That it? You're jealous."

"All mine? What are you talking about?"

"You want what you can't have." Her tongue was a rebellious thing, wilful and obscene.

Mai's eyes could have reduced to ashes anything in their path. If leaping from bed and throttling Thu wouldn't have ruined Mai's game of pretending to be ill, Thu was sure she would have done so. Instead Mai chose the worst way to be hurtful. She said in a forced whisper, "You really are insane. Just like your mother."

Thu hadn't felt sad until she entered Mai's room. Maybe it was simply the darkness falling that made her miss Birago more.

Birago was fond of saying, "The night is more foolish than the day." Everything would seem better in the morning, she told herself.

"Look in a mirror," Thu retorted.

The silence thickened.

"Do you hear me, Mai? You've been brave—ever since Birago started visiting." Thu stood up from the rocker. "You get so angry. Whenever you don't get your way." She stomped from the room. Clonk-clonk-clonk. Bi-ra-go. She scraped her shoe *Biiiiii*-ra-go on purpose.

Cong lay at the head of Auntie's bed on the pillow, which had smelled of medications ever since Thu was a teenager. Thu fought the urge to crush her head against it. Instead she flopped down onto her own bed, so close to Auntie's she could stretch out her arm and touch Auntie's rimpled skin, and sighed. "I haven't seen Birago in a week." She kicked off her shoes, picked at her toenails. Part of the Bataillons d'Afrique, he was often given assignments no one wanted. Thu didn't think his boss liked him very much, his immediate boss, the captain, anyway. His captain as well as the men in his barracks were jealous of him because the lieutenant colonel preferred him over the others. When the colonel wasn't around they mocked his tribal scars, the blackness of his skin.

Thu, on the other hand, worshipped Birago's black skin, made blacker by the wet of the water and the blaze of the sun— they met at Long Hai Beach: both of them deified the blue mindless distraction from the polluted streets. The way he rode on the top of the wave that day, arms spread wide like the crucifix over currents and riptides, thrilled her. Asphyxiated by house-work, she felt if she didn't do something out of the ordinary, she was going to explode. His stomach was lean. She could fit her fingers into the washboard spaces while he giggled, clutching her fingers. She pulled them out of his grasp.

"Try to catch me," she said.

"What?"

"My fingers—too slow—missed me."

"Cha monkey."

"You're the monkey. At least our teacher said so in kinder-garten." She poked him playfully. "He had a picture of African monkeys and black men side by side. Catch my fingers—too slow."

He stopped and kicked at the white sand—speckles on his black toes, the grains—and the beads of ocean water in the tight black curls made rainbows of light like tiny prisms. Suddenly she felt ashamed. When he finally raised his fine head and turned to face her, he was grimacing a grotesque ape-like grimace. He raised one arm above his head and scratched his armpit in parody, hooting, "Oo-oo-oo, girl, I going to show you *go-ri-lla*." He scooped her up under his arm and loped along the shoreline. "I gorilla!" he roared. "Birago gorilla. Oooooo!" An ice cream vendor leaped back, a family tittered, hurried in the other direction with their towels. Birago padded the length of the beach bellowing, and Thu, half his weight and height, screamed and laughed under his arm and pounded on his back. It frightened her at first how hard he felt, like something not human. She could run her hands up and down his torso for hours, thinking how no one would approve of their eventual marriage, because that's what she wanted—marriage, fuzzy-headed mulatto children. His race allowed her to play the good wife while simultaneously breaking away from the role. He decorated her rice-paper hat, stolen from Khieu's stash, which Mai never would have allowed, with flowers, fresh and dried. The country was against them. It didn't help that local women had been raped by black soldiers, the cases reported in all the newspapers of Saigon. He made money on the side boxing. The matches were illegal, he said.

"Does it matter?"

"To me," he said.

"Half of what happens in Saigon is illegal," she said and laughed.

"If I want to move ahead with the military," he said, "I have to be careful."

But she knew, sensed, there was more to it than that.

"What about Colonel Janvier?"

"My captain hates me enough as is."

"Colonel Janvier doesn't hate you."

"He doesn't know about the boxing. He'd probably want to go. Or box himself. He's a sharpshooter."

"See? You should tell him. What's a sharpshooter?"

Birago shrugged. "Pistols. He won competitions in Monaco. I wouldn't be surprised if he was a boxer in his day. It's just if you want to move ahead with the military"—Birago had a funny look on his face—"you can't have everyone hate you."

Thu rolled over onto her stomach now and looked at Auntie. "We've only been together seven months, Auntie, and you know, it feels like we've been married a lifetime. Has that ever happened to you? Love, I mean?"

Crazy Auntie Number Three snorted. "I've brought up how many children and you're asking me if I've ever been in love?" Her eyebrows were raised so high they nearly touched her hairline. Thu wasn't sure if that meant yes or no.

"I love you more than I've ever loved anything," Birago said the first time she saw him fight, when she was kissing his knuckles afterward, as was to become her habit.

"You need something to love that much and I'm it," Thu said, already suspecting he had a hole, and that when he punched a man in the ring he was trying to fill it with something that had nothing to do with her.

4

Georges-Minh told himself if not for the trappings of his parents' wealth, his life would be better. He hated the opulence of the place. More lavish than the French governor's, the terrace was large enough to fit a troupe of Siamese acrobats. His father had handpicked the paintings that hung on the walls, original works depicting former emperors in royal apparel, reproductions of Goya. Georges-Minh preferred a minimalist look.

Most days he felt as though he was being crushed under all the black lacquered furniture decorated with good-luck symbols, ornately shaped ironworks that flaunted means and status. He suffocated under gold and red cushions. No matter which room he entered, his father's things and his mother's too reminded him of their grand and reckless love of spending money equalled only by their grand and reckless love of life. Georges-Minh told himself he was different. Looked for evidence that ever since childhood he'd preferred simplicity to ostentation. Hadn't he loved crossword puzzles and building blocks? He craved clean lines, how he liked to keep his mind: uncluttered, free of passion.

Yet an invisible hand stopped him from getting rid of even a single gaudy landscape, or one of his mother's flowers on the terrace, a solitary climbing trumpet vine, a nelumbo with a head the size of a showgirl's headdress, an orchid spilling pornographically from its planter. Here was a grown man, both his parents gone, smothering to death in a house with lotus buds in fluted vases.

Was it the denial of his true nature that caused him to awake one morning to clots of dawn through his mosquito net? He sat up, kneaded a lumpy head. He thought he must have a cold, a terrible, terrible cold. He couldn't remember his name. He ran his fingers through his hair: drenched. He ran his hands over his skin: clammy. He searched the rest of his body for other clues. His private parts appeared to be male. He put his hand over his chest: his heart flapped like a broken bird's wing.

He could hear a river roiling outside—but which river? Breathe, breathe. He listened for footsteps. Did he have children? Did he have a wife? Thoughts raced one on top of the other. All this in a matter of seconds.

Paintings hung on the walls: reproductions of masterworks by Giotto, van Eyck, Wang Hui. Was he an art historian? He sat on his bed drenched in sweat for fifteen terrifying minutes unable to remember who he was, where he was, or how he'd come to be here.

He massaged his temples, encouraging his mind to return. Little by little it did, with the shame of an itinerant lover. As it did so, he realized something. Sometimes the universe gives you what you want, but not in the way you wanted it. Or maybe it's that you don't know what you want until it's too late.

So, in Georges-Minh's case, it wasn't until he came out of his amnesiac fugue that he understood: in order to break free from his past he would need to start with a mind wiped clean. He yearned to return to his amnesiac state, his mind an empty canvas on which he could create anything, for that was the only way to become the man he wanted to be. To leave behind the security his father's properties continued to provide for him, polished Athangudi black-and-white floor tiles and cold, smooth rosewood carvings of lucky elephants and colourful egg plaster walls.

Yet how to do so was the question, when the income his father's rental properties brought in allowed him to volunteer at Clinique de la Dhuys, the badly funded clinic with no beds, limited to providing frontline care. And what of his home medical practice, where his father's rents permitted him to accept chickens as payments? And, dear God, just how was he expected to *think of a solution* with an imported Italian chandelier staring him in the eye?

And then the solution came to him. He would get married! As soon as he got married he would no longer be solely responsible for his parents' wealth and he would have a wife who would take charge, buy silks and furniture and vases and whatever else it was women bought for houses. The thought thrilled him. He'd be set free from the burden of living life for others, even if they were dead ancestors, and finally could begin living life as his own person. That's all he'd ever wanted. To be loosed from this feeling of having a yoke around his neck. To finally feel he had permission to live his own life. Could getting married finally allow him that? Yes, yes, yes. Now all he had to do was find a woman.

Georges-Minh had no girlfriends to speak of—the cause of which wasn't snobbery but shyness. A loner with the reputation for standoffishness, he never knew what to say to members of the opposite sex and found chit-chat an effort, even to smile so the nurses smiled back. He found no lightness in small talk, no release in it. For Georges-Minh it was work. His awkwardness kept women away: they could count on his dullness.

A girlfriend? Keep dreaming, others might have told him. He longed for a wife, a normal family.

Too bad. He liked to think he was handsome—people besides his mother had said so. A girl at the lycée, once. And a woman in the Swedish foreign exchange program who'd whispered a certain word in his ear. And third, a man, a botanist working as an academic assistant at the French Preparatory College where Georges-Minh had studied for a term. On a field trip in a banana forest, strangler figs overhead, legs entwined, words against the nape of his neck. "Your member is like a massive liana vine." Massive, he'd said. Oh, yes. No prude, the botanist. A *libertine.* And Georges-Minh too, so the botanist had thought at the time.

Not a libertine, Georges-Minh had corrected in his head, not a simple *hedonist* either, so much as a man who wouldn't let his sexual choices be dictated by the establishment. Who would have sex with another man simply because it was frowned upon by traditional Vietnamese society. He told his libertine lover none of these things but secretly prided himself on his politics and moral superiority.

Yet since his parents' death he'd sublimated his desires. In other words, he worked. All the time. Calmed by the sight of his fingers among the sutures and bandages. He decompressed by working. His only safety valve. How he coped against occasional loneliness. Occasional, well. He went carousing with Chang but their intimacies didn't count for much.

He drove to work in his Panhard Levassor and the crowd parted, many never having seen a car before, patting the hood respectfully. They pulled back their burnt palms.

His father had been laid to rest with all the proper rituals demanded by his standing, had therefore become a satisfied ancestor and not a hungry ghost. Tonight he would offer his father and mother incense and fruit and tell them of his plans to get married.

They would be pleased. Nothing was valued so highly as family, and nothing within the family so much as a son, the eldest son, who would carry on the family name.

The irony, of course, is that volunteering at La Dhuys had been a way for Georges-Minh to escape his father's influence, which he'd always felt as acutely as hands around his neck. He'd become a doctor in the first place out of spite. Rebellion. An "I'll show you" exuberance. To make a point about his worth to a father, it seemed to Georges-Minh, who measured everything against the size of his bank book.

Though Georges-Minh had long ago stopped attending the soirees of French ministers, attended by the attractive sons and daughters of wealthy businessmen, he'd always faltered before donating all twenty of his father's rental properties to the monks who begged with alms bowls, reciting sutras in the market, saying prayers for lost souls trying without success to banish the dead back to the underworld. No one would have noticed his absence from Saigon's social circles anyway. The trickle of invitations after his return from university, followed by his parents' death, had less to do with his status as a doctor and everything to do with his family's name.

On the banks of the river floated a city. Many of Georges-Minh's patients worked in brothels called flower boats, after the lavish Canton custom of strewing the rooms with flowers, decorating the deck with lanterns. He did what he could, then sent them on their way. The children who had been stolen from highland hamlets, with candy treats or thin dried slices of sugar cane for sucking—they were the saddest. Their faces, after a few months in the city, rotting before they bloomed, as when a peanut vine wilted under winter, the flowers dying before their time to open.

Other patients worked at "bamboos," so-called because they contained only bamboo beds and bamboo walls. No furniture. Maybe a lamp that burned coconut oil. He treated them for beatings, venereal diseases, marsh fever, cholera, dysentery, hepatitis, and diarrhea.

The lucky ones married businessmen. Most retired to street corners, scarred by disease, having lost noses to syphilis, and became needle women waiting to mend a tear in someone's clothes or fix a buttonhole, wearing a paper nose and big glasses to hide their deformities.

He passed the promenade café that served beer and bitters, a French theatre in the Rue Catinat—a hall that dwarfed even the Buddhist pagoda on the same street, constructed of bamboo, filled with plants and cut flowers that were replaced the instant they withered—florists, milliners, dressmakers, booksellers, jewellers, ironworkers, trunk makers, seed vendors, dealers in curiosities from Japan and China that included phallic symbols, erotic books and engravings, as well as poseable puppets the size of a man's hand made from porcelain or ivory.

An execution had taken place; the head was still on display in front of the butcher shop, mounted on a stake, stinking and covered with flies. A French official decried the nationalists, describing the slaughtered soldiers as family men, and emphasizing his point by displaying the posters printed by the military of these fathers with their children.

A flatbed cart pulled by a pair of mules transporting the rest of the rebels cantered past. Whenever the driver went around a corner the prisoners, shackled one to another by their necks and strung like the lights that decorated the street, lost their balance and leaned against each other for support. They were towed through the streets like that, the whites of their eyes bright as mirror shards, paraded, in shame.

Bystanders lowered their heads, melon sellers, cyclo drivers, lawyers with street-facing offices, shoeshine boys, those who were walking the streets, or selling kumquats at the market, or cutting hair at street stands.

The military pulled the guillotine with deliberate, theatrical plodding in another open-bed cart from the jail on Lagrandière Street to the square of the night market. More public speeches delayed the newest set of executions. Then they forced the prisoners to kneel one at a time at the guillotine. Their heads rolled into a basket, one after another. The guillotine blade was carefully wiped with a cotton cloth. Until only soldiers remained. They set the newest heads next to the other in front of the butcher shop, placed the severed ears in a dish and put them inside the pagoda.

A girl, maybe seventeen, wheezing on the clinic's back steps, wore a chemise, now ruined, a blouse with embroidered buttons, a robe whose brick colour made the dirt on the sleeves appear black, and a hat with a ribbon. The way her mouth opened and closed reminded Georges-Minh of a fish.

Her eyes were opium-glazed and she couldn't focus on his hand when he offered it to her. She seemed to be trying to measure its length with her eyes; the poor had nothing but dreams and suspicions, he thought. Again he offered her his hand, trying to trap her fingers.

"Stand up, sister."

She looked up suspiciously.

"Come on. I'll take you inside."

She shook her head no.

When he tried to take her by force, he was surprised by how cold her hand was, like a cement wall at night. She jumped up. Her anger, he speculated, must have nothing to do with him but perhaps something inside of her. How could she be angry with him when he was only trying to help her?

"Who the fuck are you?" she yelled, looking at him for the first time, utter incomprehension in her eyes. "Who the fuck am I? Huh? Who the fuck am I? Get away. Don't touch me. Don't fucking touch me."

Then she hit him and ran.

He held his cheek where her nails had dug in. A round stain clung to the tile where she'd sat. He glanced down at it, then up at her retreating figure. Should he chase her? He saw now that what he'd thought was mud on her chemise had in fact been blood, but only endless doorways of opium houses remained and little boys inching from the shadows, rail-thin beauties who'd been there all along, hoping to find favours, a lover, money.

"Bad moon night," said one of the street urchins. He had the look and confidence of a mixed-race child.

"Why didn't you catch her?" Georges-Minh said, exasperated.

Something passed in front of the boy's face. A sadness. Skin the colour of tea. Eyes like a deer's. "You coulda caught her—if you'd been faster."

Georges-Minh rubbed his cheek where the blood was flowing more freely now. Goddammit, where was his handkerchief? He dug in his pockets, applied pressure to the wound.

The boy's friends giggled. Not because of Dr. Nguyen, but because some of them were only eight or nine and one of their group was applying some lipstick and making kissy faces. They walked like women, the real woman who had escaped already forgotten, a door opened and closed, someone threw something into the street, some garbage, life moved on.

The boy looked at Georges-Minh as if to say he should move on too. "You don't even remember my name, do you?"

Georges-Minh had his hand on the door handle. "Lippy one."

"Ha, wrong."

"Slow."

"Wrong again."

Georges-Minh shoved the door open. His co-workers barely looked up. Would it kill them to smile? Did he care? No one even asked about his cheek. A couple of the nurses nodded at him and resumed their duties. He was still pissed off, about the boys with the giggles, the lipstick, the sloe-eyed one with skin the colour of tea, the doorways, the blood stain, the girl. He'd dealt with violent patients before so perhaps last night had made him grumpy—his head felt *wrong*.

The young prostitute's fish mouth and yesterday's pepper spots had disconcerted him. His temporary memory loss. The paintings' erasure, the disappearance of the tiles—his father's wealth, yes, that was always on his mind—but it was more than that. He was definitely coming down with something. Maybe a flu. His skin itched. God. He hoped whatever that man who'd also lost his memory had brought into his home wasn't contagious.

He hadn't been sleeping enough lately. People sometimes suffered bouts of amnesia in times of stress. He'd been under a lot of pressure lately. He should eat more. Take better care of himself. No wonder his mind was performing somersaults. Between the clinic's viral diseases and Khieu's poisoning plots, Georges-Minh would be lucky to escape with a mental hiccup.

He dressed the scratch on his cheek, washed his hands, and settled into a working rhythm under the gaslight's glow. Two fishermen straggled in carrying a body. One carried the shoulders and one the feet. The middle swayed between them, wrapped in a white shroud.

"Where do you want her?"

Behind the two men followed an old woman, cawing and pulling at her hair. Behind her trailed a crowd like the train of a wedding dress.

The old woman said, "Leave her. I told you to leave her."

"Heavenly Father, bless me for I have sinned," said a Catholic in the group.

"I told you, she's evil," the old woman said. "Don't look, don't touch her. Now what have you done? It's too late!" She pounded her own head. She tried to push the others out of the clinic; when they didn't budge she wailed and slavered. "We'll all be cursed."

If Dr. Nguyen Georges-Minh had not been busy trying to clear off an examination table for the fishers to lay the body upon, he might have said to the woman or such people like her, "I understand believing in curses is your way of making sense of a world that is often hard and cold. But I've never been one for genies and magicians."

But instead he said, "The only curse is here, in the real world."

To which the old woman responded, "The whore is evil."

The men told Georges-Minh they had cast their carp net into the Saigon River and fished out the body. "We couldn't tell if she was still breathing."

When Georges-Minh unwound the white shroud, a mosquito net, the smell of weeds and mud rose from her body and permeated the room.

The whole group vortexed to the clinic's centre, dizzying the doctor.

"She's only a girl," he said.

"I know," the old woman said. "I know." Her voice was not unkind now. She rubbed Georges-Minh's shoulder. "And then someone"—she shook her head vehemently—"cursed her. Not even death can purify her now."

The girl's body, necklaced with minnows, writhed. She sat up and reached. Her fingers groped, sightlessly, for something to hold. Her clothes, a silver gyration, jewel-scaled, blinded as they caught the light in flashes. Georges-Minh staggered, never having seen a mermaid. Minnows in her left eye socket, her hair, mixing with her blood and pooling in the shallows where she'd been stabbed. They slipped from her wounds onto the examination table. From her mouth when she opened it, tried to speak.

The onlookers fell to their knees. "It's an omen!"

The Catholics among them made the sign of the cross.

Others looked to the ceiling fan and wept. A woman pleading for her soul recited the Vedas.

"What will become of us?"

"What do I do with what I've seen?"

"Pluck out my eyes?"

The pandemonium rose. Two medical officers corralled the group, begging for calm in the tone of voice one uses to calm oxen during a thunderstorm. They motioned the people toward the exit.

How could her body be so infested with fish yet still hold the breath of life?

In the surrounding mayhem Georges-Minh inserted two fingers into her mouth and scooped out the minnows. He cleared a passageway so she could breathe.

"I'm fourteen," she said. Her panicked voice cut the back of his neck like a small razor.

"Tell me who did this."

"I'm fourteen."

"Do you know what happened?"

"Fourteen."

To each question she repeated the same answer. He'd watched flies paralyzed by spiders, drained of life in webs while fully cognizant. What a way to go—aware of life leaching away, unable to do damn about it. How he felt. Did the fly respect his foe or spend his last minute cursing God?

Yet such things happened all the time. He saw them. Their society, their lot, no matter how much they hollered to convince themselves otherwise.

Then, a new lucidity. "Am I going to be okay?"

"You're fourteen." Georges-Minh tamped her wounds with gauze that reddened in seconds. Gauged his losing battle by the fading meter of her heart. "You're strong."

This calmed her. He repeated it. "You're strong."

She smiled.

"I think you're going to be okay." He stopped bandaging. Stroked her fish hair and told her what she needed to hear, until she took her last breath and died on the examination table.

The vacuum of her death sucked him in. At the instant of her death he lost his breath, and in the days to come he remembered thinking, perhaps when a soul left its body in trauma, it snatched the air from the room, from the building, and the lungs of the people in it out of revenge and spite.

After a quick trip to the underworld, a hungry ghost returned, impelled by bitterness.

He would never know if she'd been beaten by her pimp and left for dead on the banks to roll into the river herself. Maybe a bamboo's sadistic matron had beaten the girl and thrown her into the river, where two boatmen had then seen her body floating and fished her from the current. Had it been an unsatisfied customer? Or had she tried to kill herself, far from home?

Georges-Minh sank to the ground where fish surrounded him, beating their tails against the floor.

If only he had a girlfriend. Someone to talk to. When he reached for his handkerchief, a minnow slithered between his fingers. He threw it against the wall.

5

Later that night a woman in an uncharacteristically expensive European jacket walked into the clinic. She told Georges-Minh, "You'd never know it to look at me but I was coughing till I thought my lungs were going to come out of my mouth!"

"Has this happened to you before?"

She waved her hand. "All the time." She'd coughed for twenty minutes until she couldn't breathe. Normally she took syrup of poppies, an opiate. Her prescription had run out. "I was afraid of having another fit. Otherwise I'd have waited till morning."

"What are you doing in this neighbourhood?"

It was forward to ask. But it was forward of her to be there. In her clothes, shoes, haircut, swinging that purse. Who did she think she was with that audacious skin? Those pupils? That grin? Those teeth, fingernails, that chuckle? Acting so flippant about her cough, tossing her hair, he could snap her wrists *like that*. Her capacity to make good choices was suspect. Certainly, in the months to come, as he questioned the singularity of his decision, he would wonder how much the mermaid wheeling round the clinic ceiling had to do with it and if the ectoplasmic blur may have tricked him into seeing silk where there was merely hair, a gait more seductive than a woman's real-life walk, teeth whiter than white, a gaze more piercing. In hindsight everything appears twenty-twenty, so they say. At the time one choice seemed all he had: one alluring smile, one stunning creature in a European jacket. The mermaid had left him with an empty hole, raw as the socket of a tooth.

Indeed, when the clinic door opened it suddenly became easy to rise from the floor, surrounded by flapping fish or not. He ran his hands through his hair and greeted her. Invisible threads, something like kite strings that had been connecting his body to the mermaid's, now transformed into silken threads and grew thinner and snapped. The circling banshee grew diaphanous, disappeared. The remaining mist refreshed them. A moment ago he'd believed he deserved to be haunted. Now he was looking ahead. Already he could hear Chang asking, "Don't you think you're rushing things?"

"Like a speeding bullet," he'd say.

He put her up on the pedestal of his examination table. This alone made her deserving. For now it was enough to idealize her shoulders. Wasn't it? Never mind analyzing the feeling. The kite strings were gone.

Funny to think how one's world unravels a certain way because someone picks this clinic instead of that, takes a stroll by the water—imagine if she'd come tomorrow instead of tonight, he would have been sitting at home listening to the *Messiah* on his fold-top Victrola.

Her collarbone showed through her blouse; the silk pussy-footed there. (He gleaned in a matter of seconds that the chuckle was a facade—but the *silk*, she couldn't make that up, that wasn't bravado, that was real.) When you left a summer house and draped the furniture with sheets, the feeling when you shut the door: this was her. "I'm Dong."

"What are you doing in this neighbourhood?" he asked again. He needed to know the truth.

"Are you cross-examining me? I saw the lights of the clinic..." She trailed off when she saw his expression. "I like the water." She stared back at him, a what-are-you-going-to-make-of-it look in her eyes. Something passed between them.

"There's lots of water"—his tone implied in other, safer places. Why was she coming down where poor people lived? Was she like him? Were they kindred? Did she resent her money? He wanted to learn how those less fortunate lived, wear it like a suit. Then he'd know who he was. When he spoke their language people would call out his name: not Dr. Nguyen, but Georges-Minh.

He didn't comment on the designer jacket, though he wanted to. He examined her. In a tone of authority asked her to lift her blouse, his voice cracking with nerves.

"You could drive me home," she added, "if you're worried." She touched his hand and he nearly choked on his own saliva. "That *is* your car parked out front, isn't it?"

Georges-Minh and Lieutenant Colonel Janvier, head of the French garrison at Saigon, owned the same type of vehicle, a Panhard Levassor, though Colonel Janvier's was the newest six-horsepower model while Georges-Minh's had been his father's and state of the art only when it came out in 1891. Still, the two men shared the distinction of owning the only two imported Parisian automobiles in all of Saigon and it was for this reason alone that Lieutenant Colonel Janvier had once summoned Dr. Nguyen Georges-Minh to his quarters at the garrison.

Janvier motioned Georges-Minh over to the shade of the cracked fortress wall creeping green with geckos and dillenia.

The colonel ran his hands against his car's open sides, the flat roof like a parasol with silver tassels, the black-cushioned driver's seat, the rumble seat. Georges-Minh was admittedly impressed.

"Notice the brass." Janvier's passengers sat not under a canopy of fabric, but beneath a teak roof, sleek as a ship's. "I make sure it's shined daily by my *gabier*, my right-hand man, whom I'll introduce you to later." Georges-Minh's yellow-painted wooden wheels a farm wagon's in contrast to Janvier's rubber tires, whose rims were painted candy red.

"It sold for thirty-five hundred francs at the time," Georges-Minh said of his own vehicle, in apology, "when it was new."

"Come, come, let's have a drink."

Janvier owned a home in the same neighbourhood as Georges-Minh but never spent the whole night in his own bed. His overly cramped quarters made him claustrophobic. He had trouble sleeping most nights and often lay down on the couch in his office, asking his *gabier* to stand guard. Because of his erratic sleeping patterns it was not unknown for him to fall asleep in the day, suddenly, in the middle of a conversation.

A highly devout man, it was also not unknown for him to wake up from a dead sleep in the middle of the night and decide to interrogate someone, but not before waking up his entire staff for prayer circle.

An amateur filmmaker, he directed his own movies. He once pulled all the fingernails off a suspect and titled the series "The Separations."

Colonel Janvier's health problems included ailments to his heart, stomach, and liver brought on by drinking, stress, and rich foods, for which Dr. Nguyen prescribed a daily regimen of medicines including detoxifiers and tonics. He also tried to prescribe regular exercise and an increase in the colonel's intake of fruits and vegetables, advice that Lieutenant Colonel Janvier followed only marginally.

Her skin was the colour of fried ginger when you first throw it in the pan. When the oil has just become hot enough to scent the air and cause tiny bubbles to appear around the base of a wooden chopstick lowered into it to test the temperature. If he placed his thumb between the second and third vertebrae he knew exactly how her flesh would feel against his thumb.

Rub marks crisscrossed her back, which smelled faintly of jasmine oil. A jade coin had been dragged along either side of her spine: the crime of traditional remedies for pleurisy on such a fine body. Abuse, if you asked him. Smooth strokes on either side of the spine moved out toward the shoulders, crimson line upon line, reminding him of the structural composition of flower petals.

He asked her to take a deep breath and watched her chest rise and fall, the outline of each rib, and recalled the cages he had seen at the market that housed songbirds. Birds with bones filled with air. Like bamboo. The chief thing was to pay attention to the task at hand. He told himself to refocus. His face flushed.

"Turn, please."

But the truth was more obvious than the pupils and lashes and the brightness of her eyes combined. The reeds could bend with every ripple but here she was, more beautiful with every inhalation, and here he was again. Blinking, looking away, reprimanding himself. He tapped her chest with the flat of two fingers—a percussion of muffled sound.

This small, subtle physical event between them, this examination, was provoking him so, to such a degree, and without warning—it must be the fish girl. There was no other explanation. Still, he was a doctor, a professional. He had to get hold of himself. Otherwise he should excuse himself. Leave her in the care of a colleague. And go home now.

The area below his stomach burned, and the heat swelled, radiating outward. Flustered by the scent of jasmine, still reeling from the fish girl, he envisioned himself asking the woman to dinner. Running his fingers through her hair the colour of spilled ink.

Torture, sheer torture, her fingers on her blouse, he could imagine them in his mouth. Then the buttons. Her hair, in a ponytail, the clinic door opening and a breeze moving the few strands ever so slightly across the blouse, across her cheek as she buttoned her blouse, one button after another, with those fingers. The wait was interminable and the sweat that dripped down his back felt like the Chinese water torture he'd heard about or read of in books, he couldn't remember which now, either way, he thought he'd leap out of his skin and wanted to scream but all he could do was sit very still with the mask of a placid smile on his face, his hands clasped, waiting for her to finish. One button after another. Was she torturing him on purpose? As for Dong she was thinking about how much longer she could stretch out each motion. Man's desperation and their footing of the dinner bill went hand in hand. As she smoothed her fingers round the circle of each button top she pictured exactly how the doctor would pull out her chair from the table (chivalrously), uncork the wine and pour it, swirling it in the glass (sophisticatedly), commenting on its flavour. He was cute, she thought. For him, dinner, then, bigger designs? She was no fool.

A man wanted to feel wanted. And in control. To make him think he'd determined everything. That was the trick. She neither liked nor disliked who she'd become. It was simply a part of life. Like the overshoes she put on in the morning.

Taking her time? How long did it take to button a blouse? Now licking her lips? Her pale, almost grey-blue lips as she nattered on about "… thank you so much for this bottle of—I really appreciate it—don't know what I'd do if I didn't have some syrup to last me till tomorrow …" forced him to clasp his hands, the fingertips turning white, then purple. It took every ounce of his power to stop himself from screaming. Inhale, exhale. Had she no idea?

But of course this was the ruse. To give off the impression that she didn't.

No, she didn't. Going on and on. Now rocking as she sat on the examination table, twisting this way and that. The smell of her perfume, was it really jasmine? He looked around. Could anyone else tell what he was going through?

The body of the fish girl still lay in the corner. Tomorrow someone would get it, the creature would be gone. Two creatures. Both magical. What were the odds? Two magical creatures in one night. Listen to him. Had he gone mad? What would Khieu think? Buttons. Buttons. How much longer? This long, when your finger lingered on the glass bead, lingered there, the way a strawberry lingered at your lips when you weren't sure whether to bite down or not, savouring the cold, or the heat, the texture, the little seeds, the way it tickled your lip.

"So? How much do you think? Should I take? I mean if it comes back before morning because I've already taken, um, how much now?"

"What?"

"Because I've already taken … three teaspoons?"

"Oh—this? You can, take—" He looked at the bottle. "Four, no, two." He'd lost himself, as with the fugue.

She gave him a few piastres and he watched her walk out of the clinic, realizing in the next minute he'd never know who she was, having learned neither her last name nor her address.

Oh, well. She knew where to find him if she wanted.

Chang, the court translator and lover of books, rapped on the clinic door and Georges-Minh, the last person in the clinic as usual, sighed as he unbolted the lock.

Chang's patient smile filled him with a guilt-ridden tenderness. One always feels badly toward the thing one has hurt. Chang's sunny disposition infuriated Georges-Minh, who was melancholic by nature, and secretly envied his swish, his walk as if dancing. His disdain for what people might suspect. What if people thought he was gay? He swung his hips, sometimes trilled when he spoke. Didn't he care if he became a joke?

Georges-Minh felt so invisible some days, a beam of light could pass right through him. If he opened his mouth no one would be able to hear a single word. He kept his armour close no matter what the heartache.

Chang was a songbird. He would sing his song whatever people might think. He swung into a room and chirped the gossip of the day. How could Georges-Minh respond any way but gruffly?

"Of *all* nights for you to come," Georges-Minh said.

"Rough one?"

Georges-Minh shrugged.

Chang often came to visit Georges-Minh and the two would talk, or read each other their favourite lines of poetry, or drink plum wine until the sun came up to stave off the loneliness they both understood. Whenever Chang frowned or smiled, the right corner of his generous mouth moved more slowly than the left.

Chang took off his hat and scratched his head as if Georges-Minh might have been trying to imply something. "Why? You want me to go?"

"No, nothing like that. Just a crazy night."

"Do tell."

Georges-Minh thought about telling Chang everything that had happened but instead said, "Some crazy whore scratched me." He didn't really think of them as whores but was angry about the child.

"Is that her, on the other side of the window, glaring at us?"

"No, wait, that's … nothing."

"Ugh." Chang shuddered. "It's not nothing. It's a hungry ghost."

"Like I said. No, wait. It's a kid."

"It's just one of those opium boys."

"Get! Get out of here!"

The missing words lodged like fish bones in Georges-Minh's throat. Because the incident, his shame, the mermaid was over, there was nothing left to say. "I think I'm coming down with a flu."

The opium boys looked in at the lights of the clinic burning after hours with longing, in particular Sing Sing, the mixed-race boy who had spoken with Georges-Minh earlier, the doe-eyed one with skin the colour of tea who thought himself separate from the herd. He balanced on a barrel next to his friend Luc, who rarely left his side. As if one day Sing Sing would rise above it all and escape the streets because of his mixed heritage. One day he'd become more than he was, have a place to go where he belonged, have a place that belonged to him, just like the doctor.

Sing Sing had felt hurt at the doctor's suggestion that he throw himself in harm's way just to capture that girl. A dumb girl. The doctor was obviously *mad*. He was just a boy, and after all, she'd attacked the doctor, a grown man.

Maybe eleven or twelve Sing Sing was, not even sure himself when or even where he was born. He'd introduced himself to the doctor once, proud to tell him his great-grandfather had been a member of the Expeditionary Corps. Yet the doctor hadn't even remembered Sing Sing's name.

Sing Sing pressed himself to the glass while the two men talked and shared a bottle that the visitor had pulled from his jacket. The two, oblivious to his presence, read from a book. Sing Sing's nostrils steamed the window as he huffed in disgust.

"Watcha doing?" Luc said.

Sing Sing shoved his friend away with his foot. "Nothing."

"What the fuck? Why you always spy on them?"

"Fuck you."

Luc tried to push his way up onto the barrel to see. "Just a couple of homos. Who gives a shit?"

Sing Sing couldn't explain. His hurt at being excluded. A privileged pain he wanted to share with Luc least of all, another opium boy, a mere street urchin, with no mixed blood. Most of all he wanted to get back at the doctor, who'd had no right to yell at him for not catching the girl who'd scratched the doctor and run. *Sing Sing*. The doctor hadn't even remembered his name.

The doctor was weeping now and the man with the brandy was stroking his hair. Kissing his face.

"Want me to stroke your pipe while you watch?" Luc mocked.

"You ass fairy."

"You're the one watching."

"Turtlehead."

"Grease rag," Luc said.

"Cream."

"Butter."

"Female toad."

"Oh, go fuck your ancestors," Luc retorted.

"You know what? You're less than human," Sing Sing said.

"You know what? You're *shameless* and less than human."

"Oh, yeah? You're shameless *and* a son of a turtlehead *and* less than human."

Sing Sing stepped away from the window and sat on the ground beneath it. "Fine, whatever, I'm done. This is stupid, anyway."

Georges-Minh took comfort where it hurt, letting Chang do what he did best. His mouth and full lips banished the crazy whore, the cheek gouged by a woman he was merely trying to help, the mermaid he'd killed, his lost memory, the report he was supposed to have made to the Centre for Infectious Disease Control and had completely forgotten.

His shame of the past twenty-four hours exploded in a paroxysm.

Georges-Minh took. Chang gave. Sometimes Georges-Minh withdrew even his taking. The confusion left Chang exhausted. It terrified him. That one day Georges-Minh would roll over, back glistening with sweat. And never turn round to face him again.

"What if I loved you," Chang asked him once. They were high on opium. Chang had brought him to a den. Georges-Minh's first time.

"Ha. You can't cage a songbird."

"Touch me," Chang said.

Georges-Minh laughed again. Wouldn't take him seriously. "Give me the pipe."

"Doctor, what are you playing?"

When Georges-Minh looked up from the bottle, Chang was grinning. "What?" Georges-Minh asked.

"You've got me in your waiting room. I'm in a difficult place, you know."

"Why are you always so serious?" Georges-Minh said.

"You're looking at my crotch," Chang said.

Georges-Minh couldn't help but suppress a small smile. "I haven't put you there. You are right about the crotch, wrong about the waiting room."

"*You're* wrong," Chang said.

Georges-Minh poked him in the ribs. "I am fond of you."

The following day, on his way to the clinic, Georges-Minh entered the humid offices of the Centre for Infectious Disease Control and, although recognizing their scant resources would have little effect in stopping the spread of anything, told them about the two men he'd seen at the clinic and the one he'd seen at his home, how he'd treated them for what may be a new type of paddy fever, and he mentioned the black-spotted rash and the lingering memory loss. He omitted mentioning the girl, the one who'd scratched his cheek, even though he'd thought about her since yesterday because of the way she'd said, "Who am I?" not once, but twice, and he also deliberately left out mentioning his own brush with amnesia. He'd never before seen a contagious disease that allowed spirits to infect the bodies of the living. But, since ignoring spirits was a matter of pride, he kept out this information as well.

As Georges-Minh had predicted, the conversation swung around to the lack of resources, the lack of infrastructure, lack of hygiene among the peasants and working class.

"I'm writing a paper," the charge physician, a Frenchman whose name was Michaut, said. *"Contributions to the Study of the Manifestations of Male Hysteria."*

The other day Georges-Minh had been sitting inside, and the burden of air that sagged on the furniture, the paper flowers in crystal vases, Chinese crepe-paper dragons propped behind picture frames like museum pieces stale with loss, temporary as the stuff from which they were made, caused him, suddenly, to run from the house. And he was weeping.

He ran to the garden and the sun was shining uncontrollably. An intense feeling of life washed over him, as if he'd fallen into the river.

He wondered now, Was he a male hysteric? How else could he be suicidal one minute and ecstatic the next? Could that be why he'd lost his memory?

6

During the following weeks, Georges-Minh tossed and turned more than he slept. He treated seven more cases: four men and three women, a banker, a coolie, a truck driver, a physician, a student, and two housewives. He wondered if children had a natural immunity for he hadn't come across a single one in clinical practice. Everyone around him seemed to be losing his memory. He tried to infect himself with the paddy fever infecting others. Why couldn't he lose his, at least on a more permanent basis than he had? Was he immune? He waited for another amnesiac fugue. He thought of reading Freud himself. Maybe he could find some clues, identify what might bring one on: part of him was curious, from a medical point of view; the other was simply craving, in the most pathetic way possible, a chance to feel new.

He searched for love everywhere: for the woman he'd met at the clinic. He was rewarded by stealing glimpses of her in the red-lantern-lit shops of the retail centre, the rice paddies, the covered market with a roof like that of a shed, the river shore in the open spaces between houses filled with arrack palms, the café, the bar populated by Foreign Legionnaires, Moroccan conscripts, Senegalese sharpshooters, and European merchants, the doorways of opium houses, the Botanical Gardens outside Saigon, which were open twenty-four hours.

A most amazing witch who could be in twelve places at one time, she appeared in an *ao dai*, then an evening gown, then with a shawl wrapped around her waist. In squares of cloth like a Moy. A brightly coloured cloak. A blue chemise. Or with her hair in different colours. Or in a head cap. Or with a swanlike neck. Once he was sure he even saw her face in the body of a two-hundred-pound woman.

Then he spotted her—at last, the real her. Her appearance stoked the fire into a blaze which had burned inside him for weeks. She entered the Cao Dai temple, where he burned incense for his father every Wednesday, by way of the main gate, beyond which the city's urban sprawl was held at bay. She passed through the garden and for an instant the bodhi tree shadowed her face. After weeks of seeing doppelgängers, he feared it might not be the real her. The incense trembled in his sweat-moistened palm. As he trailed after her through the dragon-adorned entrance he tripped on a dead mouse in the door jamb.

He forced himself to stand next to her while she murmured prayers, taking deep breaths, trying to detect the scent of jasmine, the perfume he remembered from the clinic. The temple smelled of incense and burning mosquito coils made it more difficult.

"Oh, you're the doctor." Her smile turned his knees to bean paste. She said she was at the temple to burn incense for her cat, an impish look in her eyes. Her cat had gone missing. She hadn't seen her for three days.

Of wild cats the city had enough. They jumped into windows left ajar and ate food not locked away until housewives were afraid to open their homes to the breeze. If cornered, they clawed. Rumour was they'd even killed a baby. The city's medical health officer had written a report for the regional branch of the French colonial administration, published in the *Saigon Daily* newspaper, proposing a bloody cull. "Your cat has gone missing? Well, don't worry. She'll return. You can bet on it!" he said, disguising his doubt with a loud voice.

"Cats get hit by rickshaws every day, or become stray-dog food, or are even torn apart by alley rats. I'm praying, not for her return, but for her soul." She turned away, completed her recitation.

Looking back toward him, away from the statue, she told him she had other pets. Pigeons, and a python. Her python ate rats, and sometimes rabbits. It had been quite *nippy* as a baby, but now it never bit at all. She fed her pigeons peanuts. Her father had wanted to eat them, the birds, because—of course—they kept *breeding*, but she wouldn't let him. He could buy regular market pigeons for that. "He thinks I don't know when one goes missing, but I do. He tries to do that, trick me. But I count them. I know each one by heart." Only one day the snake had gotten loose and she'd found pigeon feathers scattered about. But she had gone to the market that same day and bought two more to replace the pigeons she'd lost.

Timid under her gaze, but propelled by the fire in his stomach, so like *heartburn*—yes, that was it, a burning heart—he asked her, again, what she'd been doing in the harbour area that night the ache had started.

She laughed, in a flirty way. "Why? Are you afraid of cutthroats?"

On the contrary, he told her. He equated poverty with toughness. "I know I shouldn't but they have something I don't, some kind of resilience, you know? People who've had it soft whine, and those who've had it rough complain the least. It's not like I'd say let's trade places and think my life would be better. Poverty-equals-holiness is too simple an equation. But still. Even the children have something inside them they can pull out like a knife to protect them from life's hazards. Switchblade strength. Yes, that's it."

"Switchblade strength? Ah, someone who fancies himself a poet. I'm not nearly so artsy. It's just sometimes I need to get out of the house. My mom drives me crazy."

"Parents are supposed to drive you crazy."

"Do yours?"

"Mine are dead."

"I'm sorry."

"Don't be. I'm not." He flinched. What would she think of him? That he was cold. Maybe even callous—women liked tough guys, not sociopaths. "Death is a part of life," he said, to soften his words.

"It doesn't make it any easier. You get used to people. Even their bad habits. Anyway, mine nag."

She lit her incense sticks from the fire in the drum. "Do this, don't do that," she said, imitating their voices. The incense sticks caught the flame, which leaped up the sides of the drum. "Oh, look, you've done that wrong," she said, continuing to mock them. She yanked the sticks out of the fire drum. The conflagration moved skyward. "You haven't done this right at all, Dong," she admonished in the voice of a nagging mother. "Open your eyes."

She tucked a strand of hair behind her ear, tried to blow out the flames. They blazed brighter. She grinned at Georges-Minh. Blew again. They formed a torch. Took a deeper breath. Blew. A dangerous *flambeau*. She waved the flaming pennon and shrugged. "No wonder you did such a poor job," she mimicked. "But maybe they're right. Holy shit—I'm about to set myself on fire. I just need to get out of the house sometimes! *God damn!*"

She bowed in prayer, this direction and that, the incense sticks aflame all the while.

"Are you almost finished?" Georges-Minh asked. "I'm worried about you there."

She laughed. "Good thing I know a competent doctor."

"Cheap vendors! One day someone's going to catch fire," he said. "Someone's coat's going to go up in flames because of a second-rate incense maker with no care for his art, only concerned with profits."

"Are you always so serious?"

He let her complete her obeisance. When she was done she fed the flames by throwing the remnants of her incense sticks into them.

Right now she was working as a nanny in a French household, she said, brushing the ash off her hands, but she would like to get a job working as a tour guide or even as an interpreter at the law courts. Maybe, in time. She adjusted the bag slung over her shoulder. "My parents are overprotective. I like to come down to the harbour. Take a walk on the wild side." She winked.

"I admire the poor," he said. "Like the cork from a bottle of wine, no matter how you push them down, they keep popping back up, again and again."

"Isn't that a little romantic?"

He flushed. He'd made himself sound like an ass. He was talking to someone just as smart as or smarter than himself, not some simple schoolgirl. He'd wanted to impress her with his kind heart. Now he looked the fool.

She play-punched his arm. "Just teasing."

Peeking from the top of her bag was a volume of poetry by Phi, a revolutionary, member of the Tonkin Free School.

"I went to the French Preparatory College," she said, noticing him look.

He wondered about never having seen her there, but the place was so large, and they weren't exactly the same age. "Me too."

7

Thu had heard about Dr. Nguyen from Gigi, who turned tricks in "The Church of Rome," once a chapel used by Catholic missionaries. In the fancy quarters, houses were identified by their blue venetian blinds, and so were sometimes called Blue Houses. The houses may have had names such as "Brilliant Field of Flowers" or "Club of the Mandarins' Ducks" or even "The Dwelling of the Singing Nightingale." Lately, in order to get out of doing her chores at the inn, Thu told Mai and Crazy Auntie that she had a friend, a poor single mother, who was in trouble. It wasn't really a lie. In a sense these girls lived on the cusp of danger all the time. And wasn't Thu thinking of putting herself there, on the brink of menace just to help out her sorry little family? Maybe. Look at the clothes they wore: white, blue, and black silk chemises; green, orange, or yellow silk robes; a hat with a chiffon ribbon; Chinese varnished shoes— such an outfit would cost thirty piastres at least! One gold bracelet would set you back three hundred. Gold earrings, a silver leg bangle, a jade ring, another hundred and fifty each.

Not bad at all. Did they ever worry about going hungry? Did they ever worry about being old and poor? Maybe. Maybe less than she did.

Thu carried water for foot-washing, prepared alum solution for the girls to disinfect with, replaced the coconut oil in the lamps, or refilled the pipes with opium when the customers ran out. Madame, who owned The Church of Rome, paid Thu a few tien for her troubles but only because her leering eye was on her to soon take her place among Gigi and her friends with their pomaded hair elaborately styled into place once a month by a professional who also made for them a wooden pillow to sleep on at night with a carved-out space for their curls. For how much longer Madame would let her work Thu didn't know because Madame also had men who acted as bodyguards to do these chores.

"This dupe, this mark with too much money and a heart, all the girls have had a turn working him at one time or another— too bad he's got a girlfriend now." Gigi was a half-breed Portuguese with an aquiline nose and eyes the colour of amber. She always wore silk dressing gowns with elaborate embroideries of Asian landscapes that her boyfriend bought her. He wasn't a customer but a real boyfriend who paid for her apartment. "He never wanted to sleep with any of us. It was awesome."

"Cute?" Thu asked. "The doctor, I mean?"

"I guess. Round face, little glasses like this. I guess you could say he's cute. Like an owl."

"That's not cute."

"You know what I mean. Not *that* kind of cute. The other kind. Like a stuffed toy."

"Hey, can I ask you something? Why do you still work if you have a boyfriend?"

"I don't want to upset the power balance," Gigi said. "I need my own money. Besides, he doesn't care, he's *progressive*, bohemian, a painter. Anyway, I make more money than he does." Gigi shrugged. "If you're seeing Dr. Nguyen, if you still want to give it a try, don't go to the clinic, go to his house. It's easier to play the sympathy card on their home turf, where they feel more powerful. On the other hand, if you're going to try the sex angle, which, with his type, wouldn't have worked anyway, the clinic's the better bet, away from reminders of where he and his girlfriend last did the dirty. You'll get more than most either way—you're his type."

"His type?"

"Sorry-ass."

"Thanks."

"Seriously, downtrodden's a good angle. But bring the kids. Definitely bring the kids. Hell, borrow some if you can. He's a sucker for kids."

"What did you mean, his type?"

"Likes boys, but doesn't know it."

After a moment of silence they both laughed.

Thu borrowed Mai's children and bribed them with sweets to keep their mouths shut. She had to wait until Mai took her mid-afternoon nap to smuggle the baby out of the house; Thu figured the baby would bring her luck. Her mission was two-fold: to get needed funds but also to have Cong examined. Mai wouldn't: too superstitious, she still believed her herbs and spells would do the trick. And Thu truly believed the baby might be sicker than she had once thought. She loved the baby as if she'd given birth to him herself and if Mai wasn't going to do right by him then Thu was going to have to take action herself.

The doctor turned out to be just what Gigi had promised. He chose from a jumble of trumpets that hung on the wall and played music, to which the children swayed while sucking the sugar from their fingertips and trying to hum to the beat. "Stop that," she shushed them, tried to jerk them still. Tugged their fingers from their mouths. It was important he think she was innocent of raising wild children who were suddenly behaving like street urchins, acting as if they'd never seen sugar cane sticks or heard jazz music before. But the oldest boy still wore a topknot and there was no way around Dr. Nguyen believing she was a backwoods mother, even if only a pretend one. When the boy turned twelve, Mai would cut his topknot, and not a day before.

He listened to the baby's heart with a specialized device.

"Can you tell anything yet?"

He turned the baby over. "The symptoms are nonspecific, I'm afraid. At this point I can't be sure, it could be any number of things."

Thu felt a sinking in her chest.

The baby needed more tests, he said. Some things took time. Some things required patience.

Thu would find a way to sneak the baby out of the house again, and the other children too if she needed to. She agreed she would return, next week? But for now, was there anything the doctor could give them? Especially the infant?

He fetched a bottle of syrup from the shelf and Thu listened to the thump, thump of the bottle and the doctor returned and placed the bottle in her hand and said, "Try this. It's an all-purpose vitamin. A fortifier."

"Thank you, you're so generous."

"Normally I write a script, but I can see, in your case, a widow. This isn't from the clinic. I manufacture my own supply. I have a clinic in my house. In Thao Dien. Are you familiar with the area?"

When Thu further explained their dire situation, staring not at him but at the documents in frames behind his head, Dr. Nguyen dug into his pocket and pulled out his wallet. Then he drew a little map and pressed it into her hand. Although he was naive he was beautiful in his round glasses, and a piece of her heart began to love him. She promised she would return next week, and he smiled with just enough of a twinkle in his eye that Thu believed she may have provoked his manhood, and she knew if he wanted her to she'd have offered him and his trumpet a harbour for his soul.

8

Georges-Minh invited Dong for tea at Khieu's urging. Georges-Minh, who was used to playing it safe, even when it meant missing out on life, had to fight every cautious tendency he had. Because for weeks his emotions had ridden him, leaving him exhausted, a faceless man caught in no man's land. Georges-Minh would have thought, in his case, money would have substituted for charm and that by now wealth would have brought him marital happiness. But in fact it was exactly his father's money and the problem of its many branches that seemed to be making it harder for him to talk to the fairer sex, weakening him from the inside out.

The problem of his father's money would not go away overnight or without planning. This problem called for a practical solution—and Georges-Minh had found one. He would ask Dong to marry him. Dong could deal with the deep red cushions and imported tiles and rosewood carvings. She appreciated nice things—expensive European jacket—and when children came along, his absolution would be complete.

He chose a tea set that had been his mother's. She came, this creature he'd seen on the examination table, and then in the temple, who came on with the force of a monsoon. Too brash. And she spoke out as if words did not bear thinking over first. He was drawn to her the way one might be to the panther in the Botanical Gardens, but there were no bars between them.

She was just what he needed, he told himself. Maybe she could absorb some of the chaotic confusion within him the way a cloth whisks away spilled wine from a dinner table and you never have to look at it again.

They drank jasmine tea in the shade of a potted tree with shadows to hide in when he blushed, as when he blew into his cup, drank, and scalded his tongue anyway.

Sipping, he thought to himself: this woman has two souls. She who wore clothes tailored to fit her body, nurtured pythons, and read Tonkin Free School poetry. The other part of her, the one he'd seen on the examination table, contrasted sharply with the opinionated creature who spoke her mind out of turn: a creature whom illness had hallowed, consecrated, sainted. Opinions fevered her mind. He could get very used to her as a wife.

He took her on a tour of his estate. The house, the only one in Thao Dien with a circular driveway, had a wing in which he saw patients and another where he made his own pharmaceuticals near the garden and the cabbage palm trees. The villa boasted a dining room the length of a tennis court on the second floor, as well as one on the first. Sometimes, the sheer vastness of the space daunted him. Though his villa was his sanctuary, he imagined what it might be like with a delirium of domestic energy to fill it. The living room spanned the length of the kitchen, which was a row of planted bamboo, and along the wall stood ornamental urns big enough for a small boy to hide inside.

They spoke about the ideals they shared, turning the words *justice* and *equality* into Cupid's arrows and aiming them at each other.

Two souls: part angel, part witch. An enamel of civility coating a spirit of earth, like the enamel around an iron teapot—but she was not a teapot, why was he thinking of cookware? He was losing his head. Because of her. The realist and the dreamer. He did not doubt her intellect. Only such a woman could find elegance in market pigeons, tame a python.

"Did you know prostitutes, these Brown Hollands, are so-called after a coarse fabric of the same name?"

"No, *really*, Mr. Information of the strange and useless kind." She smiled and stretched out her leg, putting her toes in his lap.

"I don't charge anyone at the clinic."

"You charged me."

"No—I mean my home one. If they can't pay, I don't turn anyone away. Thing is, the Brown Hollands, they can't afford anything. Not really. And that's the problem. But they want what the French have, things they never heard about before or cared about before: chocolate, caviar, asparagus. Status symbols. These things cost money."

"Do I hear some *passion*?"

Dong believed that because he had never been poor, had never had to share what little he had, he could feel nothing but glee at the prospect of sharing. Which, she reminded him, was different from being actually poor and forced to share half of nothing. She was not reprimanding him. She spoke with tenderness, and with the pleasure that one person experiences when beginning to understand the soul of another. But she had never really been poor either, she made a point of telling him. Her father, born a peasant farmer, had gone on to pass the triennial mandarin examination and had become a judge. "So what do either one of us know?" she ribbed him.

"I don't mean to be harsh," she said, "but isn't it shallow to confuse poverty with self-worth? Just as it's equally shallow to call a poor man a sinner and a rich man a saint simply because they are rich or poor? Naturally, stated this way, the value judgment seems ridiculous. Anyway, what stops you from selling all this junk and just living the life you want to live?"

Georges-Minh, wanting so badly to justify himself and seem worthy in her eyes, said, "We're plotting, you know." The words just slipped out. The next thing he knew he was telling her all about their group. *Datura stramonium*. The French garrison.

It was well known within the group that still had no official name that Georges-Minh had ethical difficulties with the killing of so many men. As a way of saving lives he had suggested to Khieu killing just a single man—a symbol, a figurehead: Lieutenant Colonel Janvier. Bao, because he had a wife, and Chang, out of loyalty to his friend, sided with Georges-Minh. Those with less on the line, like Phuc, preferred the bravado of Khieu's plan—kill every last soldier in the garrison.

It has to be stated that even as the suggestion to kill Lieutenant Colonel Janvier came out of Georges-Minh's mouth, deep down he believed it would never happen. How long had they been meeting and drinking wine, playing cards, stumbling home? He said it mostly to impress Khieu. None, other than Khieu, were motivated by a desire to save the world.

Georges-Minh was a pillar of the community. A doctor. Son of a wealthy businessman.

"We hit the French at the top and send a powerful message to our people," he said, "giving our side the ideological boost they need."

Georges-Minh said the words and didn't think of them again. Instead, he thought of his friends, looked at each of them in turn, Phuc, Bao, Khieu, Chang, the lowering sun, the river outside, teacups filled with mulberry wine. Had he gotten through to any of them? Khieu took the fish eye from the cod they were sharing and sucked the gelatinous mass, excitement on his face.

"Not all of us want to run for our lives," said Chang.

"What did you think you were signing up for?" said Phuc, the pipa player. He hadn't worked for a month and lived in a hovel with barely enough space to turn around. No one in the south wanted to hear the folk music he played. He'd fled a famine in the north five years ago. Now his wife was gone and he lived in a city where pipa music was considered quaint but passé. When he'd tried to work construction, the foreman had nearly beaten him with a hammer for his clumsiness. He'd tried his hand at cooking and burned himself. He'd tried to kill himself drinking snake wine and had woken up in an alley covered with vomit. He failed at all things but pipa playing.

"It's not like they know who the members of our group are." Phuc blew one smoke ring into another smaller smoke ring. "What are you scared of? The hit's going to be anonymous."

"But we don't want it to be," Khieu corrected. "They will know us soon. This act of rebellion will put us on the map. And into the hearts of the people!"

Khieu was tougher, always would be. Sometimes, next to him, Georges-Minh felt like a bit actor in his own life. Georges-Minh's best friend had long been hooked on animistic beliefs, creation legends, and searching the sky for old earth and water spirits. He'd also reworked his beliefs to include new magical systems. For him, spacecraft in their circularity were nothing other than God. Georges-Minh envied Khieu. His pseudo-research gave him a connection to something larger than himself and a lifeline to place.

The irony was that spaceships shattered his idea of the known world—so the lust for unity became a destructive force.

It was a riddle without end, a fatal disturbance for them both. Still, Georges-Minh couldn't help but respect Khieu's commitment to a cause. Khieu was dying to be impressed.

In the evenings, Khieu would sit on a cushion in Georges-Minh's expansive living room and do research. He wrote about the famous mandarin poet Nguyen Du's *The Tale of Kieu*. Nguyen Du, an eighteenth-century Vietnamese treasure, an orphan, poet, prisoner, diplomat. Georges-Minh thought of Nguyen Du as Vietnam's Shakespeare, and yet didn't precisely understand Khieu's obsession with him, at least as far as trying to correlate Nguyen's verse patterns to spaceship sightings in the southeastern provinces.

In the Central Highlands there was a rock called the Pleiku. In the legend, Buddha raised the first peasant from this rock, but a few healers now believed the peasant was an alien. Rocks were a symbol of deep stability, and spaceships had recently been spotted by these traditional sites. When Khieu got sick he wrote in code so that his findings would be safe. The hill tribes believed shooting stars were the gods flicking their cigars. Khieu saw the stars as transportation in the ocean of night. He believed the stars spoke to him. Khieu had loved the fantastical since he was a child, but since the public guillotining had begun, Georges-Minh knew, something in those beliefs had darkened, become violent and twisted. Georges-Minh refilled his glass of mulberry wine.

"Georges-Minh never talks," said Chang, who sat right next to Georges-Minh. "There he goes again. Daydreaming. Our boy."

"He's our shy boy," Khieu said, grasping Georges-Minh's hand and holding it.

"But I want to hear what he has to say," said Phuc. "*Do* you have something to say?"

"I have many things to say. All the time," Georges-Minh said. "I'm just thinking about the best way to say them."

"Well then, why are you staring out the window? You in a trance?"

"What I want to know is, are we still playing cards or aren't we?" Bao, the horticulturalist, said, his swollen eyelids making him appear sleepy. At home his moonflowers had grown so large their blossoms bent downward like tired children, bending their stakes. He and his wife would sell them soon, at which point he would thank each and every one of them, before slicing off their heads with a razor blade.

"I'm waiting for you," said Phuc.

"It's not my turn," Chang replied.

"It's not mine," Bao said, rubbing his eyes. It was silly to get sentimental over plants. Yet what choice did he have? He had no children. His plants were his children. Nor would he have his own family until he made peace with his father—Mimi refused to have children with a man who'd given up a career in politics to grow plants.

"Whose turn is it?" Chang asked.

"Who's not paying attention now?" Phuc said.

"I think one man at the top is the way to go," Georges-Minh said. "A solid message." They were a group that had never done anything, not even handed out pamphlets. Was Khieu playing it straight or being ironic?

Khieu shook his head. "I appreciate what you are saying, my friend. And the design is we're paying the cooks at the garrison to put poison in their food."

"No. I appreciate your heart, my friend," Georges-Minh said, "but not enough to change our plan. We stick to the design. I'm the one that's making it. I've taken an oath not to harm."

"But what harm are the French pigs doing to our country?" Phuc said. "Sometimes I wonder if they're even human."

"In the end I don't know what I think," Georges-Minh said.

"It's going into their Christmas meal," Khieu said.

"Wow." The coquettishness, the playfulness, the flirty laugh, the toes in the lap, all of it was gone. "What the hell are you going to do? Or should I say, what the hell were you thinking, old man?"

Dong got up from her chair, dragged it next to Georges-Minh so they could sit side by side. "I want to tell you something. Something I've never told anyone else in my life before. Are you ready? Ma and Ba rescued me from a market stall," she said. "Ho Dong isn't my real name. Mr. and Mrs. Ho adopted me. I don't know who my real parents are."

"Your parents abandoned you? In a market?"

"Babies, unwanted, next to the breadfruit." She started to cry.

"Like a watermelon," he said, putting his arm around her.

"Like a live chicken," she said. She leaned into his embrace, drying her tears with her knuckles.

"Like a leather pair of shoes," he whispered.

"I always imagine this: my parents, from the north, escaping poverty, walking south toward hope and work."

"They could have taken home a dog but they chose you."

"Dog is lucky. Do you like dog?" She was smiling now, though her eyes were still red.

"I didn't know women ate dog. Isn't the meat too strong?"

"I imagine a restaurant kitchen, where my mother gave birth to me on the road, in the storage room where they kept the bags of rice. She lies in a makeshift bed of kitchen towels, I watch her give birth to me, bloody sheets and rags and clothing, bloody everything ... I tell myself: Be glad you were left at the market."

"Yes, be glad. Your parents left you to the mercy of the gods. They were benevolent."

"I could have been killed," she said, pleasantly horrified. "My mother could have squeezed my nostrils shut."

"Until you were dead," he added.

"Babies have been eaten during famines," she said in confidence.

"I know." Co-conspirator.

"Babies have been devoured during times of need. This is," she said, playing with him now, affecting the tone of a teacher, even wagging her finger in time with her words, "this is a documented fact."

Behind the house, they walked along the river; the night air sounded with insects. In the near dark, in the scent of the jasmine and frangipani, neither one thought of it as escaping.

When they got to the end of the jetty they sat.

"I like walking at night," Dong said. "It helps order the images of the day."

"Quiets one's thoughts."

"Look at the fish." The fish swarmed the jetty's piling under the toilet. "Pleasant thoughts replace the less pleasant ones, until all that's unwelcome lies near the bottom, just like that."

"Ugh. To which process are you referring? Wait, don't tell me, I don't want to know." He laughed, waved her next words away.

She giggled, too. Could he tell? Should he?

"The night you came in. A girl died in my arms. It wasn't the first time. But it was the first time like this. She'd been thrown into the river and when they pulled her out she was still breathing. Just a girl."

"Who was she?"

"I don't know. It's not like the police know either, or care. She haunts me. I'll never find out if she was beaten by her pimp and left for dead on the banks. It could be she rolled into the river herself. Two boatmen saw her floating by on a current and fished her out. I couldn't save her."

"What was different about this time?"

"I don't believe in magic. But after that. Her body was covered not by disease but by fish. To tell you, to say it out loud seems like nothing now. But if you'd been there. I feel like something about her infiltrated me that night. I just want to be the kind of person I can respect. Nothing more."

He thought then about what Khieu often said, anger without action demoralized, words recalled so often that it was as if Georges-Minh had swallowed them. The question was: Would he let them sit inside him or would he do something?

Somewhere between the rebel Georges-Minh's words and the foundling Dong's confession he lost his nerve and the proposal remained a fantasy. He held fast for so long he became stiff. This he was good at: nurturing feelings, ideas, even words as if in a petri dish. The lactation of language. How long had it been there, this thread of a voice winding itself around the banister like a baby's thin wail alone in a room at the end of a hall? Slowing down, examining what you say, letting it have conversations with books like the Bible, Dostoyevsky, dog-eared collections of poetry by Phi or Nguyen Du. Above all, never speaking from the heart.

He treated her for lung fever at her home on Tuesdays and Thursdays. Her family lived by the river a distance from Georges-Minh's neighbourhood but he thought nothing of the mileage the tiresome trip put on his car nor how he pulled at his collar in the heat most of the way. On these days, he knocked on the splintered wooden door that hung on rusty hinges. He drummed his fingers and fidgeted in the shade, watching the ripples under the home's stilts while listening to the coughing through the wood in the shade of a diseased cabbage palm that shielded the porch in anticipation of the splintered door opening.

While he treated her, her mother and father rattled about the house, never directly intruding, but never out of earshot.

"Mother, pass me the hammer," Georges-Minh heard her father say.

"Get it yourself."

"Buddha on an elephant, woman, can't you see I'm holding the picture?"

"Then, love, you should have thought of the hammer before you thought of the nail."

"Give us a kiss, then get us the hammer."

Georges-Minh worked efficiently but self-consciously. He stretched her onto the mat. Painted iodine on her chest. Turned her over. Rubbed her back with coins, since her father was paying him to do so. While the menagerie behind the house in cages or tied to ropes, green pigeons, golden tortoises, drongos, rat snakes, skinks, agama lizards, goral goats, slow lorises, peafowls, gibbons, porcupines, sunbirds, bulbuls, canaries, toads, langurs, seraws, and a sambar deer made almost too much noise to speak over.

Too much wind in the body. Her fever could be cured by a long sweep of the coin along one side of her spine. Then the other. The imbalance of elements in the soul. Abrading the body would return harmony. Her parents were sure of it. He was no better than a witch doctor, he thought to himself while he worked. Also that the house was shabby for a judge: perhaps the man gambled. He spared Dong the insults and said nothing.

"It hurts."

"I know."

"Ow."

"Lie still."

The coin was worn on the side. He'd found the smoothest coin he could from his pocket, though her parents had offered a bowlful—to least snag the skin, to cause the smallest amount of pain. He poured more camphor oil onto her skin. The smell made his eyes water but the coin could glide better now. Lubricated, he ran its plane edge over her flesh. Steady hands, sweeping motions, away from the heart. Blood began to flow to the surface of the skin.

She moaned.

His marks looked like the claw marks of tigers.

They would last for days, the marks: when he next saw her he would feel guilty for the damage he'd done.

He followed the ridges of her ribs and repeated the procedure on the other side, frustrated that if he wanted to see her at her home he had to carry through with this charade. Why not just make a clay figure and bury it in a jar, calling on the demon responsible for her illness to come out and leave her?

"Almost done," he said.

Across the wickerwork wall that didn't reach all the way to the ceiling he heard her mother and father.

"I smell wintergreen," her father said.

"Eucalyptus," her mother said.

"Wintergreen. It's one of my favourite smells, I should know."

It was clear to him that her parents loved her, though in keeping with tradition they did not taint their love with exuberance. The father chewed quids of betel. The mother rolled his cigarettes and lit them before handing them to him.

The mother loved in the way mothers often do, through her criticisms and admonishments. Her yelling a kind of loving. *Don't look at your shadow or you will be haunted by darkness. It's bad luck to hit your bowl with chopsticks. Making this noise is a sign of poverty. As if you're asking for more food, which is a sign. And signs of poverty herald poverty.*

The days she was ill, they brought her tea in bed, to speed her recovery. Mother washed the dishes. Mother scrubbed the floor.

But when Ho Dong was well, her mother treated her as more than a slave, but somehow less than a daughter. Her name, which meant "winter," suited her. Her fragile body may have reminded him of winters in the north and famines he'd heard the old people tell stories about, when starvation sometimes forced parents to feed children who'd died to children who hadn't to keep them alive just a little longer. Her spirit, on the other hand, was the promise of spring, the buds that pushed up past cold dirt and hard wind. He was reminded of Grimm's Cinderella, and his knowledge of the tale made him feel superior to other Vietnamese, unique, as a man who'd been educated in Europe. It gave him an outsider's perspective on his own culture. Though this outsider's perspective was also what made him feel alone.

Dong's duties included: buying the chicken, killing the chicken, plucking the chicken, cooking and cleaning up, sharpening knives, sharpening axes, polishing handles, polishing shoes, drawing the water, boiling the water, picking the tea, making tea, and washing the teacups. When he was there, he offered to help.

Mother had many quirks, the most entertaining and terrifying of which was her habit of bringing stray animals home from wherever she found them. The father protested, but the lack of force in his voice intimated he had capitulated long ago. Mother was a fat, jolly, aggressive woman with a laugh that shook the house when she got her way—until she began coughing, and then Georges-Minh saw that her stance was part bravado also, for she was stricken with the same illness that consumed her daughter.

9

Street urchins often begged at Georges-Minh's lunch table. "You're so rich and I'm so poor, a tien for me." "Buy a flower." "Gum for sale." Some stared, eyes black as lakes, and didn't say a word. Georges-Minh had learned one couldn't be too sympathetic. You'd buy a flower and they'd ask you to buy another. If you told them you'd already bought one they'd say you could afford one more. Or they'd say you hadn't bought one in the first place, even though the proof lay on the table. Or, with the proof lying on the table, they'd begin to swarm. "If you bought one from him, you can buy one from me."

Georges-Minh, wise to their ways, ignored them all.

"You got a cigarette?" said a boy, sitting down at his table.

"You're too young to smoke," Georges-Minh replied. The boy stretched out a dirty hand, which had a missing pinkie finger, and he looked familiar to Georges-Minh, though Georges-Minh couldn't place his face.

"So how's about that smoke?"

"I don't smoke."

"Ah." The boy waved him off with a look of disgust across his face that, Georges-Minh remarked, at his young age already bore the telltale signs of the opium addict: the lines around the mouth, eyes like coins sunk deep into cheeks of an old man, no elasticity, waxy.

"You should have me look at that for you," he said, pointing at the boy's infected arm. "I'm a doctor, you know."

"You don't remember me, do you?" the boy said.

"Am I supposed to?"

"I wouldn't think so. The rich really do have shit for brains. I'll give you a hint: *Sing Sing.*"

"Sing Sing?"

"Very good." The boy clapped. "Straight A's for you. He can remember my name after he's been told."

A lame beggar pulled his way past Georges-Minh's table on a wheeled wooden platform, his knuckles wrapped like a boxer's to pad his hands against the pavement. His shirt was stitched together with four different colours of thread. This was the kind of toughness Georges-Minh admired. He did like the poor. The right kind. Not this kind, the cocky kind, the do-no-work-and-expect-to-get-paid kind.

"What do you want?"

"Oh, many things. Many things."

It dawned on Georges-Minh that the boy did look familiar, from the night of the death. When the fish girl had passed away in his arms, when the prostitute had scratched his face in the street and run away. Yes. He'd been short with the boy. Is that why he was here? Because he was angry about that?

"I do know you. And I'm sorry I was cross with you, back when."

The boy's eyes at first uncomprehending, filled with a gleam, and then his features hardened. It was Sing Sing's turn to be surprised. "Oh, that. Ha." He turned his hand into a gun and fired it at Georges-Minh. "Funny." He wiped his nose with the back of his hand. "You think I'm choked about that? Nah, I want something else, some information."

This was getting ridiculous. "What information?"

"Information that *I* have"—he emphasized his inflected words with head nods—"that your *girlfriend* doesn't want, about *you* and a *man* who likes to drink *brandy*." Sing Sing squeezed Georges-Minh's thigh under the table. "I think a couple hundred tien will do for tonight."

"I don't carry that much on me!" Georges-Minh was shocked—outraged—that someone had been watching him that night, that he should fall in love and have his love threatened by a meaningless fling, that he was being blackmailed by an opium-addled boy!

"But you can get it."

"Maybe, but ..."

"So get it."

"I can't now." The boy exasperated him.

"Why not?"

"I have to work. It's not as though I can just do whatever I want when I feel like it." His tone implied: the way *you* can, you louse, even though you are twelve.

"When, then?" Sing Sing asked coolly.

"Not now."

"When?"

"After. After work."

"I'll come with you. For now buy me a soda."

What he needed was a good slap. From the dirt on his cheeks to the sweat running crooked paths through it, Georges-Minh had seen it before, this kid's life, cheap and cliché.

But he bought him the soda. As if merely to annoy him, Sing Sing took the small paper napkin that had come with the drink, unfolded it and draped it on his knee like a cloth dinner serviette. Georges-Minh followed his finger as it traced the lip of the bottle, ran up and down the glass side like the feelers of a moth.

"You complain yet you've had it so soft," Sing Sing said.

He drank the soda with slow, careful sips. Having finished, he winked at Georges-Minh. "I know where to find you." His saunter was part sway, part swagger as he walked away, shoeless.

10

Georges-Minh took Dong for a drive so they could have some privacy. He'd bought her a little gift, something he knew she enjoyed. He reached between her legs and fetched them from the icebox he'd placed on the floorboards by her feet. He felt like he had something to prove. She liked strawberries. The sweet-sour sophistication of them. The way, when they were a little tart, they bit you back. Perfect specimens, he thought, grown in the night soil just outside of Saigon, tended by Chinese gardeners along with other European vegetables and fruits, such as those found in the markets of Paris or London.

He retrieved the kitchen knife out of his front pocket. She waited patiently, cross-legged now on the cushioned bench seat like a little girl. The air of Long Hai Bay was fragrant with frangipani. He held the bowl and knife behind his back in one hand and turned up the flame on the oil lamp. Now that the light was brighter he could show her.

"Ah," she said. "The exterior of them, the seeds like whiskers on a man who's forgotten to shave."

"Or," he said, "areolae. The small swellings around the human nipple. From a certain angle, this fruit introduced by the French, sown by the French, grown by the French, distributed by the French, resembles a nipple. Promiscuous."

Dong's hair was sloppily brushed away from her forehead and into a ponytail, which was then twisted into a tilted chignon, falling out of a tortoiseshell comb. In that moment he realized with an undeniable feeling in his stomach that his happiness was now wrapped up in his ambition to be with her.

"Do you know what it's like to be invisible?" he said. "My father looked right through me. My friends were paper masks, kites, animal-character hats. They seemed imbued with personalities, they even talked to me. Yet reality told me they must be factually bereft of any souls as they were made in a factory, of paper and glue. Every night when I went to sleep, I felt so empty. I wore six tunics to bed. I still shiver! Yet you, you make me feel like I'm here."

She laughed. "When I was a child, anything shiny delighted me: spoons, serving trays, dinner plates, buttons, bracelets with clasps, my mother's thimble, a windowpane's reflection, a water spill on a wooden floor. I'd accept my mother's anger in return for the joy of running my fingers through a spilled cup of jackfruit juice. You, you make me feel ... shiny." She looked down, as if guilty of something. "Anyway, I have something to tell you. I lied to you at the temple. I had a job as a nanny. But I don't now. My ma and ba sent me to a good school." She learned French, arithmetic, history, geography, how to write Vietnamese *quoc ngu* characters. Some in her class now worked as clerks for the government. "But it just blurted out of my mouth. I didn't want you to think that I was lazy. Sometimes being sick makes me feel so *useless*." The French family had let her go. They'd been afraid of her coughing. The blood on the kerchief. "I don't blame them."

She cared what he thought? Maybe this meant something. Dare he believe it even for a moment?

She proceeded to have a fit. Her body curled forward, tensed and jerked as she coughed. Her face paled as her lips purpled. She held on to her sides, sweating. She sounded like an orangutan and barked. She rubbed away tears. The coughing turned to laughter along the way. She leaned on her elbow, looking at him. "How much longer can my adopted parents go on supporting a grown daughter?"

"You are talking too much," he scolded. "Talk less. Better yet, don't talk at all."

Finally her coughing subsided. He took the tasselled canopy off the roof of the car so they could look at the stars. "Am I a traitor to prefer strawberries to dragon fruit?" she whispered. She circled the strawberry with her tongue in the moonlight.

"Am I a worse traitor to supply you with them?"

The hem of her pants stopped two inches above her ankle bone. The roundness of her tibia in moonlight thrilled him. A few mosquitoes whined close to his head. Farther away, the usual cacophony of insects and the crash of the waves. Above them a thousand stars. She took the bowl from him and cut the strawberries into thin slices in the dark. The leather seat grew warm and sticky through his clothes. She bent forward and rummaged through her bag, returned with something between her hands.

"Don't cut yourself."

She giggled. "I can do this with my eyes closed."

"You might as well be blind."

"It's *easy* to be blind."

He squinted. She appeared to be dipping the strawberry slices into something. "Don't look." She turned off the oil lamp.

"What are you doing?"

"*Feeling.*"

Georges-Minh could hear the scraping of something by his feet, granules against the floorboards when she dipped the fruit into the bowl.

"Relax." She tittered and pulled off his sandals, put strawberry slices between his toes. The heat of his body made the sugar drip. She placed slices between each toe, strawberry-toe, strawberry-toe, until every gap was filled. "Lie still!" She bent forward and her hair tickled the tops of his feet. He trembled but tried hard not to move too much. Just as he tried not to laugh. Just as he tried to pretend he knew what was coming next. What if she left him there? Anything spilled became a feast for red ants; he'd be covered in a matter of minutes.

She put the sugar bowl on the rumble seat behind them. He listened to her lick her fingers. She pushed him back and climbed astride him, then, fighting the urge to cough, faced his feet, and leaned forward, her hands on his ankles. Her hair brushed his legs. It cascaded around his feet. She began to nibble the strawberry slices. When no fruit remained she began to lick his toes.

He fought the urge to laugh out loud. "Shhhh." The sensation reminded him of a pet Pomeranian he'd had as a child who used to eat from his hand and when the treat was gone continued licking. She took each of his toes in her mouth in turn. With his eyes closed she could be anyone. "Dong …" They got undressed. Her tongue travelled from his toes to his head via his private parts. His body filled with stars.

The following evening, Chang took Georges-Minh to a party, saying he knew someone there who would pay them not to poison anyone, a wealthy businessman in whose interest it was to keep the French colonialists happy.

"Have you been talking to people about the plot?" Georges-Minh said as they walked down the street, passing a performer crooning for pennies on the corner, his hand outstretched. "You're a traitor to the cause." Everywhere people bumped into each other. Were they drunk? Infected? Or was it his imagination?

"Come on, lighten up. We can just go in for a bit and drink his free wine," Chang said. "Have you started to believe you're a real revolutionary? When has our group ever done anything besides play cards?" He laughed at the shock he saw in Georges-Minh's face. "What? Think about it, do you honestly think we're actually going to poison people?"

"So you're going to take this man's money?"

"No. He's kind of handsome. I might sleep with him to make you jealous. Oh stop—I'm joking."

Chang wondered if there would ever come a day where he and Georges-Minh would walk into a party as a couple, greet the host, order some drinks. Probably not. The reason Georges-Minh would never truly love him, Chang reasoned, impressed by his own philosophic calm in the face of such disappointment, was that in the first place, Georges-Minh was in love with Khieu. Second, Georges-Minh wouldn't admit he preferred men to women. Third, he was now hiding behind a woman he might possibly marry. Fourth, more than once at meetings Chang had seen his pupils no larger than pinpoints; Georges-Minh claimed long hours at work. Chang knew better.

As they walked to the party, Chang was satisfied simply that Georges-Minh had finally agreed to accompany him somewhere. Even though he knew if it hadn't involved the poisoning plot and Khieu's well-being, Georges-Minh would have refused.

Georges-Minh wondered where Chang had met the man. His apartment, from the outside, was nothing special. A brick deal above the Bridgeworks, Canalworks, and Railroads offices.

Inside, however, he had to admit the place was posh, the rooms elegant, plush, spotless. As were the guests. Georges-Minh got himself a glass of wine from the bar, where the host had hired someone to serve as a butler. He recognized an executive from the cement factory. The man waved and Georges-Minh waved back. What did Georges-Minh care what Chang did? Chang grasped the hand of the man who would pay them to halt the poisoning. Pulled him in close so their groins nearly touched.

He'd expected to feel angry, betrayed on behalf of the group. The man was good-looking, suave—in a ranting, rhetorical way. Maybe Chang liked that sort of thing.

Georges-Minh's head burned. Must be the cheap wine. He got another glass from the bar, drank that, got another, and drank that, too. He pretended to admire the furniture. Chang would be the one left with no family. Unmarried, no eldest son. He'd be the one looked down upon by society. A pansy. No one to carry on the family name. No one to perform his rituals when he died. He'd become a confused spirit, a wandering spirit, a ghost with no tomb to call his own. Popping out at intersections, scaring cyclists.

He forced himself to laugh. Maybe he would become a common thief in the afterlife. Living off leftovers, stealing plums from iceboxes, dancing by the light of votive candles on the roadside. Cold porridge. Even going hungry. Georges-Minh would have the last hurrah. He would not go childless, not without an eldest son who would perform his death rituals, burn his paper money, send him properly into the afterlife.

Chang came padding across the thick, expensive rugs, his face flushed. "He wants to meet you."

"Who, our host?"

"Who else?"

"No, thanks."

Georges-Minh waved to the man, their host, across the room, held up his wine glass, smiled cheekily, and took a sip. The man raised his glass and sipped as well. "I don't want to. My head hurts."

"Another flu?"

"Or the same one, I don't know."

"Maybe later, then," Chang said. He either didn't get, or was deliberately not getting, the fact that Georges-Minh was going out of his way to insult the man. Or maybe Chang, as a good friend of Georges-Minh's, was used to his funny moods. As if zeroing right in on the point, he asked, "So what's with you and Dong, anyway?" Chang crossed his ankles and leaned against a door frame.

Georges-Minh glared at Chang. "What do you mean, what's with her?"

"That's what I'm asking, what's with her?"

Georges-Minh let his scowl linger.

Chang finally raised his eyebrow and shrugged. "Lie to yourself all you want. It's no skin off my nose."

"How do you know I'm lying to myself?"

"You're a world-class liar. A cute one, but still. Look," Chang said casually, taking a swig of his drink, not even looking Georges-Minh in the eye but rather checking out another handsome man in a red bow tie across the room, "everyone can see it but you. It's not just the Dong thing, it's the whole revolutionary thing. The whole I-love-the-poor thing. You're no ascetic. You're a pleasure-seeker, a bon vivant. At least you used to be until you returned from university. Why don't you drop the act? Or the act-*s*."

Georges-Minh patted his pockets for his cigarettes. His devastation, on realizing he'd run out, couldn't be measured. He crumpled the empty pack and flung it to the floor. "Maybe I'm lying to *you*," he said. "You ever thought about that?"

"I don't believe you," Chang murmured.

"What makes you so sure?"

"A man knows these things."

"My sleeping with you is simply a political statement," Georges-Minh said.

"That I doubt. You're a reprobate. Pure and simple."

"Only women really count."

"I don't count?" Chang's face crumpled.

"Not really."

"You mean since Dong?"

Georges-Minh looked across the room. *Was* it because of Dong?

"Whatever." Chang tossed his hair, rumpled his fingers through it. Sighed, then smiled. The smile seemed forced at first, then he eased into it. He reached for Georges-Minh's neck to rub it. "Why so hostile?"

"I'm not, I'm just ... I've been under stress at work."

"You're always stressed at work. That's nothing new."

"I've been ... there's something going around, a new sickness."

"Really? Do tell. Is it contagious? Are we in danger?"

"We might be."

"Oh, my god, is it something spread skin to skin?" Chang edged flirtatiously toward Georges-Minh.

How could Chang, Georges-Minh wondered, be so quick to forget, to forgive?

"I don't know. The Centre for Infectious Disease Control has more questions than answers right now. I saw three cases in three days and then seven more in the next week alone."

"How is it spread? Show me?" Chang pouted his lips and edged even closer.

"That alone might not seem so bad, but each of them lost their memory afterward. Complete amnesia." Not all had lost their memory completely; Georges-Minh exaggerated to shift the focus away from himself.

"Complete amnesia? My god."

"They ended up in asylums. What a waste."

When they got to Chang's apartment after the party Chang tried quickly to put his words in order while opening a bottle of wine. Georges-Minh had told him he'd been with other women, but somehow he'd never believed that his friend had felt any attraction for them. Yet since Georges-Minh had met Dong, their "love nights" at the clinic had dwindled, then stopped. It wasn't that Chang had stopped visiting, but when he arrived, Georges-Minh had displayed less and less interest in touching him.

Chang couldn't bring himself to believe he had meant that little to Georges-Minh. And Georges-Minh continued to glance at his lips, his ass, his fingers, his forearms out of the corner of his eye.

He wanted to talk but instead put his hand on Georges-Minh's leg.

"Chang." Georges-Minh laughed but left his hand where it lay. "There was never an 'us.'"

"Does it matter?" Chang, caught off guard by Georges-Minh's candour, hardly knew how to answer.

"Well, it means nothing we did was planned. It means ... it doesn't mean anything." Georges-Minh stood, crossed the room. Opened a window. Stuck out his head and breathed a long breath. "If two guys get together—something happens. That's it. That's the beauty. There's no—*this*." He stepped back into the room, waved his hands. "As soon as you bring *this* into the equation, it's ruined."

Chang wanted to cry. The reasonable explanation was that Georges-Minh was confused. If Chang didn't want to be judged, who was he to play judger? And if Chang loved Georges-Minh as he said, he should offer him his arms, not his admonishments.

"Come here." He sashayed across the room, trying to make light of the moment, and stretched open his arms.

"Stop. What are you doing?"

"Don't push me away," he whispered into Georges-Minh's ear as he embraced him. "You were right, I was wrong. That's it. Just relax."

It was only a matter of time before Georges-Minh had calmed down enough to allow Chang to begin stroking his hair and a second or two more before Georges-Minh had allowed him to take off his shirt and loosen his belt. Soon Chang was sucking his cock.

"See, doesn't that feel better? Not planned. Just something that happens. Now relax. In a minute all this will be ancient history."

Georges-Minh went to the Centre for Infectious Disease Control the next day. He wanted to talk to the French doctor. Outside a man was selling dead cobras in jars of rice wine solution. "Cure all your ills, buy some snake power, drink some tonic, bloom and flower." The plasterwork-grey building had turned black where the shade of the hopea trees had caused a mossy fungus to grow and the plaster to crack.

Inside, people bustled behind a wooden counter where Dr. Michaut sat sipping a coffee and reading a newspaper. Light filtered through a single dirty window. Behind closed doors, people could be heard speaking in other offices.

Dr. Nguyen Georges-Minh had drunk too much the night before and his head hurt. In no mood for pleasantries, he leaped right in. "Dr. Michaut, I'd like to bring up a theory of sorts. At some point it might be interesting to collaborate. I'm going to propose, because using this better facility, but anyway, to the point, then. I haven't yet treated a single child for the new paddy fever. None at all." He patted his forehead with his handkerchief. Why was it so bloody hot in here? "They've all been post-pubescent." He waited. "By the way, are we still calling it paddy fever?"

Dr. Michaut appeared more interested in his morning paper and his coffee than in getting up from his seat. Was he overworked? Underpaid? Perhaps Dr. Michaut had his, what was it called, *Contributions to Male Hysteria* paper on his mind. Georges-Minh forced himself to be civil. He had no choice— there was no one else to deal with. He had lain in bed last night, unable to sleep, and had spent the better part of dawn theorizing. The key lay in how developed the psyche was. The more at peace a person felt with who they were, not at war with a monster within, the more immune they seemed to be. He thought back to the words of his first patient—"I see a monster inside you"—and wondered why he, of all people, should be immune.

As he tried to think of a way to relate these things to Dr. Michaut without sounding like a raving lunatic, Dr. Michaut put down his paper.

"So, Georges, I've been working on that report some more, and I'd be curious to hear your opinion. The one I told you about, *Contributions to the Study of the Manifestations of Male Hysteria*? One colleague to another. I'm expanding the idea to include a discussion about the Vietnamese as teachers of moral vice."

"Come again?" Georges-Minh thought he'd heard wrong.

"Cochin China and social depravity."

He thought the doctor must be pulling his leg. "How so?"

"The Vietnamese as teachers of moral vice. Not meaning ones like you, of course."

"No offence taken." Of course he took offence. What was this man on about? If only he didn't need his help, his lab, his equipment, he'd pop him one in the jaw.

"I don't include you in these comparisons. You studied in Paris, like me."

"What do you mean?"

"Well, at least when it comes to French soldiers and officers who are away from home. The Vietnamese, lascivious, have corrupted the French with desires that were never theirs. No wives or girlfriends, polluted by the fiery climate, lonely, bored, they enter the opium dens. In the dens, French wills are further sapped by the drug. The heat, the exoticism, far from France. The geography of perversion. The colonists indulge in *pederasty*. Anyway, my concern is not morality." He waved the air. "As a medical officer, I specialize in disease control. Pederasty reduces the rates of syphilis." He got up from his seat, approached the counter, and looked Georges-Minh in the eye. "Between you and me, to look at the *con gai*, the traditional prostitutes, with their lacquered teeth and their red spittle, like devils, well it's no wonder. I'd choose a boy, too. Looks like blood dripping from their lips."

The Vietnamese people as *teachers* of vice?

"The worst is yet to come. They go back to France, they take these things home with them. Ah, then. Their vices."

"You may consider," Georges-Minh began, in as calm a voice as possible, "if a Vietnamese 'boy' engages in pederasty at an opium den it is merely as a means to pay for his own opium habit. Or perhaps to acquire goods the French have put him in mind to purchase, which he otherwise couldn't afford."

"But the boy has an inherent *predilection* for it," Michaut said, "which the opium only manifests, bringing his fantasies to the surface. How else is one to explain its frequency among young people around the markets and opium dens and theatres? Incurable sodomites." He stopped. "No offence."

Georges-Minh's stomach burned. He should have eaten breakfast.

"Pederasty is virtually unknown in France. While it's basically practised in broad daylight in Annam."

What about all the libertines? Verlaine? What about de Sade? Georges-Minh said nothing.

"I'm not trying to condemn the Vietnamese at all. I quite like the Vietnamese. Between you and me it's the Chinese. They brought the opium to Vietnam in the first place."

"What about the paddy fever?"

"Yes, the paddy fever. Are we still calling it that?" Dr. Michaut walked to the desk, sat down as if something had been resolved. "How many new cases?"

11

Georges-Minh stood out in his garden at dusk. The datura seed pods were the size of an egg and covered with spines. He could understand why they were called thornapples. But the scent of the datura blooms was erotic and the blooms themselves lived up to their moniker, trumpet flowers, heady as art, fit for the gods, although the leaves' fetor almost overpowered the perfume of the petals.

Careful not to prick his fingers, he collected a few of the blossoms, mainly to brighten the pharmaceutical wing of his villa, because the real poison lay in the seed pods. He settled himself in front of a long table where he had set up his old-fashioned mortar and pestle. There he began to grind. He started off with a small but respectable two grams and began pulverizing. The smell was sweet but earthy.

The lab was so quiet that the sound of his own footsteps answered the crickets outside, and the collection of test tubes clinking in the wooden rack as he walked from one side of the room to the other could have competed with an orchestra. A pipette, a bottle of methyl alcohol, and he was ready. Clutching it all in his arms like a baby, he returned to the long table and piped a small portion of liquid into the test tubes along with a measure of the seed pulp. His earlier feeling of uncertainty about who he was and what he should do had given way, since his discussion with Michaut, to the small joys of experimentation as the methanol turned yellowish while he shook the mixture. He hadn't experienced such a thrill since his undergraduate days. Not because, he thought to himself, this could kill a man or this could kill a hundred men. But because the thrill of following up on a hunch and the possibility of discovery was akin to falling in love. Or so he told himself. He labelled the experiments in brown paper on the test tubes.

12

Dong notified him of her pregnancy when she was filing her fingernails one night after visiting his house for tea and treatment. She'd been filing her nails into the shape that her mother preferred—ending in a point that could draw blood—and the dust from her nails fell into her lap. She brushed it away with the back of her hand.

The two of them landed on the thin cotton sheet she had slung over the bed frame. No more simple bed frame in the Chinese style: tomorrow they would buy a mattress.

Something about the moment's poignancy gripped him before she had even opened her mouth. He sensed he was observing a mystery at work when she placed her hands on her stomach and sat, an angel mid-song, a mouth ajar in invisible prayer to an invisible God, fingers over her belly, paused mid-file. Then she said it and he felt he was gifted with second sight. "Your baby, Georges-Minh, is growing. Its head and feet. The blood and beating heart of it. Already, even now, I wonder whether it can smile. The tiny hands. The fingers. Which will one day grasp ours."

"Are, are you sure?"

"Of course I'm sure." Her voice assumed a teasing tone. "It's not like I'm trying to trick you into marrying me or something."

As with all important things in his life he consulted Khieu. Khieu answered in riddles as he sometimes did. Understanding the oracle wasn't always easy. If Khieu told Georges-Minh he'd dreamed about the wind, he might be pointing out discord, not beauty; if he told Georges-Minh he saw him covered in sand, his meaning might be he had plenty of time, like an hourglass, not that he was dirty. When Khieu got sick, his eyes grew shiny. "If you've lost your luck, it can become free floating."

"I get what you're saying," Georges-Minh said. "You think I'm not ready to have a son."

"Or it can enter another person." Khieu didn't often understand why everyone made their lives so complicated. Stigma banished the truth. Kept it from living free, out in the open. The truth was that there was nothing from which to run. Not even Dong. Georges-Minh didn't have to torture himself. The colonial power wanted sex to be associated with depravity and disease, but Khieu believed that if one truly wanted to broaden the expanse of human liberation, one needed fewer boxes to slot one's living into. Pleasure wasn't meant to be analyzed and pigeonholed. In the real world, birds didn't live in holes but spent most of their time flying around in the open sky.

"I get it but don't worry. Dong is honest."

"This can happen with bad luck, too, do you understand? One person gets sick, while the other gets well."

For weeks he'd been paying Sing Sing however many tien he asked for.

"That pretty thing, bringing you sweet biscuits on your break." Sing Sing examined his filthy fingernails in the restaurant where they'd been meeting for sodas. "Imagine. Cheating on her—and with a man, no less!"

It was just something that happened. In the same way as he had once petted a dog, or stroked a cat. Or like visiting a swimming pool. Just because he swam didn't mean he was a swimmer.

On Sing Sing's last visit Georges-Minh had apprehensively taken a large and heavy crate of contraband goods into his possession.

"No more," he'd told Sing Sing, the crate clanging, and he strained to lift it, hiding it along with the medical supplies. Sing Sing, whose infected forearm was getting worse, sweated constantly. Today his wrist was swollen to twice the size.

Georges-Minh tried to put out of his mind how long he'd be tasked with keeping the crate. Whatever was happening between him and Sing Sing put at jeopardy all he and Khieu had worked for, no matter what paternalistic feeling he was developing for the boy.

"You should let me look at that arm."

"I'm fine."

"You're high."

"I can handle it. You can't control the world. Control yourself. I look after myself. Like you should. Partnerships are stupid anyway. Everyone always lets you down. Why would you do that to yourself? Lean and lean. Do that and you'll fall. It's why I keep having those bad dreams. Got to figure out a way to stop the cops from finding me. But the dream loops around. Why on earth would anyone expect him to help? He's only saving his own neck. Something good might happen. But it won't—"

"Sing Sing, stop it."

"—his own neck from the chopping block. That's how it goes. Everyone looking out for themselves. No one's ever caught me. When I fall, I mean. So I learned. You know?"

"What are you talking about?"

"Just don't fall. Goddammit. Don't stop now. Get up. Getting up makes you strong. You've always pulled yourself up." His head was in his hands now. "Don't stop now, don't stop. Don't be the person who waits to get caught. It's a trap, stop waiting."

"What's a trap?" Had he had a fight with a friend? A lover? At his age?

"No one will ever catch me."

A pimp. Of course. It all made sense now. These boys were just as vulnerable as the girls. "Who's trying to hurt you, Sing Sing? Do you have a pimp I should know about?" Prey to the scourges of the French. The diseased infrastructure. Their foreign presence had created it.

He could not let everything he and Khieu were fighting for go down the drain.

"I don't give a shit 'cause no one's ever given a shit for me."

He touched the boy's hair.

"We're alone in this world." Sing Sing looked up through his tears. "You know that, don't you?"

13

At the next meeting, Georges-Minh confessed to the group with no official name that a boy was blackmailing him. This group that, had it not been for Khieu, may have drifted apart long ago. They were like the spokes of a bicycle wheel, with Khieu holding them together at the centre.

All the members, save Bao, sat cross-legged, on the bed as usual. Chang fiddled with the buttons of his expensive suit. Phuc tried out the new strings he'd bought for his pipa. Bao, whose lion-hearted aspects came out when he'd been drinking, paced the floor.

"It's not about the money," Georges-Minh said sheepishly, trying to defend himself against Bao's boorish defence. He had no need of it. Felt embarrassed. "It's more of a principle thing."

Phuc and Chang looked at each other. Looked down.

As Bao paced, bicycle-chain belt rattling, he waved his glass, pointed it at Georges-Minh. "Don't let some little shit get away with that."

Chang focused on the floor, scratched his head. He was

seething at Bao's emboldened-by-drink plea. *Wine in, words out.* The fool.

"I don't care what he's got on you. That's just wrong." Bao's emphatic pointing caused him to spill his drink, splashes ending up as far away as Georges-Minh's dresser. "Who is the little shit?"

Georges-Minh felt all this shouting was drawing terrible attention to the group. The French-style villa was distanced from the neighbouring houses by a property considered expansive, even for Thao Dien, and guarded by the noise of the river out back. But as the men got drunker, their voices got louder, and soon even the river wouldn't hide their anger. Not to mention the lack of focus when they should be concentrating on the poker game.

"Shouldn't we act when one of our group is targeted?" Bao's oily hair thrashed about.

"Don't worry yourself about it," Georges-Minh said quietly.

"I'm not going to let this kid screw with Georges."

"Please, sit down."

"To what end did you tell us, then?"

Chang said, "We should show him we won't take this."

Everyone looked in Chang's direction. Mouths dropped.

"Chang?" said Georges.

"We take care of our own." Chang reached over and squeezed Georges-Minh's hand. Chang thought it was a terrible idea. Do something to the boy? And make themselves vulnerable to police? If it wasn't for Georges-Minh, he probably wouldn't even be part of this stupid group, but he was Georges-Minh's knight, not Bao.

Instead of telling Bao to sit the hell down and stop spilling his wine, Khieu put his hand on his shoulder. "We'll talk about the kid later." Georges-Minh felt a sinking feeling at Khieu's lack of concern. Bao's drunken defence had overwhelmed him. He hadn't meant for his business to overtake the discussion. Or had he?

Wasn't that part of his dysfunction? Never knowing what ranked where in importance? Especially in matters of the heart?

"Meeting! Everyone!" Phuc clapped his hands together. "Let's stop acting like children."

Georges-Minh paid his order no mind, used to his litany of complaints. Phuc compared everything to something else. Whatever existed before him by its nature could never be as good as whatever existed out of sight. He constantly waxed poetic about the north. The better light of Thanh Hoa, the more gifted sensibilities of the people, the finer-tuned ears of the audiences, even the larger restaurant portions.

"How much have you given him so far?" Bao wanted to know.

Phuc cleared his throat and muttered at the same time. "Selling ass to feed mouth."

"What did you say?" Georges-Minh asked.

"Nothing."

"I want to know what you said."

Khieu said, "He's only suggesting you might be surprised at—"

"Maybe she'll be more understanding than you think."

What had Phuc and Khieu not told him?

"Can we please focus on the meeting now?" Phuc asked.

"We should kill him," Bao said.

Chang burst out laughing. "What's this criminal 'we'? You suddenly a gangster?"

"Try me," Bao said.

Khieu said, "To what end *did* you tell us?"

Phuc, scratching his belly, let out a burp.

"What do you know that I don't?"

"Maybe you shouldn't worry about Dong's reaction," Phuc said.

"Tell him," said Khieu.

"Fine. I saw her," Phuc said. "She was working down at the harbour. There. Now you know."

"Working. As in …?"

"Yes."

Georges-Minh stared. "No, I don't believe you. You've mixed her up with someone else."

Phuc shrugged. "Believe what you like."

Khieu, who'd been reading detective stories of late, said, "I insist on finding out the truth of this matter for you." His tone asserted he already knew and had known for a while, for that matter since the day Georges-Minh had gone to his place and they'd talked of clocks and sand and luck. "What does it matter what someone does for a living? What's all the fuss? I'll get you proof, if you promise we can get back to the meeting."

"So this is why you told me I shouldn't be a father," Georges-Minh said.

"A father?" Phuc said.

"Congratulations," Bao said. "I'll supply the flowers for the shower!"

Chang's face stove in. Georges-Minh had gotten that whore pregnant? Who knew if the kid was even his? Could this day get any worse?

Georges-Minh's eyes flickered to the floor.

"Always know who the hell you're dealing with, that's what I say." Bao took a sip of wine, shook his head. "I tolerate many things, but lies, hypocrisy. Bah. Not among them."

"I am sure." Georges-Minh said. "I am sure who I'm dealing with."

"*I'm* sure who you're dealing with, but you're not," Bao said, "I can tell."

"Then I think I'll just ask her."

"Ri-ight, and she'll just tell you," Khieu said. "Just like you'd tell her if she asked you, So how many male lovers have you had, Georges-Minh? How many female ones, for that matter?"

"Anyway, why'd she be working on a flower boat if her dad's a judge?"

Phuc laughed. "A judge?"

"Come again?" Khieu joined in the laughter.

"Yes, a judge. The Ho family? Her father used to be a farmer, then passed the triennial exams. She told me so."

"My family knows all the judges," Chang said, shaking his head, "all the magistrates, everyone who passed the triennial exams. Khieu's right. Listen to him for once." He never thought he'd find himself agreeing with Khieu.

Georges-Minh went down to the harbour that same night and spent two hours wandering and asking after her. He didn't know if he was angry with or grateful to his friends. After all, their concern came from a place of caring and love. Still— how could they be so mistaken? How could those he trusted be such fools?

After scouring the harbour, satisfied his friends had been wrong when he found no one, no girls, no foot washers, no oil-lamp tenders who knew a Ho Dong, he went back home and told Khieu, who'd been waiting for him. Sitting on Georges-Minh's bed, Khieu checked his pulse, hand up to his neck, noting the beats silently, as if, to counter the bad news, he needed to calm himself with the predictability of his body's rhythms. It was vital for him to find patterns where none existed.

"I'll find her if she's out there, my friend," Khieu said. "And bring home the proof. I care what happens to you."

Chang went to the temple to contemplate whether he was causing harm by continuing to love Georges-Minh now that he and Dong were together. Chang lit incense and inhaled its scent. He'd loved Georges-Minh first.

He prayed Buddha would grant Georges-Minh the courage to confess to Dong what he and Georges-Minh had once shared. He prayed for Georges-Minh to fall out of love with her. He prayed for Georges-Minh to love him back.

He thought about their evenings at the clinic, and how even then it hadn't sufficed for him to be just Georges-Minh's after-work delight. Why had Georges-Minh abandoned him?

Most of all he prayed Dong would lose the baby. A child would only add unnecessary complications when they got divorced, which of course they would.

Chang doubted a child is what she'd wanted when she met Georges-Minh. He could go and tell Dong himself. He could prevent so much future suffering here and now.

14

Khieu found Dong, who went by the name of Ly, in a flower boat and returned to tell Georges-Minh so. Returned with the boat's name and added which nights she worked so Georges-Minh could go and see for himself.

"You're talking crazy," Georges-Minh said, refilling his own wine glass, but when he found her, having gone down to the harbour to see for himself, he had to admit she resembled one of the poseable ivory puppets from the night market, as erotic as any prostitute, a stranger to him. The lamp lit a floor strewn with flowers. She sat behind a mosquito net and because she hadn't seen his face said, "Half a piastre," before she'd turned around.

"Dong."

A sharp intake of breath. "God."

"What the hell, Dong."

"A whole piastre for the whole night?" She shrugged, trying to make a joke. "Oh, come on."

Georges-Minh began to pace back and forth.

"I followed the advice of a supposed friend," she said. "Just wanted to find work. Respectable work, but I ended up in a godforsaken dance hall, serving drinks, forced to dance with customers. Hell, one thing led to another, here I am—Will you quit pacing?" She held open the mosquito netting for him, but he didn't enter the bamboo bed. "You know, my mother has the cough, too. Her health hangs on a change of climate said this other doctor we saw in Danang. We haven't the money to move. But I'm determined to try something. Anyway, who are you to judge? Who's never had it hard."

He was stunned.

She glared at him. "Don't look at me like that. Won't you at least say something? God. I'm not going to hold the mosquito net open forever. If you're going to be my friend, fine. If not, get the hell out. Which is it?" She let the net fall. "In fact, if you're going to have to think about it, get the hell out now."

"I'm sorry, Dong." He went in and hugged her, then hugged her harder. He almost said, *I forgive you.* "Forgive me?"

"Yes."

They clutched each other, two bodies on a bobbing boat. There were more rooms upstairs and the floors squeaked and men grunted and the sounds carried through.

"So, what do we do now?" she said.

He shrugged. "What do you want to do?"

He confessed to Dong his marriage plans, the ones he'd been saving since the afternoon he'd invited her over for tea. He'd never felt her equal, and something about the bobbing of the boat and the scent of the flowers gave him the courage he needed.

"Let me get this straight," she said. "You want me to spend *your* money on the house, and buy furniture and plants …?"

"And books," he added. "And bedding."

"And more pets, and pet food. And absolve you of … how did you put it, your guilt at having inherited all your parents' money?"

"Well, yes. My guilt, and my self-disgust at my cowardice at not being able to do anything about it."

"Oh." She grew serious. Looked at her hands in her lap. "Is this a proposal." She didn't ask it like a question.

"Yes?" He posed it.

"Hmm."

"And soon, we would have more mouths to feed?"

"Which would ..." She scratched her head, because now there was an extra component to deliberate on. "Make it easier to spend even more money."

"Yes, not to mention breed an improvement over the prior generation. Our children could certainly be no worse off than us, I hope. My political duty to my country being to give it sons who will stand up to the French." Sons who would become heroes.

"Hmm."

Her hmms worried him. What on earth had he been thinking? What foolishness had possessed him? But didn't she say she was worried her parents would no longer go on supporting a grown daughter? What options did she have?

PART II

Sleep

15

A month later, on the hillside where Georges-Minh and Dong sat side by side looking down at the forest, she presented him with a cigarette case, a box of tobacco, and a jar of betel. The jungle spread out before them as they gazed across the unmoving treetops so like the crests and valleys of the South China Sea. "A child is a testament to the parents' love," she said.

"A child is a political duty," he said.

She slapped at his arm.

He kissed the top of her head.

Later, in their bedroom, her things on his—their—dresser where before there had been only a collodion print of his grandparents in a brass frame: a tortoiseshell bracelet, the cigarette case, the jar of betel, now empty, but he had saved the jar, the things she had offered in exchange for his taking her as his wife, he kissed her again.

His villa clamoured now with the domesticity he had once only imagined: the long dining room had been taken over by the pigeon coops, the python cages, Dong's cats. Her mother and father had filled it with gardening equipment, clay pots, and mounds of earth. He had expected release. But his days oppressed him and he volunteered more often at La Dhuys, where he witnessed case after case of scourges caused by the colonial evils which he told his wife about each night, because they continued to talk, as husband and wife ought to, though she accused him of spending too much time at work. Or in his home office. Or manufacturing pharmaceuticals in his laboratory just to get away from her, and from the rest of her family. "Are you working or *hiding* in your practice?" she said, taking *the tone* with him.

Now, at times, she wondered, thinking back to how they had first met, the ghost of the mermaid, the unplanned pregnancy, the rush of the marriage, if she was competing with the ghost. His baggage. Or, more properly, why she should. There were other fish in the sea. She was young and beautiful. Why was she still hanging around?

At first, before their marriage, they'd had sex all the time. Now he barely touched her. Since they'd last made love: fourteen times the ants had ridden down rainwater streams like tiny villagers past coconut husk and rotting papayas on boats made of fallen leaves. Thirteen times she'd listened to tamarinds hitting the roof during windstorms. Twelve times he'd gone out to collect them and eleven times he'd forced her to come, too pregnant to be useful at anything but holding the kerosene lamp.

After supper they retired to the veranda, as they did every night, and she sensed his boredom and his distance from her. "Georges-Minh, where are you?"

The purple sky smelled of wind and the calm before the storm. He'd eaten too much opium. She pointed out the beauty but he couldn't see it. For him there was no night smell of the earth's steamy heat and rich fallen fruit. No smell of wet palm leaves or rainwater dripping from the eaves. Just a swelter of jungle. A circular driveway revealing itself like a snake. Petals lost among the dirt.

"You never touch me anymore, Georges-Minh."

"How can you still want it? You're pregnant."

"How can you say that?" She tried to keep her tone steady.

"Sex fiend."

"We used to like each other."

He continued to charge no one at home, turning no patient away who couldn't pay. He saw paddy fever patients, lotioned their blackened arms and legs but remained untouched himself. Patients took advantage, claimed to have not a tien to their name, and then went drinking with his fee. Thanks to his father's equity, which continued to bring in money, Georges-Minh could afford the luxury of not feeling duped.

The widow named Thu continued to visit with her four children, needing money. He played the trumpet and the children danced. She tugged at her children bidding them behave, though all they did was sway to the jazz.

Women who needed money, they came in daily, whose need made them desperate. They all wanted what he couldn't give them: hope.

The opium he did in the pharmaceutical wing of his villa melted away the tension between him and Dong. Also, the things Chang had said the night of the party, the fact they might be true. Anxiety about his true nature, his hypocrisy. After the bitterness on his tongue subsided, only dreams remained. Smoking the paste smoothed the experience too much; eating it was better. No wisps of sweetness from a pipe on his tongue this way. Only bitterness. Pure acrid taste to jolt him away from his delusions and into a better world. What he deserved.

All his doubts about himself faded from a blare into a distant hum. He hallucinated about the den he'd been to with Chang.

Men and women with sexless faces, everyone in silks, silhouetted by candlelight on flower boats that bobbed in the water. He closed his eyes and slept, but it wasn't true sleep. Everything was lovely in this world where he could be anyone but himself for a time. He floated above his own predicament and viewed himself with a detachment and a sense of humour.

Since the light hurt his eyes he would walk, heavy-limbed, to the windows and draw the blinds. If it was night, and most often it was, for he waited until Dong was asleep so she wouldn't know about his growing habit, he would extinguish all the gas lamps and illuminate the lab with one single candle. As the drug turned him into someone else, the candle appeared to burn brighter until its halo seemed as bright as a sunlit window he could let himself fall into.

He could become a child again. A baby.

A nobody.

The opium lent a beauty to everything. The datura blossom of his garden, by moonlight or daylight, it didn't matter, its egg-yolk hue. He saw beauty in the oscillating toothed margins of its petals, in the reflective surface of his glass test tubes, in the shape of a bottle of ethyl alcohol, in the orange flames of his Bunsen burners when he was coherent enough to perform experiments and create new and better poisons to kill the French. Everything was new and magical. The blossoms released their fragrant scents for minutes or hours—time lost all meaning—and a world of possibilities, with or without the French, gyrated for him like an exotic dancer.

Addicts in opium dens gave themselves up to perversions. He soared to revolutionary heights. Young boys like Sing Sing refilled pipes and submitted to men with weakened moral wills. Georges-Minh became a hero.

He'd gone to such a den before he'd gotten married, coerced by Chang, and ever since he had held a secret disdain for all opium boys. He'd tried to banish from his memory thoughts of what he'd done.

Chang certainly had wanted a different outcome. He'd told Georges-Minh he loved him. Spoken of songbirds. Put his hands on his body.

Georges-Minh had laughed and pushed him away.

Georges-Minh had lain down and inhaled from the pipe; the sweet honey air rested heavy on his limbs. Lewd scenes surrounded him. His dreams spilled and scattered like seeds from the trumpet flower pods on a white sheet. The opium made his nose itch and his private parts tingle. So quickly did he have an erection in his thin trousers that he had no time to hide it from the boy refilling his pipe. His desire ambushed him. He was an innocent victim of his own genitals.

In the low light of the den it was almost impossible to tell apart the women attendants from the boys, their long hair and slender hips. Georges-Minh raised his head, grown so heavy, from the mat. "What's happening to me?"

"Go with it," Chang said.

Mainly soldiers and a few officers filled the den, attended to by their boys. His own "boy" became more alluring to him. He lay down his head, suddenly occupied by a thousand sexual fantasies, some delightful, some grotesque. He watched his boy's beautiful hands, the fine, neat fingers at work adding more opium to his pipe, and without realizing it started stroking himself. The next thing he knew he could feel his boy's caresses and he was giving himself up to them. The boy, no more than eleven or twelve, smiled so sweetly. Before long, Georges-Minh held him in an embrace and the child submitted passively to all Georges-Minh's whims. Their romp ended in a barbarous convulsion. Georges-Minh left the opium den without saying goodbye to Chang.

He never returned to a den. His desires when on opium

became less frequent over time until fantasies took over completely. What replaced true desire was the idea of desire. When it came to Dong, his erotic fantasies were twisted but his means were weak. He still became aroused from time to time but his body had long ago ceased to cooperate. He'd smoked himself to impotence.

To help with the anger he made new and better poisons in his lab—he was up to Poison No. 27 now—and he ate increasing amounts of opium to forget.

Outside, other people, victims of paddy fever, continued to forget as well—their names and birthdates, the number of children they had, their professions and lovers. Some forgot their favourite foods or the months of the year. Others professed to forget the Four Noble Truths and other Buddhist teachings. Some omissions seemed more convenient than others.

Even Dong forgot things: one day she forgot to take in the wash and left it hanging out all night. As a result, a ghost crawled into one of Georges-Minh's best shirts and it took two days, 150 tien, and three priests to get it out of the house. By the time it left, it had broken four vases and sucked the flavour out of every single mango.

In exchange for her carelessness, Georges-Minh ordered Dong from one room to another, past windows that cast curly wrought-iron flower shapes. Dong, who'd once walked into his clinic and given him clear moorings. It could have been anyone, but it had been her. The euphoria of her was gone, replaced by a weight on his shoulders, head, and heart. Barking or cajoling, entreating, whispering, wheedling, shouting from the cool of the lush garden to the heat of the service courtyard, pinching her moon belly, but always demanding something.

The monster inside him told her to hull the rice and wash the rice, and after she'd cooked the rice he grimaced his disapproval. The duties weren't new—she'd always picked out stones with her bare hands—but the orders he gave made them seem so.

He played with his poisons, the opium and datura, in his lab.

He, too, began forgetting things. One day he forgot to wear his hat to the clinic. Then he forgot to wear his tie. One day he forgot to get out of bed and to his surprise a colleague from the clinic showed up and asked him if he had a cold. His co-worker gave him an examination, concerned at the pallor of his skin, and the next day Georges-Minh's boss requested he take some time off work.

He imagined a hurricane on the horizon. The wind tangled around his limbs. He dreamed his bedsheets were eating him and he woke in a sweat. He shouldn't have gone back to sleep. Dong had covered the bed in pillows with embroidered cases from Paris and linen sheets imported from the best European shop for such things—he had to admit, the first time he'd slept on a sheet, he'd loved the cool of the fabric, but did she need so many frilly accessories?—and he'd paid the price. He'd slid off the pillow as he slept, a fussy elaborate thing, rooster detailing at the centre, and a spirit, sensing his opportunity, crawled into bed with him. When Georges-Minh awoke, he was next to one of the most hideous ghosts he'd ever seen. It had black eyes and fangs. Its breath smelled like corpses.

Again, it took as much trouble as it had the last time to rid their villa of the spirit that, once again, had been invited in by Dong. Everyone, including children, knew spirits were tempted by extra pillows on the bed, and could only enter a house when asked.

Perhaps the rising conflict within him caused the stranger's face to greet him in the mirror. He no longer recognized his smile. Couldn't conjure his good-time face, as if his mouth had disappeared. And when he viewed himself at an angle, something about his silhouette seemed odd, as if his whole demeanour were contrived. Not only that, the voices he heard were unfamiliar. Were they in his head? Or in his house? He stopped, listened, pressing his ear to the door. He drew back. They were in his house. Beyond the door.

However, when he listened with more attention he could detect only the voices of his mother- and father-in-law, and their daughter—his wife. Patience, patience. A mystery to unravel here. For instance, were they in fact who they claimed to be? There was a gap in his understanding. A hole in his head. How had he, in fact, got to this place, with these people? He couldn't remember. Who *were* these people in his house? *Did he really know any of them?*

The remembrance of his previous fugue rose like an object from the water and sank back down again. Had he been given the opportunity for a fresh start? Khieu would see it as life presenting Georges-Minh with new possibilities. Khieu wanted to hurt the French dogs. As soon as he thought it, his stomach flipped. Georges-Minh had not yet decided if he possessed the strength to kill.

Yes, something was happening. Now, in front of the mirror—he was sure of it. He paused, closed his eyes, concentrated. Unbelievable as it sounded, he could *feel* the change— he could will it, right now. If only he was sure what he wanted to change into.

"Dong!"

He stepped away from the mirror, cold, clammy panic rising within him.

"Dong!"

He retreated back to his bed for safety and watched his room shrinking until it was exactly the size of his mattress.

"What's wrong?" Her hair fell about her face and the sweat above her brow framed her expression, concerned, slightly irritated, as she peeked at him through the doorway. The rice flour on her hands had left a smudge on her upper lip, from wiping her face, from moving away a strand that had fallen.

"Look at my face. What do you see?"

"A whisker."

"No, look closer."

A sigh. "Your breakfast is going to burn. A chin. Brown skin. Red lips. More whiskers." She rubbed his cheek with the palm of her hand. "You should shave."

He bared his teeth. "Can't you see?" His frustration was building, mixing with his affection for her.

"Your smile. What's wrong with it?"

"It's not the same as yesterday."

She frowned. "Neither is my stomach. So, does this happen, like, to people when they get a certain age? Are you under some kind of pressure?"

He knew of no such precedents, though he knew of a man who'd killed himself on the eve of the birth of his son.

"Our country is in crisis," he said. "Men abandon their families and leave their wives in charge of feeding the children. The women have no money and they do what they must to survive. This country was the possession of the Chinese, and now is the mistress of the French. For a thousand years we've lived under the dominion of others. It's why everyone's going mad."

She kissed him on the nose, and left the room with wide eyes.

When no one was around, namely Dong and her mother—and he double-checked to be sure—he made himself some tea in the foreign country of the kitchen. Its white tiles ran the long side of the house. Here, the women would fortify their bastions against his growing insanity.

He listened to the pump drip, concentrated on his fingers' movements, centring his consciousness to the singular, focused point of the teacup, the tea leaves, the teapot. He steeped his mind in blue-painted porcelain, tried to focus away from his approaching fatherhood.

The last time they'd talked as lovers do under the bas-reliefs that decorated the windows had been months ago. The columns of white stone around the main entrance carved with flowers, leaves, and a human face had missed their presence as they fed each other strawberries grown in the night soil of Saigon's outskirts by Chinese farmers to pamper Europeans and tempt the natives.

Dong never cried, but she never gave him the satisfaction of complaining, either. She complained only to her mother and held her tongue in his presence, so she wouldn't have to meet his eye over the dinner table when he gazed at her with annoyance.

He was no better than other Vietnamese husbands, but no worse, either. His growing taste for opium caused him to withdraw from her and, perhaps since he'd always secretly regarded himself as superior to other Vietnamese because of his education, he felt himself better than her as well. Her pregnancy caused two things to happen: her lung fever to go into remission and her outrage to strengthen her constitution, so that when he ordered her to pick pebbles from the rice, her hands moved with the ease and speed of hummingbirds, and when she was done she could look him in the eye and say, "What next?" She completed every task he gave her. And, unlike Georges-Minh, deluded by the false sleep of the drug, she slept in sweet exhaustion every night. Sometimes they held each other, but this was all.

Most men drank, cheated, beat their wives. Abandoned them. Kept other families. Returned at will to their first wives. Free to help or not. Contribute at whim. This was his proud culture. No, Georges-Minh wasn't so bad. And if he sometimes acted out in ways he knew he shouldn't, at least he could take comfort in knowing that he was better than most. Still, there was a time he'd loved her. There was a time he'd seen more. Wanted more. "Your hair's the colour of a moonlit river. I could drown in it." She had once stirred him.

Dong was on her cleaning rounds when she found something in his office. A postcard submerged deep in the pages of an anatomy book made the image of a half-naked man in his swim trunks more suspicious than Georges-Minh's blushing face.

"Why are you saving this?"

"A postcard from the Côte d'Azur?"

"I can see that. I'm not an idiot."

"Stop yelling."

"I'm asking."

"Then why are you yelling? You said you could read."

"That wasn't my question."

"So why are you asking what you already know?"

She circled around to face him. No matter where she stood, trying to capture his eye was like trying to stand in front of a revolving door. "Is this the ghost I'm competing with?"

"Do you have a point? If so make it because some of us actually work around here."

"Fine. I think the postcard reminds you of a time you could actually still get it up." She wanted to say more. To talk of libido and youth—*his* lost libido and youth. That maybe she represented chains in his mind, and that the postcard represented some kind of freedom Georges-Minh believed she'd stolen. That perhaps Georges-Minh had wanted to prove to himself he could merely get a wife like so many other little boys. But simply wearing the ring didn't mean it fit. What she did say was, "If you weren't so high, I bet you could get it up."

She wished she could pluck desire from her chest and throw it out the way Georges-Minh threw out the used bandages and swabs at the clinic.

He was shaking. He was found out. Chang, and their secret parties; the blow jobs, the anal sex.

"Hah. You thought I didn't know. Your lack of desire? The fact sex was great and now it's not? Face it. You're an addict."

He'd seen the guillotine blade coming down, then he saw her mistake. Quickly, he had to mount an offensive. "Goddammit!" It was all he could muster. He walked to the window. Stared out.

"Chang. Him and Khieu. The meetings."

He lit a cigarette, wished his legs would stop trembling. "Okay, shit, you're right," he said. "We'll talk, but later."

"You have a problem." She meant the opium. The revolutionary leanings.

The brown water of the Saigon River coursed by. He shook his head and after taking only two drags tamped out the cigarette in a plant pot.

"It's the stress of the clinic. It's been getting to me. Just need a little help. Soothes my nerves."

She reached for his hand and held it. They stood silently together looking at the river. "But it's getting worse."

Marriage to Georges-Minh was paddling upriver. Dipping oars into brown water, her arms tiring of the work, shoulders burning from the sun. The lies hurt worse than the journey. "What's going on with you? I just want the plain truth."

"Nothing."

"Do I still make you happy?"

He thought of the children at the clinic. He'd often pictured their faces as buds pelted by a sudden winter, rotted on the vine. "Here's what you're not. A flower that's bloomed before her time."

"You never talk to me like that anymore."

Her voice brimmed with pain—knowing he was the cause made it hard to answer.

"I'm sorry," he said.

16

Thu came often to visit. He took her out for lunch and as they walked through the market, they window-shopped. The children ate lemon grapes and banana candies, unable to believe their luck, filled their bellies with duck embryo, banana-flower salad, mooncakes, steamed buns, yam fritters, sizzling crepes with turmeric and coconut milk, spring rolls with dried shrimp and jicama, catfish, field rats, clam rice and tapioca pudding for dessert. Even the baby had stopped crying in Thu's arms.

"Go on," he said, pointing to the expensive jade comb that lay on the jeweller's display case. "Try it on."

She blushed. He was too extravagant. Did she dare? She smiled at him and felt her cheeks grow even warmer, because of the way he gazed right back, his eyes piercing through her coyness with something approaching hunger. Yes, he was like a wild animal stalking its prey. His smile was warm, but suddenly she was frightened by him—yet in a delicious sort of way. She lifted her eyes to meet his again and then shook her head, laughing.

"I don't need anything like this." She pushed the comb across the countertop, back toward the jeweller, using the tips of her fingers, feigning a look of disinterest. "If I didn't know you better, I'd think you were trying to bribe me." She lifted one eyebrow suggestively. She'd found an easy "mark," as Gigi called them, men with money smoothly parted from it, certain ones without even demanding sex. She returned once a week for vitamins, once a week for money.

"You deserve pretty things," he said.

His voice had an odd edge of desperation, she thought.

"Will you also buy one for my daughter?" she said, touching the girl's shoulder. Her voice was still coy, playful.

"I'll buy you whatever you wish, whenever you wish." He chuckled and asked the clerk to wrap two combs.

On the way back from the doctor's, with the vitamins in her purse, two jade combs wrapped in red tissue paper, money, Thu felt better, as she always did, for having done something. For having tried while Mai just lay in bed, malingering, and stared at the ceiling.

17

Dong's resentment—whatever modicum remained after her muscles burned—she channelled into ancestral ceremonies for the dead. Believing she had hidden her true purpose from Georges-Minh, she lit incense for her dead birth mother, asking for her help in getting her husband back. Her offering of the frangipani flowers that she'd picked behind the villa on the riverbank would bid her mother come to her aid now.

It didn't matter that her mother had abandoned her as an infant. Her last act before dying—having hauled her failing body off the migration route to give birth—was to find the breadfruit stall and place her baby in it and say a prayer to the gods.

Her mother would accept the flowers. Would have to accept them in exchange for future services, forced by the rules of the ancestral ceremony, summoned by her daughter through ritual, whether she'd actually wanted to leave the spirit world or not. And after having taken the flowers (forced to, by ritual), she would hear Dong's prayers and become her ally.

Perhaps Dong's alive and betel-chewing adopted mother would not stand by her side against her new tyrant of a husband who must be going through a personal hell to be acting this way. But an ally from beyond the grave was better than no ally at all. Together they would drive out the curse that had befallen them. Where it had come from, Dong had no idea; all she knew was that evil had taken up residence in the villa—in Georges-Minh himself—and with her dead mother's help, everything would return to the way it had been when she'd first fallen in love with the man whose seed she'd begged for inside her.

18

Thu scurried home with the children before Mai missed their presence, the taste of duck embryo lingering on her tongue. A limping dog trotted with a dead rat in its mouth and the body looked like a furry black piece of sausage. Little Trang gave it chase.

"Get back!"

"I want to pet the dog."

"Come back here now." The older daughter, Phung, pointed to the shops where mannequins wore apparel imported from Lille. "Women could win hearts in clothes like that," she said. Boys with large round baskets waited in front of the market for women to come out with their purchases so they could carry them home for a penny. "Let go my hand." Phung almost yanked away from Thu, who clung on while the girl pulled toward the shops. It'd be a miracle if she got home intact.

"Come on. And remember, don't tell your mother a thing. Then we can do it again. You like the candy?"

"Can I keep the jade comb?"

"Don't be silly. Do you know how much food we can buy with that?"

They approached the intersection. A man in uniform, a drunken soldier, lay on his side, almost on his stomach. Thu was having trouble holding the baby while clutching the hand of the youngest boy, who wanted to pet the stray dog, and while making sure the girl didn't wander away to gaze at dress displays. The midday cannon detonated, signalling the time for afternoon nap. It startled Trang, who thought he saw a rickshaw in the road, and in an effort to leap out of the way, was hit by a real rickshaw.

His body lay crumpled under the wheel. Thu's mind went blank. She lifted him and put him on the sidewalk next to the drunken soldier. Her next thought was to find someone. She left the children and not knowing where else to start, put one foot in front of the other, blood on her hands, and yelled, "Mai! Khieu!"

Only then did she notice the others, also hollering. So many people. An old man bellowed on the corner. So did a turtle vendor, a fishmonger, a letter writer, a little girl with a basket of bread on her head. Their limbs, as if they'd been burned, were covered with ash-like flecks. They wandered, immune to the physical pain of their pocks, their eyes like rain. A young deliveryman glanced at the breasts of a woman next to him, drank deeply of his beer, placed the half-empty bottle on a stack of orange crates, and yelled. A child shrieked to the heavens from the centre of the road. How had she not seen them before? The city was full of them, these invisibles. And now that she was one, she felt clouded by it all, the child's beauty, his closed eyes, his tongue held out as if to catch the sweetness of raindrops, wanting, waiting for more. She heard men screaming for fallen comrades, women for missing husbands; children, lost friends, people repeating their own names. Everyone searching for something they had lost.

Thu tried to press through the crowd that had gathered around the man who had hit Trang. It sounded like he was trying to defend himself against accusations of being drunk. She felt herself caught up in an angry wave, pushed on all sides and pulled against a storm. In the melee she lost the combs Dr. Nguyen had bought for her. Enough, she thought, and turned back. Let the furious mob deal with him.

She leaned over Trang and stroked his cheek. "There, there." An older woman squatted next to him, held a bowl filled with water and had been trying to administer careful sips to his closed lips. "Give me that!" Thu took the bowl and moistened the boy's forehead with the drops that fell from her fingertips. She splashed a larger amount across his whole face and finally dumped the entire bowl on his head. This made the bloodstain that had started to grow on the sidewalk expand more quickly. The old woman jumped back and Thu started to panic. She shook Trang, and kneaded his arms and legs. "Wake up. Wake up! What are you doing? Come on, honey, we have to go home. Your mother will begin to worry about us soon."

Fathers, uncles, aunts, mothers, daughters, sons petitioned gods, hometowns, memories. She scratched her pocks. They wanted forgiveness, understanding, retribution, castigation. This was a mania that could be tasted. This flavour, unlike a drink of deep, sweet water, parched and burned the taster. It was a thirsty kind—drinking of itself, eating and eating, remembering freedom, until it left only bone and parchment behind. "Khieu!" she called, trying to overpower the wishes, regrets, hopes, and destinations of others that rode the scorching air, the smell of oranges in crates, the sharp drone of mosquitoes, and the menacing hiss of cyclo wheels. "Khieu!" They screamed, she screamed.

On a day such as today one could pass a mirror and not recognize oneself. Bump into a friend of twenty years in the street and not know his name.

Love itself is an oblivion, a forgetting, a fugue, and its inevitability does not cloud our anticipation or change what we hope for. Would that she could find a love that fed; it would be benevolent, ripe. A warm and swelling thing that made the fullness in one's own heart want to offer itself, to belong to everyone who had also ever hungered. "Khieu!"

19

The police entered the clinic and ordered Georges-Minh and the nurses into a corner and left the patients shaking in their gowns where they stood, bleeding if they were bleeding, crying if they were crying. An old woman wearing tattered clothes kept her head down, as if the police would find her guilty of something if she dared meet their glance.

Georges-Minh's chest felt like it was being crushed by a hot and heavy stone, yet he called from where he stood, "What can I do for you? Can I help with something?" They'd already found Sing Sing's box under some bandages, vials of camphor, and flats of coriander seeds, and ignoring him, pulled it down from the shelf. They pried the lid off with a folding knife.

"It's not mine, whatever's in there. Just so you know."

The two officers rose immediately, at the ready, shoulders squared, one slightly in front of the other.

"No, no, the thing is, I, I know this boy?" He raised his hands over his head. "In fact, if you look in the alley he's probably there now, this junky kid, it's his, the box."

He thought about it later, when he realized what he'd done. Maybe that was part of why he'd turned Sing Sing in. Sing Sing was not to blame for what Georges-Minh had done the night Chang had taken him to the opium den. Could he even say the words? Assaulted a boy. But looking at Sing Sing, dealing with him, forced him like a leper to look at his own sores. No one wants to see that which they've hurt. *Who.*

Sing Sing's sidekick had set him up. Pimp or no pimp, infection or not: Georges-Minh didn't owe him anything. That's what the boy's outburst the other day had been about, his guillotine-talk and his bad dream. He'd been running from the police. They'd been on to him and his buddy had led the police right to Georges-Minh's clinic. Goddamn him. Whatever fatherly feelings he may have begun to cultivate for Sing Sing were now gone.

"So what do you know?"

Georges-Minh wasn't going to let his group go sliding like a ring down the drain. Everything they'd worked for. The plot. His relationship with Khieu. Until Dong, his whole life had been that one man. Working to build himself up in that man's eyes. Hands up in front of him, palms out, Georges-Minh said, "I can tell you the whole story. This kid, he saw me up to something." He smiled in a way that he hoped conveyed "man to man," and added a slight lift of the shoulder, a sheepish but not too apologetic shrug to indicate contrition at the same time as knowledge of his rights, and how sadly fate intervenes and we sometimes get caught—but by no means are we wrong, just unlucky. "You see how it is. How it *came about.* So, he forced me to pay since it was something I know my wife might not have appreciated. I know now I should have taken care of it," as if to say this is what a better man would have done, asserting his manliness, was it working? There were grunts and nods, possibly of approval, and if not, at least they weren't sounds of outright dissent.

He worried that his words would trip from his mouth at the wrong speed or in the wrong order. For that matter, had he brought any opium to work today? Usually he kept it stashed at home, but every now and then, especially if he was feeling unusually stressed, he wrapped a gram or two in hell money and slipped it into his sock, where his body heat warmed it slightly and made it the perfect consistency for melting into his tea at lunchtime. After a while being in there, it became so pliant he could no longer feel it, and at this precise moment he couldn't remember whether today he had brought some with him or not. He began to worry that he'd get searched. He'd better hope he didn't stutter.

"So, fuck me, I've got a soft heart and I let him put that godforsaken crate in here. I wasn't really thinking about it. We were swamped with the junkie vermin we get in here. The lousy whores. I treat them for free, you know. Because I want to stop their spread of disease. I didn't even really see him bring it in. I mean, I did but I didn't—so busy you know dealing with this riffraff"—he thumbed his patients, huddled in various parts of the clinic, looking at the floor—"and then I kind of forgot, till you came. Anyway, take it and I'll show you where he is." Thank goodness he'd spoken clearly.

He grabbed his overcoat before they had time to think twice about it and before he knew it he was leading them down the street and praying Sing Sing would be in his usual spot.

The boy was too high to run. Georges-Minh pointed at him, leaning up against the alley wall with his friend. Sing Sing's arm was leaking a putrid substance, and he stared at the doctor, dog-eyed and weary.

Georges-Minh knew it was the last time he'd ever see the boy, and the boy seemed to know it too because when he gunned down Georges-Minh with his finger, his trigger finger was slow and sleepy and sad.

Sometimes Sing Sing would press himself to the glass watching Georges-Minh at the clinic, and Sing Sing remembered how he'd dream of being asked to join them. Just once, for a plate of sausage and baguette.

In the next life, he and his friend Luc would have a house. They'd have four walls. Imagine making yourself at home, never having to watch your back. Imagine, the doctor had two such places: his house and the clinic.

I'm the boy who looks to the insides of things,
Because I can speak with the Emperor Duy Tan,
Because our beautiful Buddha comes with me,
Because we will go up to heaven.

20

The first thing you do is reach around for your sunglasses on your head. If they're broken, the other person started the fight. If they're intact—you did. Birago rolled onto his back on the hard sidewalk, squinted his eyes to shut out the sun poised above him like a flamethrower. He didn't think he'd killed anyone but couldn't be sure. His head hurt. He was alone—apparently—apart from the circle of people staring down at him, including two kids. His battalion buddies had left without him. The thought of the walk back to the barracks made Birago spit. He rotated his neck and wrists, flexing muscles, checking himself for injury. Nothing seemed broken. He had a terrible itch on his back and he felt a bit feverish. He was close to the harbour. Nearby were some Hindu shops, wealthy, shrewd owners, moneylenders or pawnbrokers, too, well dressed always, how he wanted to be someday in handsome linen jackets. And ooooh, their women—full of *refinement*, those ones, hair piled on top of their heads.

A broken doll asleep at my feet.

Birago's bloody hands.

When he looked up he saw the shops and the fine Malacca women. When he looked down, the boy doll by his feet, blood more black than red. A split canvas. Unreality.

It couldn't be. Was it his imagination or was the group of people standing over the doll's body by his feet growing tighter, corralling him?

... and I don't remember a thing. Two kids staring at me, my hands bloody.

He wasn't going to stick around to find out who the doll belonged to.

He got up and ran.

21

"What's all the racket?" Crazy Auntie limped down the stairs. Mai followed, rubbing her eyes.

The boy's body lay in the entrance hall. Blood pooled from his head and stained the hardwood floor beneath him. Mai ran the rest of the way and Thu closed her eyes.

Mai rocked the boy in her arms: "You're going to be okay, you're going to be fine."

Crazy Auntie tried to calm the children who leaped and pounced on each other in their shock. Thu couldn't bear to witness a scene of spontaneous human combustion, too brightly lit, the horror of something exploding and burning up from the inside out.

"It's not my fault," Thu said, but no one heard.

A rank odour of rotten potatoes emerged from between the floorboards. Two shoes rose along with the smell and circled each other as if duelling. A planter flew from the shelf and kindling sticks joined it, spiralling from the wicker basket near the stove, and more items followed the shoes: a pillow, a plate, a half-eaten melon, all trailing after the shoes as if on parade. A water glass, the water still in it wet and cold as eyes, the liquid danced, the beads in turn, each one a pupil, watching; then a book, a chessboard and all its pieces, a statuette of a dancer with a red grass skirt, a photo in a frame, an oil lamp, a pipe of Khieu's that Mai had not had the heart to throw away with all the tobacco burnt and in the air, a pair of Crazy Auntie's slippers all spun around the room. A vase hit Thu, knocking her unconscious. Crazy Auntie shrieked and held her hands over her ears.

PART III

Names

22

On his lunch break, Georges-Minh liked to observe people. Today, having bought Thu and her daughter jade combs, while letting the extravagance of his feast settle, he watched two men sitting nearby, waiting for a soldier to get up and leave before they tried anything, and Georges-Minh wondered about their faces, what they hid behind their expressions—what needs—before accosting the soldier as he was thronging with the rest of the pedestrians.

Lately he and his friend Khieu had taken up amateur detective work because their duties with the group required them to be vigilant at all times, to make sure they weren't being watched, to determine they weren't being followed, and as a sort of hobby.

Personally, though, Georges-Minh felt attracted to the pastime because he wondered about people's pasts and what voids they might be trying to fill, and detective work seemed as good a way as any to find out. What things they regretted doing or wished they'd done might be revealed by looking closely at what they wore or tracking their movements; the ways they acted said a lot about who they were, what they'd been through, and where they were going.

Now he prided himself on spotting a flash of something under their table: a knife. What action Georges-Minh would take when they attacked, he'd not yet determined.

The soldier's head pitched from his hands and rolled forward onto his table. He was too inebriated to know the two muggers had been talking about him for the last ten minutes, since they'd observed him lunge across the marketplace and tumble into a seat, an easy target.

One of the muggers laughed and wiped the blade on his pants, put it back in his pocket. Georges-Minh glanced around. A common robber, but as part of his hobby Georges-Minh made note of his every aspect: he wore shoes a size too large and had lime powder on his palms; his peasant's pants were loose and dark blue; atop his head he wore a bowler hat. The other mugger wore dirty beige pants and a jacket with only an undershirt beneath it. Georges-Minh's heart beat faster: no one else had noticed the knife, or if they had, they ignored it.

A moment later the soldier pushed his chair away from the table and the two who had been watching him did so also.

The soldier was still weeping as he stumbled into the lane. The men walked behind, closing in quickly. The knife glinted in the open now.

Georges-Minh hopped up from his seat, hurried into the lane.

"Brother," he said, reaching the soldier before the two men. "Long time no see." He hugged the man. He looked familiar.

"Who the hell are you?"

"Hey, don't you remember me? I'm your long-lost relative from Thao Dien. Don't tell me you don't remember."

"I don't have no relatives in Thao Dien."

Georges-Minh hugged him again and whispered into his ear, "Those men are following you." He slapped him on the back and said loudly, "You drunkard, you do have relatives in Thao Dien. You got to slow down on that stuff. The reunion? Uncle Quy? Don't you remember?" He shook his head for all to see. "You don't remember."

The men had retreated to a print shop, keeping a low profile under New Year's banners and paper monkeys as well as other cut-outs in various shapes hanging from the ceiling in reds and golds.

"They've been watching you for some time. They've got a knife."

The soldier looked around.

"Don't look now!" Georges-Minh hissed.

"How do I know you're not some part of their fucking scam?"

Georges-Minh tipped his head. "They're right there. Just a heads-up." He slapped the soldier's shoulder. "So good to see you! Come by the house and visit the wife and me. It's been too long. And lay off the sauce!"

23

"I'm a balloon-body," Dong told her dead ghost mother. "A misshaped pumpkin. I've got stick-thin praying mantis legs with the balance of a stool or water jug some days while other days I tip over easily. There's no telling which will happen. Buddha forbid I try to pick up a shirt from the floor."

"Oh, honey, you and every other pregnant girl," her dead ghost mother consoled her.

Georges-Minh stood still before the window, watching. Butterflies cut as if from a bolt of rainbow silk soared over the breeze, over the river, tumbling in the wind. They mocked him outside the window of his practice.

Dong's adopted mother and father tramping through his house annoyed him. Too much of one thing and not enough of another. Putting his books back, but not in the correct place on the shelf. Buying his newspaper, but the weekly instead of the daily.

One day Dong would succeed in picking up a piece of taro root fallen from the chopping block. The next day she'd tumble collecting kindling in the yard. Even when her parents insisted on cutting the firewood she pushed them away and persisted vengefully in her chores. A contest of strength, because she could not allow Georges-Minh to one-up her.

He rubbed the binaural stethoscope as if it were a talisman, watching her. Fighting with her moon belly, she grasped the shard of wood that had flown away from the axe handle. Hands on her knees, taking a deep breath, she straightened herself up and put the pieces in a woven carrying basket, the same one she used when she went to the market to buy pork belly or live chickens.

As always he knew his irritation was wrong, but he couldn't help it, couldn't make his emotions fall in line with his intellect. And there was a sweetness in letting one's feelings run as free as street children. The opium had begun to affect his digestive tract—why did everything affect his *stomach* so? he whined to himself, to God, to no one in particular. He never wanted to get out of bed, yet the river kept flowing by, reminding him of movement, of all there was to do, and he thought he could well imagine how the patients in the asylums felt, strapped to mango trees for their own safety, crazed by the screaming in their heads, while fresh air blew around them.

Her fingers aimed and then flailed at their mark. Above her swung her songbird in a cage. Should he go out to help her? Aiming and flailing, failing, aiming again. He was relieved of the responsibility of having to decide whether to help or not by a patient entering his practice.

The week before, Dong's father had asked to speak to Georges-Minh man to man. Her father had offered him a quid of betel his wife had rolled, and the two of them sat side by side on the porch swing rocked by the breeze under the trellis. Above them squash vines crept greenly and the foot-long fruit hung down

like bells, also swaying in the breeze. The vines needed pruning
and the garden beds cried for attention, too, pungent with mint
and basil.

The prickliness between them was tangible. Sunlight shone
down between the squash vines and the light hurt his eyes, he
may as well have been looking at sun flashes, knife shafts
thrown from the sky. Dong's father wanted to offer advice. He
took Georges-Minh's hand and held it. Georges-Minh recoiled
inside.

"There are two kinds of women in the world. And you can
tell them apart by the way they treat their men. Their husbands.
Every woman treats her husband the way she treats her father.
Or how she treats her son. Act like her father and you will get
respect. Act like her son and … well. You think I'm here to tell
you to treat my daughter better. But—I'm here to say don't
become the kind of man whose wife has gained the upper hand.
But be kind about it. Do you understand? Don't become the
kind of man who's treated like his woman's son. Or," he paused,
chuckled, "postpone it for as long as you can." He squeezed
Georges-Minh's hand. "But, be *kind*." He took off his glasses
and wiped them with a dirty rag from his pocket. He rubbed
his eyes, smiled, and sighed. "Only illicit lovers are treated as
men. And that's the hard truth."

Georges-Minh muzzled the sound of the man's heart with
his stethoscope; magnified thusly, the sound of its beating
almost overpowered the creak of the door as it opened. "What
do you need?"

"What do *you* need? From the market?" Dong asked.
Without sounding as though she particularly wanted an answer.
"Anything?"

"Nothing I can think of." He could think of things if he had
the time to think. "Right now I'm a little busy."

She drummed her fingers against the door frame, leaning there. "I should go to the market." She paused, as if just for a moment she'd forgotten why she was standing in the doorway of his office in the first place. "*Should* I go?"

One could train oneself to ignore anything. "Go if you want."

"If *you* want anything, I'll go."

"I'm fine," he answered. One could ignore anything, but at what price?

"I *could* wait."

"So wait."

She cocked her head, thinking some more. "But if I don't go now, I won't have time to hang the wash later."

"So go now."

"Well, I could go now. Do you want anything?"

In her absence he'd think of her, long to be with her. He'd want to reach out and embrace her. Tell her how he loved her ears, her eyes, her smile. But why, oh why—couldn't she see he was working? "Mung bean cake, then. Hurry back." He turned back to his patient as quickly as possible.

She closed the door. His chest panged. Had he heard her quickly murmur "I love you" before the door shut? The steel cup of his stethoscope had marked his patient's chest, leaving a red ring. "Sorry about that," he said. When Georges-Minh pulled at the back of the man's hand, his skin remained raised, Georges-Minh's fingerprints remained behind on the tent of parchment as if the man was made of rice paper: possibly dysentery, or perhaps cholera. "Does this hurt? Does this?" Georges-Minh massaged the man's abdomen in a circular pattern with his palm, trying not to feel guilty he hadn't said "I love you" back.

Within minutes he was lost in work.

An hour after Dong's departure to the market, a teenage mother carried a squirming baby into Georges-Minh's office. His cheeks were mottled by tiny red lesions, the same colour as the cheeks of the model in the sandalwood soap advertisements that decorated almost every corner of Saigon. If it was paddy fever, it would have been the first case in a child. On closer examination, the rash, though similar in its constellation, presented in a different colour. While he was thinking about whether this may be a mutation of paddy fever, the door opened.

When Dong came home Georges-Minh did not say "How was the market?" He did not say "I'm glad to see you. I missed you," or "When I'm working I love you. Isn't that amazing?" Though these feelings burbled from deep within him and began to rise as words, he just looked at the tiny lesions under a magnifying glass and noted the shaft of light the open doorway made.

But when he did raise his head, there was something askew about her like a familiar picture on a wall having slipped on its nail. Just crooked enough to make you feel you might be looking at a completely different picture. Or the same one through new eyes. She struggled to hold a smile on her face but it appeared more a grimace, someone in pain trying her best to be stoic.

The first thing was her hair. The pieces in it—bits of something, the stub of an old lottery ticket, maybe. And the hair was slightly tangled. The way it sometimes appeared when she'd tossed and turned at night.

Second thing—if he hadn't looked closely, he might not have noticed at all—something stiff in her posture. As if her body itself was holding a secret. Her muscles keeping something in. Keeping something from him?

"What is it?"

Finally, she said, "I need to talk to you."

He examined her himself. She was not bruised. Hardly dirty. Her left cheek dimpled when she tried, again, to smile. The soldier hadn't touched her jewellery. Did the French not like jade? Or the amber Buddha around her neck? He must have been a Christian. It had been broad daylight when she was at the market. Georges-Minh said lamely, "You were raped in broad daylight. At the market." His wife, lying on an examination table lit with yellow. The baby's contours jutted defiantly, a triangle created by an elbow, an oval indicating the foot that kicked him through her uterine wall.

She'd returned with all her groceries. Oranges, some eggs. Sitting absurdly in a wicker basket on his office floor, undamaged. His practice now bore a Closed instead of an Open sign. The patients in the waiting room all sent home.

Maybe she'd lied about the whole thing? *I'll pull his leg. We'll have a good chuckle. That'll get him for how he's been acting.*

"His skin smelled sour. He told me his wife was in trouble."

She had followed him into a muddy alley strewn with fallen roof tiles behind an opium den, and she'd ignored the market women who were hissing at her in warning even though Dong had heard of women who'd been raped by gangs of soldiers—who hadn't?—but *his wife* needed help and she'd thought: If he's *married* he must be a half-decent man. He'd gripped her by the elbow and said, "My wife is in trouble, she's just back here." Besides, he was alone.

"He wore silly shoes, these rubber-soled things." Half running, because he trotted her along toward the alley past the boys with their baskets begging for a penny to carry someone's groceries home, and she followed him, naively, not wanting to lose him ...

"Who gets raped on a Tuesday morning?" she said. "Who gets raped carrying oranges?"

It was only afterward that she'd realized he was drunk, when he breathed on her, cheek to cheek.

"Before he had a chance to do anything ... he passed out."

The man hadn't finished?

"He couldn't get it up. So technically, he didn't even start."

Another soldier had saved her, had pulled the milk-skinned man off her. She remembered to grab her shopping basket.

Her shopping basket?

"Why lose all your shopping, have to do it again?"

Had she been to the police?

Which police? The French? "What's the point? I'm fine."

"So because there's no penetration it doesn't count?"

"I'm just tired. I only wanted to come home." She started to cry.

Burn the clothes, she'd said. So he did.

He felt as insubstantial as the smoke rising from her kerosene-sodden clothes. He poked the mess with a stick and didn't know what to do. He should ask Khieu. Khieu would know.

Every action he now proposed to himself, to kill or not, seek revenge or not, met its counter. If he bloodied his wife's attacker, he'd get bloodied. If he killed him, he imagined dying by a bright-bladed guillotine for his crime, his head rolling into a basket.

There were no guide books for plotting revenge. He fell to the ground in front of the dying fire, rocked with his head in his hands. His own wife on an examination table. Fate understood. If they could rape his wife, he could kill a man. If he killed a man it could barely be his fault.

Khieu brought a stray dog to the next meeting which wandered around licking sticky patches on Georges-Minh's bedroom floor while Khieu said, "We sit here and spend just as much time talking about what we should call ourselves as what sort of actions we should take. We have a month before our supposed action and well? Doesn't anyone see a problem?" Khieu looked around. "Are we playing? Is this a game?" More calmly he added, "It's not just a matter of revenge but of coming up with solutions, pragmatic ones, even simple ones. Small steps in the right direction. Direct action. The death of eighty soldiers, or a hundred, two hundred."

"Yes, but suppose we did. Take this ... this action you suggest." Chang made a circular motion with his hand. All he could think of was the baby inside Dong. Circular like a toad. Circular like an egg. "How would this direct action take shape? By stealth?"

"Think about it," Georges-Minh said. "Our ranks are thin. We can't afford any measure that will compromise our numbers. Like I said before, if I hit Janvier, I can make it look like an accident." Though he hadn't told Khieu about the rape, his anger about it had made him steely. Most of the doubt was gone from his mind now. He was quite certain he could kill a man. Part of him was looking forward to trying.

"Mixing deadly brews?"

"The clinic has those," Georges-Minh said, "or I could make as much as you need. See that flower there, the whitish-yellowish one? I've made twenty-seven poisons out of it. The poison is not the thing."

"Too much thinking, not enough action," Khieu said. "The poisons, what have you done with them?"

"Well, I made them."

"That's my point. Where are they?"

"In my lab."

"If I've told you once I've told you a hundred times, demoralizing."

He supposed he could have poisoned his wife's rapist. Khieu was right: at heart nothing had changed. Georges-Minh prized security above all else. Valued safety. His own interests. His own health. His own life. Khieu was speaking to the group but really he was peering into Georges-Minh's soul. Diagnosed his weakness.

If Khieu's wife had been raped, Khieu would be in jail by now for having killed the son of a bitch.

"Let's ring an alarm bell!" Khieu shouted. "We're a nation of sleepwalkers."

"We *are* a nation of sleepwalkers." Let him stand up for himself now. "Demoralized. But how will we know if it's the right time to make the hit? What if the people don't stand with us when we need them to?"

Khieu looked at Georges-Minh as if to say, *I expected as much. And will you find yourself a backbone?* "Maybe that's our reason for being. Our gift is our capacity to lead, the burden of the father." He chuckled, pleased to view himself this way. "So then ... to light the first candle, strike the first sword."

Phuc said, "Okay. Let's say we go ahead. Georges-Minh gives us the poison, we kill the soldiers. Then what? We kill a handful of French soldiers. This makes them leave the country?"

"I know," Khieu said suddenly. The energy within him bubbled up like gases in hot springs. "We'll do both!"

"What?"

"Kill both, yes! All the men at the garrison *and* Lieutenant Colonel Janvier. The act will inspire so many. Wait and see how our ranks will swell." He ran his hand down the stray dog's back. "By the way, it defeats the whole purpose if we make the murder of the colonel look like an accident." He glanced at Georges-Minh the way one looks at a silly child. "Our group takes responsibility. Georges-Minh, you will sign our name! Long live MPYM!"

"Wait," Phuc said. "I don't think it was completely decided yet. The name, I mean. I had proposed Fighting Dragon. I still like that best."

"Well, what about Mysterious Scent of the Mountains?" Khieu said. "That was my vote."

"Mysterious *Perfume* of the Yellow Mountains," Georges-Minh reminded everyone. "I thought that's what we'd decided on." He sighed. Could it have deteriorated back to the ridiculous so quickly?

"Long live Vietnam! You have access to him. You can get into his quarters." Khieu raised his hand. "I know. I have it. Listen. After you commit the murder, paint this in its entirety on the walls in blood: 'The Mysterious Perfume of the Yellow Mountains Shall Rise, Long Live Vietnam.' What do you think? Is that too long? Maybe just 'We Shall Rise'? No, too vague. Maybe just 'MPYM.' In blood. Yes."

"Fighting Dragon," Phuc said. "MPYM is even more vague than We Shall Rise. If we're discussing vagueness positionings."

"I say we put it to a vote," Georges-Minh said.

"Good. All for MPYM, raise a hand."

"No, I mean who to kill."

Over the coming weeks the debate over whether to murder Lieutenant Colonel Janvier as the figurehead of the garrison or all the soldiers continued to rage.

Now that Christmas was approaching, they voted by casting ballots into a teacup. The sigh of relief Georges-Minh breathed when the count came up in favour of poisoning just the colonel was short-lived, for his satisfaction at knowing that fewer lives would be lost was followed by a shudder. The administration of the poison, the suspicion, would fall on his shoulders alone.

24

Birago shadow-boxed in a jungle clearing surrounded by hibiscus hedges. Thu sat on a bamboo stool drinking basil tea from a tin cup. He hadn't told her he might have killed a boy: he jabbed the air trying to forget the smashed mouth, the bleeding eyes. The doll haunted him; he kept secret his wakeful nights, his nightmares when he did sleep.

He'd blacked out. So was he supposed to turn himself in? Go to his superiors and tell them the story? Ask his buddies what the hell had happened, the ones who'd abandoned him? Besides, his "buddies" weren't really his buddies. It wasn't like that.

He couldn't tell Thu. Not a woman.

For the moment Thu's mouth was busy with a cup, thank God, because otherwise she was an expert on everything. "Birago, I don't want to speak out of turn ..." "Birago, I know it's none of my business, but ..." Her eyes would pretend to be angry with him but she would kiss his swollen cheek in that way that only women could express love and judgment together as one emotion. She'd taken on the unofficial role of his manager after his last fight against Ca Ong, "Sir Fish" after the ancient whale sharks that grew to immense size on the muddy beds of the East Sea.

"You *orgueilleux*," his father had said, before Birago had joined the Bataillons d'Afrique. *Proud.* "You like to be *gblazhou*, spending so much money on clothes. A dandy man in *zouzou*— how you buy a purple silk tie for thirty francs when you don't have five francs for a toaster?"

Maybe he was arrogant, even vain. The truth was he'd been thinking about retiring from the ring long before his losing streak began. He considered his verdict neither fatalistic nor defeatist: giving up boxing simply didn't mean the same thing to him as it did to Thu.

He viewed his fights as simple money-making performances. Sure, he relished the elephant ka-pow of a knockout, the satisfaction of a cheering crowd, but ultimately he was an actor; the ring, his stage.

Before each match, he combed and styled his hair. The mirror was his true audience. He played for it, posed for it, preened and pranced, saying his own name over and over while he flexed his oiled muscles, which were every day taking a bit longer to warm up, his joints constraining him from deeper within. Ever since he was a kid, when he felt bad or sad he would remind himself of himself, say his name, and it would bring him back from whatever chasm the bullies had pushed him into.

After he'd lost to Sir Fish, Thu had poulticed his bruises while discerning his flaws and prescribing remedies. "Birago, it's not your fault you lost. Now if you just look at it like an army general would ... I know it's not my place to say, but ..."

"You know what, girl? You got no idea when it comes to boxing."

It wasn't that he loved Thu less in the ring. He just couldn't take her nagging anymore. Birago, Birago, Birago, he said. His stomach, an octopus with tentacles, hunted from the inside, clouting his centre. Moreover, she always acted the lion in bed: tossing her mane, roaring so loud. Why couldn't she have chased his octopus centre away when she made love to him? Roared it from him, bitten it from him, fucked it out of his body.

Could have if she wanted. But she didn't. She left a little piece of that octopus jelly behind. What could she gain by letting a jelly piece live on?

Did she leave a piece of nervous jelly because she was inept: an artless doctor who on finishing surgery forgets the scalpel? Did it on purpose like the witch doctors in Senegal so she could control him like a dog? Train him, teach him to stay close, stay alert. Straight, true. Heel. Yank him on a chain. Tie him up. Let him loose. Whenever she felt like it?

"What are you thinking, Birago? Why are you so quiet tonight?"

Punch, punch, jab. He shadow-boxed under the growing shade of the hibiscus hedge. Jab, jab, straight. The bare field of plain water across from where Thu sat reflected the setting sun and made her face glow green.

He wouldn't lose his rhythm, not because of her.

"Me so quiet?" he said. "You the one who sitting there not saying a word." Apart from the chiding, she'd grown into herself lately, cat-eyed, critical, hyper-focused on his mistakes but unwilling to talk, to open herself the way she used to.

She wiped away strands of hair that sweat had glued to her cheek, and the bangles on her wrist tinkled.

A hook, a cross.

"Birago?"

Women. In a way he was glad. The last thing he needed now was heavy talk.

A cross. A hook.

She touched his shoulder.

He jumped. He pushed her away. Couldn't he demand a little respect? He wanted it in the ring. From his woman, too.

Who knew why the French needed Saigon, a nothing town with two dirty streets that ran the length of a river. Maybe its strategic position at the water's mouth explained something.

Still, it was enough for Birago to know the country he was fighting for, even if it wasn't his own country, had to have it, and that they were on a mission along with a shipful of seamen and cannons and field rifles and engineers to replace the soldiers presently holed up in the garrison and dying of marsh fever. He'd do what they needed him to. Artilleryman today, captain tomorrow.

He'd journeyed over from Shanghai with Lieutenant Colonel Janvier. Once ashore, he'd become Janvier's go-boy. The colonel had called on Birago to complete all sorts of personal chores for him, and Birago had done everything he'd asked, including polishing the brass on his automobile, even unclogging the mechanism of his favourite fountain pen to get it working again.

"I wouldn't bother," Lieutenant Colonel Janvier had said, "but it was a present. My daughter's in France, as you know."

Birago found human skin blocking the ink.

"Can you believe he stabbed his own neck? I was getting a confession. Right there in front of me. In the jugular. What a mess."

Birago got the pen working again. Anything as a stepping stone to a promotion.

The chores forced him to miss other duties in the barracks, and this, added to the favouritism shown to him by the colonel, caused even more resentment among his fellow soldiers than did his black skin alone. His captain was not immune to feelings of wrath due to this preferential treatment, either. Everyone hated Birago. They suspected the older man of having a gay affair with him. They suspected the younger seaman, the dandy, of having seduced him.

Nothing but evil could come of such an unholy union. Such liaisons were not unheard of in the French Navy—but among men of such vastly different ranks, and between two such different skin colours?

Birago felt a spiritual bond with Lieutenant Colonel Janvier because of his skills as a fencer and as a sharpshooter (Birago once won a competition in Monaco, though he kept silent to the colonel about his boxing, knowing the sport was illegal). Birago found the colonel had the most exceptional hand-eye coordination he'd ever seen, which made him not only an excellent torturer but explained his wonderful dart throwing.

Every time Birago glanced at the colonel's rank insignia he told himself the only thing that separated him and that man was respect—so Birago made a deal with himself. He'd do whatever Janvier asked of him, even if it meant wearing an apron and scrubbing his dishes, because each day he did so was a step closer, he figured, to having the same rank insignia on his own chest.

"Birago, I need to tell you something. I don't feel like myself. I feel fuzzy. Like my head's been hollowed out. My head's like a cavern. I feel like I'm watching myself do things from a distance but I don't know who I am. Do you ever feel this way, as if I can watch myself from space, and nothing makes any sense? None of what I do makes sense, makes any difference. As if there's no point to it all. I may as well be a corpse, a walking spirit. Invisible—I sit in a crowd and I feel I'm invisible. I know that others can see right through me. That nothing of what I do will have any consequence, therefore I can do anything. I have been given the gift of invisibility. Of being able to do whatever I want. Of invincibility, because nothing I do matters. Because I do not matter. Because I am nothing. I am no one. I have no memories. I am not real."

Thu scratched at her arms and continued, "Are you real? Are you a person? I am not a person. Right now I am not real. That's how I feel. So I can do anything. I can kill someone. I can eat someone. I can make love to someone. I can turn into someone else. I can fly. I can jump from a building. I can be a boy. I can be a girl. I can stop eating. I can stop breathing. I can stop sleeping. I can sleep for days."

"Hell, girl. What?" Crazy. Heavy talk. "What you telling me this shit for *now*? I got to fight."

Before the fight, Birago tried not to hear the beating of his blood. He tore the tape with his teeth, fraying the edges before flattening it down around his wrists and knuckles. Men climbed into the palms and fastened gaslights to the treetops. As he shadow-boxed in the ring, trying to keep his muscles warm and ready, Birago could see spectators from the corner of his eye snaking down the rugged road strewn with mulberry leaves, carrying chairs, beer, wine, food toward the makeshift ring. It never mattered where the fights were, in a gymnasium, in a courtyard, in a hastily drawn circle in the dirt shielded by spectators who themselves watched out for police, he'd always felt at home in a fight. The same way he felt when he rode on top of a wave and the sun reflected on the water and time stopped, and for a moment the world felt right. The bushes hid poinsettias that peeked here and there the same colour as Thu's lips and the way her face looked when it glowed green in this light, in a stand of palms reflected in the pond water, made him feel some kind of right too, if only for an instant.

He remembered a conversation they'd had on the porch of Mai's inn where she lived in one tiny room no larger than a broom closet. Her room would have been too small to fit both of them, along with Crazy Auntie, who treated him like a son even though they'd only met a handful of times. They lay on the crumbling porch that Birago had often offered to fix and Thu had never obliged him to repair. A blue cottony mist perfumed the afternoon: the cat, skulking along the stone path that led from the door to the gate, smelled the approaching thunder on it and wrinkled her nose. An impromptu thunder shook the cabbage palms and the cat scurried under the house and a heavier rain bathed the ground which began to steam, fog rising. Birago sang a popular refrain into Thu's ear while she watched the clouds draw in.

"I like the sound of your singing," Thu said, taking off the morning glory sandals he'd bought her, and she let the rain fall on her feet. Her toenails, cut straight across, were dusty.

"Is that why you like me? Because I sing?" He lay down on the wet wood.

"You like me because I'm black. I'm the forbidden fruit."

He could see her blushing, even as the light slunk away. Thu, the rebel; he knew she was embarrassed to admit that she loved his blackness because it made her sound shallow, as if her love were skin deep.

"And because you are a rebel," she replied. "Your people are like my people."

"A rebel? Like, which people?"

"Black people. Trod down."

"I fight for your people," Birago said.

"Not *those* people, I'm not talking about the soldiers. I'm talking about the rebels in the hills. The ones in Dak Lak."

He didn't want to discuss politics with her. He'd rather know if they were going to have sex or not. He sat up and his body on the porch slats left an outline on the wet wood, like a face pressed to a mirror.

"I don't think I really know what you're talking about." He put his arm around her.

She raised her voice. "The nationalists are very brave," she said. "The women polish rifles alongside the men and the men sew buttons alongside the women. Everyone shares in the work. What? Why are you looking at me like that?"

Most nights he got beaten or spent his time beating others and it was nothing he'd tell Thu about—what could he say that she wanted to hear? She should know what the barracks were like. But maybe because she'd once again leave that octopus jelly piece inside him, or because he felt uncertain, like a nervous schoolboy, he said, "They share and share alike, your nationalists. Your revolutionaries in the jungle hills. Everything will become communal someday—even husbands. Is that what you want? You want to share your men and pass around women? You want me to sleep with everyone?"

He relished her shock, the hurt. He had no idea what the rebels were really like. Only talk he'd heard among the soldiers. It was probably all propaganda they were being fed from above, but at that moment he'd wanted to pass it on. Had wanted to be nasty, without really knowing why.

Birago had no men in his barracks to joke with, always got ready for his dates with Thu alone. No one slapped him on the back. No one punched him in the shoulder or stole his hair oil. For his dates with Thu, he wore civilian clothes, a silk suit and tie, and he splashed on some jasmine cologne. His commanding officer looked at him and said, "*Très chic. Très féminine.* I believe you like being the centre of attention, *n'est-ce pas?*"

In the battalion men took "wives." He was embarrassed to have been one. Like the fact he'd broken a doll, this was a secret he'd take to his grave. Not for Thu's ears, his forcible maidhood, sewing the shirt buttons of his fellow soldiers while they circled him ready to pounce, among other things. That trying to fight back had earned him black eyes, cuts and bruises. He tried to complain to the captain.

"You're *comme tous les Africains*," the captain said. "Whining too much, wanting too much out of life. *Ton* idea of military service doesn't match *la réalité* of military service, and you need to get used to it. *Tu as* problems, you're probably asking for them. The boys are just having fun with you."

He thought now, in hindsight, Thu had brought up politics on purpose, to elicit a disagreement, in order to deliver the following speech. "Your lack of ingenuity, Birago. Your lack of smarts. You don't think about things. You have no inner resources. You live for the moment. That's why you'll never be able to shape life to your will. Are you listening to me? This is what stops you from having things go your way: ignorance, weakness, frivolity." Using what his mother had called five-dollar words, and to what point? To prove she was more intelligent? To make him feel less of a man? To force him into a corner, like a boxing opponent?

"Does analyzing me make you feel smarter than me, woman?"

"You are careless, Birago," she said.

"Yes, woman. I am," he said. "And proud to have no cares."

"Childish."

"Child*like*."

"Do you know many have already left? How many conscripts are fighting with the nationalists? They've made rebel camps in the mountains. You'd move forward in life if only you opened your eyes."

"Maybe I am innocent. Better than those minds who care too much. Or who care not at all."

"You think you know so much. In reality what do you know?"

She closed her eyes and sat across from him while he counted the seconds, five, six, seven, before she opened them again, her body quivering with rage.

"I was *joking*," he said, trying to salvage something. A night together. A chance to touch her breasts, perky as pears.

She ignored him.

"You like the sound of my singing, right?" He reached for her arm.

She yanked her arm away.

Finally, she stood up but avoided his gaze by looking at the porch slats. She picked up her shoes and went back into the house.

"I was just *joking*," he hollered.

For two weeks she pushed him away each time he touched her.

He knew a secret. The red blouse like a bloodstain that day they met. She hid her arms, the slash-mark scars on her wrists. They walked avoiding razor-sharp palm fronds hidden in the sand.

With the innocence only children and the kicked-around possessed, she told him her secret. "Have you ever hurt so bad you wanted to die?"

He told her what he thought she wanted to hear. He thought she meant a heart in pain and nodded. Said he understood.

She shook her head. Explained the man who ran the brothel had beat her so bad she could hardly walk. "I physically hurt that bad. So I tried to kill myself. Isn't that ironic? But I got up. I got up and ran away. *The rich sell their pets. The poor sell their children.*" She laughed. Only her eyes cried out save me, save me. "I was eleven."

He told her then he was a boxer.

He looked around the makeshift ring, at the gaslights, the gathering spectators. For the last while he'd boxed only because of her. The excitement of her lips, not the ring, not the lights. Her lips on his skin. Not the audience—her.

For the last while he'd done it in spite of the losing, boxed for her, because of her, just for her, the way she kissed his torn knuckles every time, even when he lost. The way she admired his stamina. But now he would quit boxing if he had to, and he wanted his woman to agree with his choice. Understand him.

He just wanted her to shut her eyes, because he wanted to keep her and he wanted to go out a winner. He wanted his cake and to eat it, too. Why not? He was willing to be a man. He just wanted her to be there for him. So far he'd let her keep that little jelly piece, wrapped in paper, on a chain. Shown her he could be domesticated. Maybe he'd been playing a game with her. It was almost as if he'd never been tested before. Maybe he'd never loved her. Maybe he'd never been put to the test.

Two things could happen to you in the ring: you got sharper, or you froze. Acuity was all about fear. Fear could be your friend because it made a knife blade of all your senses. Honed them till they were keen-edged. On the other hand, the opposite could happen. You could lose it. You could get so worked up about this or that, you wouldn't know which way to turn. This is how women made you, if you let them. One was fear, one was worry, Birago wouldn't let Thu do him this way. If boxing had taught him anything, it was that fear sharpened, worry paralyzed.

Yet the unpleasant tangle of his ambition was somehow wrapped up in his lust. Or love. Had he ever been in love? He wasn't sure. So he didn't know if he'd recognize it, if it ever happened. A maid who liked to put on airs with existence, but who, like him, had nothing to protect from the world's hazards. All he had was his black boots. And his fists. He'd never been good at anything. But maybe he'd be good at living the high life.

This fight would be his coin flip. Win, he'd keep fighting. Lose, he'd go after all things good.

"I don't want to go out a loser," he mumbled. It meant taking his jelly piece back from her and putting it where it belonged. It meant being a man.

"What do you say, Birago?" She entered the ring, too. "You don't know what being a loser really is. Making a mistake, that's for keeps. Really screwing up. Do you know what that feels like?"

"*More* a loser than I already am. I'm going to quit, Thu."

People watched a man and a woman arguing in a boxing ring in a jungle clearing, a light shining on them.

She looked at him like she'd been hit by a streetcar.

"Anyway, what's it to you?"

Her eyes reflected two separate images of himself: Birago the soldier and Birago the boxer. Birago in a sloppy uniform, Birago with his black skin glistening. Birago the conscript, Birago with a bare chest.

"Prove to me your love," she whispered in his ear. "Show me."

He nodded, less because he cared, more to get her off his back.

Women had prepared their men quids of betel and rolled them cigarettes, even lit them, and a boy sat atop a palm keeping watch for soldiers and a man with a loud voice wearing a chain for a belt took bets and the crowd, grown restless waiting for the match to start, chanted, not the names of the boxers, but the names of the towns they were from.

"Sai-gon, Sai-gon."

"Hai-Phong, Hai-Phong."

The fight began. No gloves.

Smack, a right, then a left, then a right. A right, then a left, another right. Birago delivered two more blows. The other fighter's name was Jack Lee. Already his legs wobbled. Jack Lee's sweat smelled like sandalwood and his black hair reflected the gas lamps in the palm trees.

The doll floated behind Lee's right shoulder. The doll laughed, and a rambutan's white pulp spilled from his mouth. Birago's legs quivered. The boxing match turned into a brawl.

Birago swung but missed. Lee landed a hard left hook.

Next round Birago opened with a combination inside. Birago knew since his losing streak he'd been sitting down on his punches a little more. The broken doll floated in his sight line and he wanted to punch that, too, but part of him simply wanted to stop fighting.

His opponent wouldn't stand still, wouldn't allow himself to be hit. Birago threw another bad left hook. The crowd tittered; someone threw a mango. It bounced off the ropes and glanced off Birago's arm.

But Birago learned something new from every fight. Some bodies crumbled. Others moved toward pain. Tonight something awaited, a different power, on the mat. It had to do with the mango, how it had bounced off his skin, and he could see it among the spit and blood. He picked it up, not for Thu, but knowing somehow he would not sew another damn button at the barracks anymore.

His opponent flicked his jab. Birago swelled with a familiar but newfound strength, the feeling akin to being down in the dumps and running into an old friend on the streets, taking heart from their heart. He landed a wide right. The crowd roared. Then Lee landed a short right and a hook to the ribs. Birago punched his opponent. Lee backed up.

Lee began pumping his jabs. A good one-two. Double jab. Birago docked three rights.

Lee backed up.

Birago got him with a straight left.

Lee jabbed but his jabs were short. He wobbled.

The crowd cheered, "Birago!" Lee threw a three-punch combination.

Birago spun into the circle of spectators and when he regained his balance Lee got him with a straight left to the chin.

Now the crowd cheered, "Lee. Lee!"

Double jab. A left snapped back Lee's head. Lee bled from under his eye. He tottered.

They were still trading jabs when Lee went down.

After the fight Birago craved a shower. His skin burned. During the fight he could have flown to the stars and back. But now he just wanted to rinse off the sweat that prickled his skin. He'd won, and ironically, now that the fight was over, he suddenly cared little about whether he would keep boxing or not. He just wanted to wash and forget.

25

"Not another blasted ghost. Whadja do this time, Dong? Leave some nectar on the doorstep and the window open?" The knocking had taken Georges-Minh from the river he'd been dreaming about.

If it was a ghost he could ignore it. Maybe it would go away. The knocking grew louder. "Shall I get it, dear?"

Dong rolled over, covering her head with the blankets. "So go already," she mumbled.

He pulled his sleeping coat around him. What was wrong with a little respect? Georges-Minh had made three more experiments in his lab, each more deadly than the last. At times like this, poisoning his family didn't seem like a bad idea.

His stomach growled. The smell of burnt rice still clung to the air—if he tried he could still see the cloying smoke layered just under the ceiling. At dinner she'd burned the bottom of the rice pot. How was it possible that, since she had become pregnant, she had forgotten how to cook rice? Even he knew how to cook rice. Though the rest of dinner may, in fact, have been edible, he'd pouted like a child and refused to eat any. He'd gone to bed hungry and now he was starving.

"Coming, coming."

He opened the door to a man with ridges that ran across his cheekbones.

As he woke up a little more, Georges-Minh recognized him as the drunk soldier he'd warned earlier. And then it clicked. He was the same man, the *gabier* he'd seen a few times at the garrison with Janvier.

"Come quick," the man said. "Colonel Janvier's dying."

They drove to the garrison while the man named Birago explained that Janvier had eaten a large dinner of duck and red wine and had woken with chest pains. "Like from a heart attack. I'm scared. He didn't look good."

"He's lucky to have you for a friend."

"We should hurry."

"He's lucky you were there."

Georges-Minh drove as fast as he could and tried chit-chat to calm Birago down. "There's only so much you can do when someone won't improve their diet. I keep telling him." He got Birago to tell the story of the first time they met. He asked him for details, to distract him.

"I met him because I was the only one with a bird in my hand. I found a stupid bird in his bunk." Some days now Birago wished he'd killed the bird. He'd caught it, and rather than kill it, he'd cupped it in his hands. He'd climbed to the upper deck with the bird still clasped in his palms, pecking to be released. He'd opened up his hands and the bird had flown free right in front of Lieutenant Colonel Janvier, whom Birago hadn't noticed standing by the starboard-side anchor chains.

"Ah, like a magician!" The colonel had laughed.

"I don't know why he takes such a shine to me. That's all I can come up with."

Birago said nothing else the rest of the short ride, looking out at the scenery, the blind nothing.

The colonel was pale and moaning when they arrived. "Am I going to die?" he asked from the floor, looking up at them like a scared boy.

Georges-Minh examined him, took his pulse, which was steady and strong.

"Belly gas can feel worse than death. Put this pill under your tongue. And you should lay off the duck, which is what I told you in the first place. Will you listen to me now?"

He groaned and rolled onto his side, pulling his knees toward his chest. Georges-Minh stroked the sweaty hairs off his forehead and told Birago to fetch a pillow to place under his head.

PART IV

Ghost

26

Mai and Thu summoned a rickshaw to head into the fray of Cholon and careened through the streets. "We don't have enough to eat and you're taking us to a soothsayer?" Thu accused. "How do you plan to pay?"

Mai had taken her boy's broken body into her bed. She'd taken the money kept beneath the vase in the front room with her also. She'd been shattered upon the shores of his death.

The children avoided the room and huddled with Thu and Crazy Auntie. Their mother had been possessed, had slipped into madness as one slips into a channel of water, her boy a stone around her neck.

She let the loss lie next to her. She stroked it, held it, wept into the crook of its neck. Khieu had not once returned since the birth of the baby, so let her do all she could to prevent him from mourning the boy's death. Thu and Crazy Auntie argued through the closed door of her bedroom that Khieu had a right to know about the accident and they should go out into the streets to find him.

The money she'd once upon a time let Khieu steal she would no longer let Khieu steal. What she'd once left hidden under a vase in the front room she clutched between the corpse and herself. She realized that love *was* about sacrifice, what you were willing to accept, but it wasn't to be wasted on a man. It was a woman's burden not to speak out. This was the measure of love, the open country and the jungle of it, what you were willing to suffer for it and how you suffered it—but you could not measure strength this way for a man. For a child, yes. Oh, yes.

Only she deserved his blessed blood, the sheets redolent with it, the gathering flies, the privileged suffering of his scent.

"I'll kill Khieu if he comes," Mai hollered back, "the instant he sets foot in this house." Let that be the universe's poetic justice.

Days later they did wash and bury her son. But coming out of her room involved believing that her suffering had been *for something*, that her cup of grief was no longer filled with loss alone but something holy. The heavens aligned chaos, like the stars.

The practical furniture in the soothsayer's shop—a low table, an oil lamp, a mosquito net, a rolled-up sleeping mat—contrasted with the lavish paintings that decorated the walls, of the royal family on bamboo-leaf paper, mountain landscapes done in vegetable dye, other assorted masterpieces in garish colours. Thu waited in the doorway bouncing Cong on her hip. He squirmed, feverish, fussing. The old woman squatted next to some rolls of dried-up sugar cane.

Dust streaked the widely spaced floorboards through which one could see to the earth below, rats chewing on piles of rotten mango. Next to her, a wooden trunk.

Mai kneeled. She bowed in respect. "It's my baby." She pointed at the doorway. She explained everything, told the soothsayer about her alcoholic father, her mother's suicide, the vengeful ghost she'd become. If her mother had it in for her family, the soothsayer needed to know.

"Where is your husband?" the soothsayer countered.

"My husband? But I think it's possession."

The old woman lifted the lid of the trunk. From it she pulled a bag of sand and a map. She spread the map on the floor.

"You mean today?" Mai said. "At work."

"Five baht for me to tell you if he's safe. Ten baht if you want me to tell you his exact location." She waited. Her eyes were dark blue lenses, a little milky.

Mai answered by reaching for her purse—she was here now, after all—but she shook her head as she passed her the coins.

Mai knew she needn't have asked the woman to do any divining at all; she could have answered all on her own: with his Portuguese, somewhere in Saigon, kicking around in a brothel. If she'd wanted to do the legwork she could have hunted down the address herself. Rumours abounded. It was just a matter of plucking one from the flotsam.

The old woman threw a handful of sand onto the map. She studied the pattern of its falling. On her haunches, she circled the piece of paper, looking at the sand design from different angles. Finally she smacked her hand down on the paper, making the sand bounce. "The Central Highlands," she said. "Dak Lak."

"Dak Lak?"

"Where the Forest People are."

"Who are the Forest People?"

"Monsters of the green corridor." She pointed to where the sand had gathered in a rivulet. "Take the sea route, then cross overland. He'll be somewhere near there, where the Montagnards bang sticks together to talk to the gods."

"What for?" Even Thu looked up from where she waited in the doorway.

"Take a knife." The woman sketched a new map and drew an *X*. "Before you call out his name, throw the knife into the wind. Take this knife for only twenty more baht. Such a good deal. It will guide you." She wrapped Mai's hand around its bamboo handle. In answer to the question in Mai's eyes, she added, "Listen closely, listen again. Throw this knife into the wind. Call his name before it hits the ground. Where it sticks into the earth's belly, where the shadow falls, a crooked shadow, where sunshine balances on the darkness, you will find your husband nearby."

"Look, I've already lost one son. I'm not going to lose my baby, too. Thu, bring Cong." Mai motioned. "This is why we're here, you haven't even seen him yet. Thu, come here!"

"I know. Find your husband. Your baby needs him."

Mai swallowed hard. "But how will I know where to look if he's hiding?" she said, reaching for more money, knowing she would have to ask Thu to add water to the soup tonight. "How? He'll just … appear?" she asked.

"You'll have to dig," the fortune teller responded, as if she was just as puzzled, and asking questions of whomever was spooling out her answers from above. She shook her head.

"For a body?" All Mai could think of as she paid for the knife was her dead son, his clothes and little bloody shoes. Even as he'd grown rigid, she'd not let go. She wasn't the type of woman to let go. "I know he's alive."

"Who's going with you?"

"My sister." Mai looked toward the door. "She'll come, if we decide to go."

"What do you mean *if* you decide?" the old woman snapped. "You *have* to go. Or the baby will die."

27

"Why can't you do it?" Bao said.

Phuc's best suit hung loose about his shoulders. His fingernails, trimmed and filed, stuck from sleeves too long and sheened with wear. His bicycle, propped against the wall of the flower shop, dripped with falling rain, as did the pipa case in his hand.

"You don't play until tonight."

"Set-up. Rehearsal."

Bao nodded toward Mimi standing behind him in the kitchen over a dish of steaming noodles. "It's Christmas Eve," he whispered. "How'd you get this gig, anyway?"

"Their regular guy got food poisoning."

"Just go if you're going to go." Mimi glared at both of them in the doorway, the steam rising from the plate in her hands. He'd seen the defiance in her eyes before. "I've already poured the sauce on." She lifted the plate. "Now they'll get soggy, but what do you care."

Phuc waited in the doorway, desperate. "It's a personal favour for a friend of Khieu's. It has lucky money for the children."

Mimi slammed around the kitchen. "You were the one who wanted to celebrate Christmas. I don't even see the point in it."

Phuc said, "Look, we've never played together before. If they like me, it could lead to something." From the rat trap of his bicycle he took the package wrapped in brown paper. "If it wasn't for the rehearsal, I could make the delivery myself."

"I thought you hated the French." Bao leaned against the door frame.

"Money's money. Please?"

28

When Dong went into labour at three in the morning, Georges-Minh was preoccupied with the poisoning plot. So much so he didn't hear Khieu break into his office to steal vials of toxin.

Nothing had alerted Georges-Minh or his wife that her pregnancy would advance in an atypical direction. Dong would stay pregnant for the right length of time. Her morning sickness and cravings, her aversion to strong smells, her aches and pains would lead to a birth with just the right amount of agony.

"Georges-Minh," she cried hours before he was to slip poison into the colonel's cognac.

She stood in the bathroom, stooped over, one hand on the small of her spine. Could it be true labour two months early? He ran to Mother's room, roused her.

Mother steeped roots in ginger tea for Dong.

Khieu had insisted Georges-Minh poison the colonel on Christmas Eve, for he'd said everyone would be too busy with the festivities to notice what was happening until it was too late. It seemed a reasonable assumption.

While Georges-Minh's wife continued to scream and, between labour pains, concentrate as best she could on her deep breathing, a flute player of some renown had come knocking on Phuc's door.

Within the hour Phuc was begging a favour.

Bao ate Mimi's long life noodles. Then he took a cyclo and hand-delivered the brown paper package with lucky money for the children.

In the nick of time a package arrived for two cooks, who mixed datura into the soldiers' coq au vin.

Georges-Minh went to Lieutenant Colonel Janvier's house to gamble.

In the mess hall, someone had decorated a jade plant. Homemade streamers and foil decorations said "Joyeux Noël," making the garrison cheery. Two hundred soldiers sat down to eat: garlic and morels, glazed carrots with parsley, a rich brown sauce made of chicken blood. Not every soldier liked the Brussels sprouts and pushed them to one side of his plate. Some ate these diligently, remembering their manners. Some dove in, devouring the entire meal.

A soldier rose to his feet and, clutching at his gut, stumbled to the washroom, swayed, and fell into a puddle of his own vomit. Other soldiers tumbled one by one, clutching their stomachs, too. They writhed on the floor, moaning, spitting up blood.

As the soldiers thrashed and jerked on the garrison floor, two cries were heard from within a villa, a pair of razor yelps.

By then Georges-Minh, in another house, with Lieutenant Colonel Janvier and Artilleryman Birago, had reduced himself to a nervous wreck, watching the two men drink and play cards, wondering when he should slip the poison into their glasses and how.

Once a week, the doctor and the colonel played cards, only on this particular evening, Birago was in the colonel's den as well.

"Mix us some drinks," the colonel told Birago, who obeyed with a quick nod and walked stiffly into the kitchen. Birago appeared humiliated. Something about the way he turned, the way he held his shoulders.

God, how could Georges-Minh kill him, paint the walls with his blood? When Khieu asked him why he hadn't done it, why their group hadn't been credited in the newspaper, Georges-Minh would look Khieu in his one green eye and say not even Khieu could have done it had he been there. His friend was passionate, he had deep convictions, but God, he wasn't the clearest-thinking man. Paint the walls with a man like Birago's blood? What was this? Theatre? Khieu's emotions were a horse that dragged his logic on a rope behind it.

Georges-Minh waited for his drink in Lieutenant Colonel Janvier's expansive and handsomely furnished library while the elder man took up his fencing sword and began to joust the air in front of the bookshelf, thrusting the tip toward copies of Byron and Proust. Birago returned with the drinks on a tray. Georges-Minh leaned back in his chair and, trying to act casual, gratefully sipped his cognac. He desperately needed something to take the edge off. He tried breathing deeply. He tried clenching all the muscles in his feet and then relaxing them.

He'd concealed the poison in his front pocket, held his hand over top of it, which grew sweaty there. He realized if he didn't release it from his grasp, he ran the risk of clumping the powder, which might then refuse to leave the envelope when he tried to sprinkle it out. He quickly removed his hand from the envelope and pulled his fingers out of his pocket. The haste of his movement caused the colonel to glance his way.

He forced himself to relax, cross his legs, slouch into his chair. He took another sip of his drink and polished off the entire glass by accident. How could he distract the two? He hadn't thought that far. Could they play charades, close their eyes? Could he get them dancing? His vision blurred. He should slow down with the drink. He felt unnatural. Out of body.

He had to remind himself that what he was doing was just and true.

Anger without action was demoralizing.

He needed to engage. He needed to be all business.

Birago took the tray back into the kitchen and threw it into the sink. The noise made all the smaller muscles in Georges-Minh's body go numb, as if he'd spent too long in the cold. He had the capacity to move large muscles, but those for lighting his cigarette, for instance, had stopped working. He put down his lighter before Birago, back from the kitchen, noticed. Thankfully, Janvier was too busy jousting to notice Georges-Minh start shaking.

He'd only agreed to kill one, not two. The deal was off.

"You're a married man, aren't you?"

Georges-Minh nodded.

"You like a little on the side?"

Georges-Minh laughed to mask his worry.

"Join us, Birago. You like women. Tell us about some of yours." Janvier motioned for the black man to sit down. "Pour yourself a drink."

What if Georges-Minh's nerves gave him away? What if they found the poison in his pocket? If he got caught, what would happen to Dong?

"I like big women." Birago motioned breasts with his hands. Janvier laughed.

Georges-Minh could run but another part of him knew if he did he'd never stop. To plant his feet and strike from where he stood, to focus his thoughts, to trick himself into visualizing Janvier as nothing more than a robot—that's how he'd get this done. Flicking the contents of an envelope over the liquid in a glass was just a fucking motion, for God's sake, like waving goodbye, tipping your hat.

"And you?" Janvier poked him with the tip of his sword.

"Little ones." He winked. "More than a champagne glass is a waste, as they say."

Janvier said, "I propose a toast." He raised his glass. "To women."

"To women," Birago said.

"Women," Georges-Minh said.

"Most Vietnamese aren't like you," the colonel said. His shirt was damp with sweat. He put down his sword.

From Janvier, it didn't feel like a compliment. "I was educated in Paris."

The doctor and Birago and the colonel gambled and drank and Georges-Minh played cards and knew if he could get the colonel and Birago to drink another and another, he could more easily sprinkle the poison in. Get them drunk. The ironic part was Georges-Minh's medical advice to the colonel had been to cut down on his liquor. Would the colonel notice Georges-Minh's lack of admonishments? No. His type would be happy for any excuse to drink more than his allotment.

The colonel shuffled the deck. "A franc picked up on the road gives us more satisfaction than a hundred worked for, *n'est-ce pas?*"

The colonel was trying to drink Georges-Minh under the table. Georges-Minh was pretending to drink as much as he by pouring his own into the potted jackfruit next to the colonel's desk. The plant was large and the planter stood on the floor a mere foot away from Georges-Minh's thigh; he hadn't planned the seating arrangement, but pouring the drink out bit by bit between pretend sips had worked so well that

Georges-Minh dared let himself believe for a moment the plan was meant to be.

Beyond the window, the steady humming of cicadas. People sometimes knew in moments of truth what they were capable of and what might kill them. Suddenly, Georges-Minh realized that until now, he'd been acting the part of the murderer, the plotter, the spy. He now realized he didn't have to pretend. A part of him truly hated this man before him. Blood ran inside his mouth where he was biting.

The longer Georges-Minh waited, the worse the waiting got. He needed to make his move. Georges-Minh leaned forward, tossed in his francs.

No one man wanted to be shown up by the other, so more rounds were had. The cognac bottle had long ago been brought into the den and ice dispensed with.

Birago and the colonel had been singing all the songs they knew and had been for the last half hour.

The only answer, as far as Birago, was to become someone else. Only a monster could kill an innocent man. To allow that door to open, even for a second, would mean he'd have to step outside of himself and become one. No more thinking. Just doing. The two men weaved, knocking the desk.

The door would be ajar only a moment.

"I got to piss," Georges-Minh said. "Hey, the bottle's empty. I'll get a new one." In a motion, reaching for the empty bottle, shielding their drinks from view, he dropped the poison into their glasses. "Luck disguises itself as genius, gentlemen, but it's only luck," Georges-Minh said.

Lieutenant Colonel Janvier had raised the stakes by putting in twenty more francs, thinking about his daughters back in France, soon to enter university. Unfair he'd missed so much of their growing up. His own father in a nursing home back in Provence got to see them all the time. Life was a fast-moving stream. All you could do was capture small moments from the outward flow.

Georges-Minh watched them vomit. He watched their eyes. Georges-Minh feigned illness, too, lest Colonel Janvier pull a pistol and shoot him. Angry eyes grew scared, then empty: too sick to fight, the men convulsed on the floor, reminding Georges-Minh of minnows.

When they were dead he penned a note. He left it on the desk. He considered its contents, thought again, placed the paper beneath the colonel's hand.

If they believed the colonel had murdered Birago over his shame at an affair between the two, then Georges-Minh's action was revolutionary, too.

29

Georges-Minh froze. The tipped-over basins of water, the blood, the carnage of sheets. And Dong twisted tight as a pretzel in the crooked bed where she lay, staring blankly at the wall. His mother-in-law sat in the corner of the room, shaking her head, her eyes closed, hissing at Dong to take her child, love it how a mother should.

He reached out to touch Dong, overcome by an urge to make love, to be alive inside her. He thought back to the powder dissolving in the cognac, the looseness with which Janvier and Birago drank, limbs full of trust. Alive one second, dead the next, their bodies thunking to the ground, the jackfruit spreading its green leaves in the hot wallpapered room. His ironic urge for Dong's life to surround him now made him wonder about death and desire: nothing was strange on a day like this, opposites could tie together.

Dong rolled onto her back, trying to affect a casual tone, but her words came out thin, strained. "I'm tired, leave me alone."

"She won't hold him. Not even hold him." Dong's mother

held up a head of black hair for his inspection. The baby squawked. "She hasn't even fed him yet, I keep getting her to try." She put her finger in the baby's mouth. "Put him on the breast, I said. He needs you, I said. I don't know what's wrong."

Her father approached the bedside with a tea rag soaked in eucalyptus water and stroked Dong's forehead. "Shh, Mother. Leave her be."

"Maybe it's because you weren't here. I never saw a mother treat her baby this way before, except for once, when the child was unwanted ..." She frowned at him. "Where were you, anyway? Drinking with the boys? You should have been here."

"Enough, now," said her husband.

Georges-Minh took the baby, placed him on Dong's chest.

Dong, stony-faced, let a tear trickle down her cheek. She pushed the baby away and crossed her arms over her chest. She wept and her face swelled. The tears came in a torrent. Once she started crying she couldn't stop.

30

Georges-Minh stood on the veranda of his villa and listened to the crickets, looking out at the black and imagining the dangers that lurked in the countryside.

"None of the soldiers died," the messenger said.

"The soldiers?"

"They clenched their guts, vomited blood, and maybe even prayed for death. But none of them died. The French general declared martial law. The cooks are in jail. The officials're waiting till morning to chop off their heads. Both cooks are Catholic. They've asked for a priest. I think they want to confess."

"But soldiers weren't supposed to die."

"What do you mean?"

"Someone got their wires crossed."

"An order was sent out."

"Then someone made a mistake. Someone gave the wrong orders."

"No mistake. The cooks received the poison."

"But I never sent the cooks any poison."

"They received it."

As soon as the messenger left, Georges-Minh went to his lab and saw that his medical cabinet had been jimmied. The thieves had left their crowbar behind. It lay black and sullen looking surrounded by broken glass. His experiments had been stolen. Powdered and liquid, pill form and paste. Pieces of the brown paper in which he'd wrapped the bottles lay torn among the shards of glass. He'd been double-crossed. By who?

If the cooks confessed, it would be only a matter of time before the jig was up. To wait now might cost them everything. He'd have to pack. Run. To hike, travel by rail, boat, navigate river ways and jungle paths.

He banged his head on his knees to stop the reeling. Where was his whisky? He found the bottle, took a swig, then another. Before he knew it, he'd finished it all.

He'd do some opium. Once the edge was gone, he told himself, he'd be able to see things more clearly. He smeared a piece off from the larger chunk and ate it. More than usual, but Christ, his lab had been broken into and his wife had just given birth. He'd murdered two men. Dong didn't want her own child. Who was tracking amounts at a time like this? The opium rushed over the ocean of whisky. Ah, he breathed. Now he could focus on the task at hand.

He went into the bedroom where she lay. His wife had stopped crying and dozed. He put a pillow against the baby so he wouldn't roll off the bed. With his back against the pillow, the baby closed his eyes. So pale, so fragile, so thin. Within a few seconds he was snoring. Georges-Minh staggered to the window where beyond a single pane of glass crickets continued to chirp the way they did on any other night, and beyond the porch swing rocked by the breeze the river ran, and squash vines crept greenly and the foot-long fruit hung down like bells and swayed in the breeze under the trellis.

Yet everything had changed.

31

When Birago came to the next morning he smelled blood. He reached for the sunglasses atop his head but there weren't any. Then he remembered where he was and his gut clenched and the events of the previous evening came flooding back. He tried to roll over and felt a knife stab of pain. Slowly he managed to get himself onto his hands and knees and from there he pushed himself to sitting. Colonel Janvier was where Dr. Nguyen had left him. Bastard.

Birago tried to stand and his legs wobbled but finally held him. He checked the colonel's pulse. Not only was he dead but his arms had jelled in place and blood had pooled to the front of his nose, making his normally imposing features appear comical.

He slid the note from under Colonel Janvier's stiffened arm and read it. Not the colonel's handwriting but the doctor's. Birago lay his head down on Colonel Janvier's desk and considered his situation.

Things didn't look good. No one at the barracks liked him. Now his superior was dead and the doctor was trying to make it look like a murder-suicide. He was smart enough to see how this was all going to play out. The Navy would try to quiet the circumstances of Lieutenant Colonel Janvier's death. For the garrison, the murder would confirm that a gay affair had taken place. He would simply have to defend himself so loudly against these accusations that people in Thailand would hear his protests.

Then it dawned on him. Maybe this was how he could get his promotion. The thing to do was simply go to the doctor, extract a confession, and bring him to justice. When he uncovered the reason behind this murder plot and revealed the connections the doctor had to revolutionary types who were planning other operations against the French regime, oh yes, then the garrison would respect Birago. Respect him enough to want his cologne at their meetings. Birago would show them. He'd show them all he was no *zouzou*, *tikatika* man. He was a see-what-he-wants-and-takes-it man, a no-holds-barred man. A fuck-with-me-and-I-kill-you man. That's what kind of man he was. Promotion today, high life tomorrow.

He was shocked when he returned to the barracks to discover that two hundred men had been poisoned the night before. Eighty of them remained tucked in between hospital bedsheets, their faces nearly as white as the material that surrounded them. But as he rubbed his own stomach, which was feeling better but had not returned to normal, it didn't take him long to come up with a theory. And he was careful to explain to the captain who'd taken him into his office for questioning.

"The poisoning of the lieutenant colonel and the poisoning of the soldiers must be related somehow." He told the captain he'd seen the doctor sneaking off before he passed out. That the note was an obvious forgery.

The captain scratched his chin. "You don't believe he killed himself, then."

"No sir."

"Maybe it's a set-up—you and the doctor."

"Why would I want to kill the colonel? He was good to me."

"Maybe you were jealous of him, of his wife," the captain said. "His affection for his daughters. That you couldn't have him all to yourself."

Birago allowed his body a single reaction of disgust: a loud exhalation.

"I asked you a question," the captain said, leaning over him. "Why were you jealous of his wife? Perhaps you wanted the man as your lover?"

"Why would I be? They don't even live in this country. Besides, I want to find his killer."

"Maybe you want to flee before I press charges, is that it? Are you going to run before I file charges against you?" The captain waited, his cigar smoke screening his taut and shiny face.

"*Are* you filing charges?"

"No, I don't think so." In an instant his voice changed. "Shame for fighting with the nationalists! Shame for causing the death of a colonel, a husband, a man with two children. Shame for poisoning all the soldiers."

32

Georges-Minh packed while Dong slept. He found a bag of salt fish in the pantry, a small axe, a half-carton of matches. The opium calmed him as he gathered emergency candles, kerosene, herbs and roots in glass jars from the wooden shelves. The opium helped him divine each object's true worth, focused his remaining fear. All this took place in silence. The rhythm of rooting and rummaging, finding a knife, wrapping the blade in kitchen cloth, then tying it round with twine.

Georges-Minh ran across the driveway to his office to fetch a textbook that might be needed and worth its weight. On second thought he probably didn't need the book. Yet he clutched it as he walked back to the house. He might never return to his home office again. He paused between the house and his office, looking at the book. His hands, in this light, looked covered in blood. What had he done. The garrison cooks had been arrested. So far, no one knew he was involved. But his anonymity wouldn't last: they'd soon make the connections they needed and his medical career would be over. He didn't need the book. So why was he loitering halfway between the house and his office with it? He had no plan. No plan of action at all. Maybe he could ask Dong what to do. He hadn't a clue what to pack and a wife who as yet had no idea he was a murderer and a baby whose life he'd put in jeopardy. And he would ask her for advice? The moon glowed and swelled and ballooned and popped. Stars rained everywhere. He raised his arms over his head and hurried for the house as fast as he could with the book in his hand. No, how could he get her involved. He must leave. She'd had nothing to do with his craziness.

He glanced at his wife's sleeping figure and then scanned the bedroom for more things to take. He was stalling, he knew. A professional photograph of his mother and father-in-law on the dresser to the right of the Giotto painting and one of his own parents in front of the justice of the peace in Saigon. Also on the dresser, her jade earrings, his cufflinks, side by side. Stockings on top of hair pomade. Echoes of laughter in the high-ceilinged rooms. Sighs. Laps. Lips. Stories. Eyes, dry and wet. Their spirit buoyant on the possibilities of years to come. Calling the images back, over and over. Every which way. He looked at his pocket watch.

Dong woke up. She saw the suitcase. "What are you doing?"

He explained.

She began to throw things at him. Things for him to put in his suitcase. Socks, a sheet, shirts. "It was Khieu, wasn't it?" A towel, a mosquito net. "You've gone ahead and done it. He told you to do it. The thing with the blood and Mysterious Perfume of the Yellow Mountains! Vietnam! Vietnam! On the walls."

He placed the items in his suitcase. Only its swelling slowed his progress.

"It *was* Khieu, wasn't it? You wouldn't have done it except for him."

"That's not even our name," he mumbled. "Perfume of the Yellow Mountains."

As he packed, Dong held her hand over her eyes and did not look at him.

"Think of the baby," she said.

He continued to pack, said nothing.

"Don't go," Dong said, now passing him things from the drawer—a belt, suspenders, sock garters. "Couldn't you just wait a little while?"

He placed those items next to the others.

"Stop. I'll turn you in."

"Dong. Now is not the time."

"You are not leaving me!"

"Not *now*. This isn't a game."

"Or what? You'll poison me?"

The dawn's rays tumbling through the window made the teak floor blaze. Dong struggled up from bed. He may as well have been looking at flashes of the sun made by a signal mirror. Georges-Minh shrank inside.

"You can't make me stay," she said. There was hurt in her voice—a shaking within her, a fire at the core that would soon erupt—he sensed it. "This isn't the Stone Ages, I can go wherever I want. Fine for Khieu to set you up to this, who has abandoned his family. Did you ever think of us?"

"I made up my own mind."

"You can't. You're incapable."

He felt as though she'd slapped him.

When he was finished packing, Georges-Minh buckled the suitcase closed and tested the weight of it. Less said the better. Not to mention her despair. The turmoil he'd put her through couldn't be denied. In what way would their emotions guide their debate about what to do in the days that followed?

"If you leave, you'll never know."

"What?"

"Anything." She crossed her arms over her chest. "Anything might happen to us. Whatever at all. And you'll never know. Maybe I'll leave the baby in the market, for all you care."

If he left her here she'd let the baby starve.

He'd be responsible for yet more deaths.

He deliberated.

"Fine, pack some things." God, he hoped it was him and not the opium and whisky talking.

33

The sun had yet to set below the fence when two soldiers bound Birago's hands with twine. The captain stood with a cigar in his mouth and a corporal stood next to the captain doing nothing in particular.

"What's going on?" Birago said. "I don't understand. I've told you everything I know." He let his feet go limp so the soldiers dragging him to the yard would be forced to pull his weight. "Why are you doing this to me? I'm a good soldier. You can't do this to me." When he lost hope that the execution might be a joke orchestrated by his peers to scare him, he kicked, he bit, he spat, he screamed in Senegalese. A line of five soldiers raised their rifles at his head. "I'll do whatever you want, sign anything, go anywhere. Untie me. Come on—"

His head slumped forward when the shot rang out and he fell.

34

The rumour was true. The two Catholic cooks had called for a priest from their jail cells. They confessed names, places, dates. Unburdened their consciences of everything. Thus cleared their heads before they were lopped off.

Khieu hopped onto Georges-Minh's kitchen counter. "Congratulations! Two months early, isn't he?" Khieu, the fool, had been drinking all night. Now he'd shown up on Georges-Minh's doorstep, minutes before he was to leave. "You *are* the new father, right?"

"Those cooks signed our death warrants, thanks to you," Georges-Minh said. Khieu had gathered everyone, Chang, Phuc, all except for Bao. Georges-Minh eyed his suitcase.

"Relax. Cigars all round. Come on, boys. Let's jubilate a little."

"You broke into my lab," Georges-Minh said.

"How serious is our situation, Georges-Minh?" asked Phuc. "Should we all flee? Two cooks have been guillotined. Maybe three. Chang, you said a seaman's been shot."

"My point exactly." Khieu cocked his head and narrowed his eyes. "I thought about it all the way over. Two cooks have already been arrested, as well as a seaman. I'd say the case has been closed." He lit a cigarette and crossed his legs, blowing out the smoke. "Besides, aren't we here to congratulate Georges-Minh on his sudden fatherhood? Welcome the new baby to the world?"

"From what I've heard," said Chang, "the shooting of the seaman wasn't only to do with the poisoning. My contacts say he had enemies. The poisoning might just have been an excuse to get even. So saith my grapevine," he said, licking his thick lips.

"See my point?" Khieu said. "So long as they don't pin it on me, I'm good. They'll find a scapegoat. Let it not be me." He crossed himself.

"You think the military is going to drop a case like this so easily?" Georges-Minh said. It wasn't like Khieu to act this way. "What about once it hits the papers? You're all a bunch of fools."

"No, *you're* a fool. And the military think *we're* a bunch of fools. That's our golden ticket." Khieu's eyes became lucid. "They think we're incapable, a pack of drunks who couldn't organize a successful revolt if we tried. They have no respect for us. No faith in our intelligence to stage anything. That's our saving grace. Don't you understand? *That's* our cover."

"You're drunk."

"Wine in, words out," Phuc said, reciting an old proverb.

Georges-Minh looked around the room. "Where's Bao? Why isn't he here?"

"I *am* drunk. Drunk with power. Drunk with grief. What's your point?"

Georges-Minh shook his head. There'd be no talking to Khieu in this state. "I'm going. If you guys hadn't shown up we'd be gone already. Bao's got the right idea. For all we know they're already on our trail."

"They don't know anything." Khieu flicked his cigarette, the ash barely missing Georges-Minh.

"Wait," Chang said. "I'm going with you."

"Listen," Khieu said. "I want to have a drink with you and say, 'Dad, way to go.'" He tried to grab Georges-Minh's shirttail.

"Quit pulling at me," Georges-Minh said.

"Okay, fine. Have it your way." Khieu waved his hands around. "You're not in the mood, I can see that. They think we're idiots, so do you. Don't worry about it."

"Let go." Georges-Minh's opium high had worn off and had left him with a pounding headache.

"Leave him alone," Chang said to Khieu.

"Sit down, have a drink. You're running from nothing."

"Don't be so naive," Georges-Minh said. Khieu was scared. That's why he was drunk. Why he himself had gotten high. "Do what you want, but I'm leaving."

"How long?" Phuc said, visibly shaken. "Do you think we have, I mean? Before they start the hunt?"

"Did you at least go by Bao's place on your way?" Georges-Minh asked.

"Of course. Empty," Khieu said.

"I've been meaning to take a vacation anyway," Phuc said, lighting a cigarette off the end of his last one.

"Him and his wife left town is what I heard," Khieu said. "Saw her at the train station."

"I'm leaving now," Georges-Minh said.

35

The morning of his execution, Bao remembered his dream. His own name in red ink on yellow paper written upon the Ledger of Heaven. Le Bao Victor. Age 28. And after his name, three words: A good death.

If he'd gone into politics rather than cultivate a thousand red petals of peach blossoms, followed in his father's footsteps, he wouldn't be here. In the jail on De la Grandière. If only he'd listened to Mimi, he would never have met the cook who opened the door, took the package he'd delivered on Phuc's behalf. He'd be in Mimi's arms. He'd been so bullheaded. He punched the wall, balming his regret in pain.

The cook had recognized him. "Children's Moon Festival. Mr. Le. Victor!" He clapped his hands. "The chrysanthemums. The scent clung to the bedding even after they died. And what a memorable yellow they were!"

Bao passed him the brown paper packet, explaining it was from Khieu.

"Please. Take a drink." The man called into the house. "Tran. Some rice wine. Look. It's Mr. Le. From the flower shop."

"I'll find some bean cakes to fry up," the wife said.

"Don't trouble yourself," said Bao, embarrassed by the fuss, for now a skinny boy was pushing a choice of chairs around a rickety table. Guilt forced him to join them for one glass before finally removing himself and heading home, never thinking the package contained not *li xi* but datura, and that within hours the police would come to his door, that he would crack under torture and name his friends.

They would cart the guillotine into the square where a crowd would be waiting. His wife.

Mimi had wanted children, but none would mourn Bao's death. Tie a red thread at the family altar. Pay astrologers to conspire for a date or geomancers to select a location for his funeral. Who would light incense? Inform his ancestors he'd passed on?

Maybe Mimi wouldn't even come to his execution. And who could blame her if she didn't? He knew she'd visited a pyromancer at a rocky point in their marriage to ask if she'd chosen the right man, if she should stay or go. The pyromancer carved questions into a turtle's shell. Heated the cracks and deciphered the answer from the way they split.

"If you knew you were going to die tomorrow," the pyromancer questioned, "what would you do? Power is acting from a place of knowledge." This was her riddle to take home, understanding that the right man was someone she'd want by her side even then.

At his grandfather's funeral, a procession of a hundred porters had been led by two elephants and mourners in blue. A mandarin in a silk robe had swatted little barefoot boys away from the coffin. Such a soul would be led to the River of Forgetting, where his spirit would mount the Dragon's back and, bathed by those perfumed waters, be washed of his sins.

He walked up the three wooden steps to the guillotine platform, hands bound behind his back. The men at his side steadied him, held him when he stumbled. He turned to look for Mimi. Saw a bloody wicker basket. All he could think of was how he had wasted his hours at Georges-Minh's while Mimi cooked and cleaned at home. He drank and played cards while she worked. He plotted with those misfits, and he could have taken his place next to the junior cabinet minister of Annam, his father. Because of latent adolescent anger, he was dead: all children rebelled, but they didn't all ruin lives, try to overthrow the government.

He saw her then, met her eyes.

They forced him to kneel over, pushed down his head; the wood crushed his neck, rasped his skin; he stared into the bloody pannier.

A crowd had turned out. It tittered, shuffled. Some people had come in support of Bao. Most had not. When the blade fell it made a whooshing sound. He saw the basket, the wicker weave, felt his eyelashes blinking against it. He felt no pain. Was surprised, even shocked, that at first no darkness fell and that hearing remained. Enough to make out Mimi's voice, not calling out his name, but howling the battle cry of revolutionaries, offering forgiveness, absolution, and mercy. "Vietnam, Vietnam!"

36

In the end, Khieu didn't wait for the police to knock on his
mistress's door. Nor did he wait to see how his fellow Perfume
of the Yellow Mountain members would hold up to interrogation
under duress. After he sobered up, he thought about how the
cooks at the garrison had been taken into custody and had confessed, and he waited until his mistress fell asleep after they had
made love. He waited until she had turned over in the bed of the
small apartment they shared and he lifted her thin opal-coloured
arm off his thigh, kissed her eyelids one-two-three times as she
snored, oblivious of the part he had played in the drama unreel-
ing itself, and he wished it was a film such as one they'd talked
about seeing that he could put back on the spool, start over.

Why hadn't he said anything about Bao? He didn't know.

"Goodbye," he said. He wanted to add, *I hope we meet again*,
but he felt like a character in a book and looked around,
self-conscious, as though someone had caught him mid-
thought, already hunted. He took one last glance before shutting the door.

In the south of the country, resembling two rice baskets at either end of a pole, each had fought the French invaders in a dozen quiet ways, or had wanted to believe they had, had soothed themselves with this thought. For the last twenty years, the French had failed to suppress the Montagnards of the Central Highlands, who returned like a rash that could not be controlled. The French would extinguish one outbreak and the rash would reappear on another limb, just as virulent as before. The forests were too deep, too dark. Neither the French nor the Chinese had ever conquered any of the ancient wandering tribes in whose direction Khieu would now head, hoping to find some shelter, some prospect, for what he didn't know—he travelled blind, lost, had no direction, clothes, supplies, no idea what would become of his life.

The tribes spoke their own languages. Lived in houses on stilts high above the ground, so he'd heard, and still hunted with arrows and crossbows. They wore loincloths or went naked. He'd run to the hills and hope their people would take him in.

37

A soldier knocked on the door to Dr. Nguyen's villa. He looked beyond the river at the brambles and tapioca vines edging the opposite slopes. A canal system ran between houses not situated directly over the river. Only the rich could afford to be right over the river, and residents on the smaller, artificially built tributaries—in houses such as the one he'd grown up in, such as the one his parents still lived in—used the water that flowed between their smaller, more primitive houses for drinking, bathing, and washing, as well as going to the bathroom.

In the villa he found only an old woman and an old man. On each side of the door bougainvillea spilled onto the ground red as blood. A songbird sang in a cage above them in the entrance hall. The old woman told him about the blessed event, the birth of the child yesterday, and said that Dr. Nguyen, accompanied by his wife, had left to show off the infant to relatives in another province.

38

Mai heard the gate clap shut. She struggled up on one elbow from her bed to see Thu's open basket filled with catfish, rice, soursop, beansprout: where on earth had she gotten the money?

Mai wished many things: that Cong wasn't sick; that her husband wasn't vagrant; that her son wasn't dead. Mai let her head fall back onto her pillow. Mai knew that bitch Thu was dying to accuse her of dramatics. Mai could see it every time Thu came into the room. Thu loathed anyone in pain.

Maybe night simply made her miss her husband more.

A star. Could he see it, too? White. The colour of mourning. At this moment, she felt he was training his gaze on the same star as her. By looking at the same star in the same instant, their spirits were becoming one.

She rose from bed and drew a tunic from her wardrobe. As she put it on, the fabric shimmered, reflecting the oil lamp's glow. The way silk mirrored light the same way a black lake did stood as a metaphor for something. Had she less sadness to dwell on she could have put her finger on it. Husband gone, son dying, one more in the grave.

At night even childhood heartaches came back. Tragedies, because of their size and bulk, should have erased them, the sad little moments, the tiny mournings, the nothing pains. Yet the moment-to-moment sufferings, the unkind looks, the harsh words were a burnt offering unto them. They fuelled the memories of the shores upon which she'd been shattered. Kerosened them. Stoked them.

She had clutched Trang's body and refused to let go. She'd become what surrounded her, the stinking space, the sheets covered with dried blood, the mustering flies.

Even as part of her knew she was wrong, a more powerful part claimed control and said, You will do what I want.

As if she was riding a bull, a bull she couldn't control, after a while it had become easier to stop trying, to let herself go and pet the boy's hair if that's what the bull wanted, if that's what felt right. To cuddle up to his body, even as it had grown rigid, because— because after all, who was Thu to suddenly speak of rights?

She let the loss lie under her body, beneath her softly, so she could sleep and dream.

In her dreams she saw Khieu shave. The water dripped from his fingertips into the bowl beneath the mirror. His hands on his chin, his neck, pulled the skin taut. She loved its smooth tea colour. The gleam of the straight razor.

A drop of blood, red as a pomegranate, bloomed on his cheek. He blotted it with his index finger and then licked it. As he shaved the other cheek, the blood mixed with the water like rain on a windowpane; it meandered a path in the wind.

She dreamed about his arms. She leaned her head against them, cupping her head in the nook of his chest. How deeply she inhaled, dizzying herself with the memory of his cologne. She could still smell him. Some part of him must have been left behind, in his books and his papers, his clothes and his shoes.

Their baby was dying. Was it Khieu's hand smothering him and not her mother's? She clutched his body, rocked him to her chest.

Loss flew through the persimmon trees.

Mai forced Thu to agree to search for her lost husband. Never had the decency to pose the "Come, now?" as a question but said "Come, now!" as an order. Made her cross her heart and promise to gouge her eyes if she told anyone, even Birago, especially Birago, they were leaving.

The two women stood in the front room that absorbed sound, creating an amniotic sort of silence. Thu clenched her fists, ground her molars. Outside the other children were shaking water off the trees because the branches were wet from the rain. Children who'd have to fend for themselves, with Crazy Auntie upstairs, while she and Mai were gone. Who did Mai think she was?

On the table, in the room that hadn't heard any laughter since the day the dead boy had lain on that floor bleeding from his ears and eyes and nose, stood a teak-and-china bowl pushed up against the wall filled weekly with cut flowers. A fool's chore.

These days it was even worse than disliking cut flowers: it was no longer just a matter of seeing the waste in it, watching the greyish water stain underneath the bowl expand and thereby mark how long you had been filling it with something like hope; no matter how well tended, the blossoms yellowed and rotted and mildewed and stank and died. The sentimentality of trying to keep them alive churned her stomach in even her best moments.

These days Thu couldn't look at a bouquet unless willing to face her greatest fear. She'd start crying. Not because flowers were inherently depressing, but because the buds looked so beautiful, their heads bowed. Beauty had been popping up everywhere, it seemed, since Trang had died.

Mai said, "It's not as though the gods haven't told us where he is. Besides, you owe me."

"Meaning?"

"I have to say it? My son was alive when you left, dead when you came home. My baby is dying, Mai."

The only pure joys were echoes now.

Dragon shadows danced in the corner by the ceiling. Thu shook her head to banish the dread of impending loss. Birago was just a man.

How long before lonesomeness made him decide to fill the empty hours where she was not? Just a man who would succumb to a man's temptations. What man would wait for her? What man, given her absence, would remember her, a plain Jane, after she left the room?

He would find a lover, but not in sorrow, nor to fill any empty hours or arms. He would find her from a selection of others, the way one found a new pair of shoes, without fanfare or forethought—not to fill a hole Thu had left behind, but for fun, in a moment of frivolity. That's why Thu's presence near him at all times was imperative. She was the kind of woman who was easy to forget and she knew it.

Thu would have to send Birago a letter explaining what had happened as soon as possible, whether Mai liked it or not.

She would send a postcard from every single stop. Every town on their journey. Each postcard, poetry. Birago liked poetry. Dirty poetry, erotic verses. In place of her presence, at the very least she could supply him with carnal tidings to remind him of who she was, the kind of woman easily forgotten, therefore willing to fulfill his wildest dreams, do anything he asked, without hesitation.

"I'll go with you for one week," Thu said. "If we don't find him, I'm coming home."

39

At the station Georges-Minh and Chang pressed into a siphoning heat, children trying to ferret Georges-Minh's pennies by hawking bags of peanuts or offering to shine his shoes. Sweating in the dancing waves that rose from the tile floor, he passed his money through the wicket and bought three tickets to Hue. Dong, dressed in a conical hat and loose pants, looked like a schoolgirl; the baby boy could be her brother. He fed himself with the hope that Dong and the baby would be protected travelling with him because those investigating the poisoning plot were searching for single men, not a family.

Georges-Minh had told his mother-in-law that he was taking them to visit his uncle in another province. "So soon after the birth?" Mother had enquired with a furrowed brow. Yet she knew better than to press, for even those strong by nature realize by instinct when not to push.

He wiped his brow with his already soaked hankie while Dong waited in a cooler corner with Chang and the baby. When the girl behind the counter said, "Where to today, sir?"

for a moment he had stared, not recalling his name, and when his senses docked like a ship in port he found himself stuttering, "Hue," for no reason other than the man in line beside him had spoken it, and when the teller in front of him asked him to repeat it he found himself saying the single syllable again, "Hue."

His wife waited with suitcases at her feet in front of an altar furnished with lotus flower and mooncakes. He patted his brow. The shadows were so heavy they seemed clothlike, starched.

Bread sellers, coconut vendors, civil servants, and conductors rushed by. They moved through the streets as wind, putting him in mind of a mystic who was preparing a potion to turn his men into an invisible army. "In the mountains there's a general," Khieu had said during a meeting, "and his followers practise 'flying scissors to the neck' and how to fight with their hands. They say he's making an army of ghosts. They'll march into Saigon." He moved his hand like a banner. "Invisible, they'll attack the French and succeed. Because who can fight the wind?" Georges-Minh had thought Khieu was having them on (to believe it himself!) or perhaps wishful thinking was making Khieu lose his mind. But now, in the corner of the train station, he longed for such a cloak of invisibility, thought of the mystic general while French police and soldiers sauntered past.

The trip from Saigon to Hue would be four hundred miles—eighteen hours. Besides all the mundane supplies they would need for the trip, he had also packed Dong's medicines. Her eucalyptus oil and her Tiger Balm, her tincture of opium and capsicum, her rubbing coins, which he'd wanted to leave behind, though he hadn't said so, afraid of hurting her feelings when she'd insisted on bringing them, tears in her eyes because they reminded her of her parents.

After they boarded the train, the sky greyed to the colour of congee rice gruel. People rushed with the determination of millipedes with their shopping baskets, or sold mangoes and hairy red chom-chom, as the peasants called rambutan, bananas and star apples, durian, pineapples, pomelos, lychee nuts, papayas, persimmons, egg-shaped sapodillas, and jackfruit.

He looked out the window, suddenly sombre. "What'll we do?"

"What *can* we do?" Dong said.

Georges-Minh shivered.

"Don't cry," Dong said.

Georges-Minh kept shaking his head. A tear fell from his nose onto his lap. He wiped his face with the heel of his hand. He felt so cold. He wondered if he was having opium withdrawal.

Chang wished Georges-Minh hadn't brought Dong. The military hunting them might have provided the best chance their relationship ever had: united against persecution. The two of them, against great odds, on the run, all alone, against the world. Georges-Minh would break down in the hotel, and Chang would be there to stroke his hair.

"Hey, who's hungry? I'm hungry." Chang dug through one of their cases. "We have salad rolls, spring rolls, duck meat, eggs. What would you like? Some guava juice? Coconut?"

Chang's enduring infatuation was too much to fathom. Was he acting now for the sake of the baby? The little innocent who'd done no harm to anyone, and thus deserved none of this suffering?

Reclined, they had each sucked a pipe at the opium den.

Chang had reached out. Said, "I love you."

"You're just high," Georges-Minh had said. The den's smoke obscured the hand, the mouth Georges-Minh pushed away.

"So?"

"Love isn't a songbird. You can't cage it."

"You're afraid."

"Set it free."

Chang passed Dong a few items on a napkin and she handed the boy to Georges-Minh. His head smelled fresh. They passed rice fields dotted with white birds. The rice plants swayed and mountains rose in the distance beyond the fields, the mountains a darker green intersected by dirt roads that, from a distance, looked like snakes. An unfamiliar feeling surged through Georges-Minh with the force of a monsoon. Suddenly he and the baby were a world of two. He felt anchored to something real, sure that an earthquake, a tidal wave, the sands of time couldn't have moved them. In a thousand years the two of them would still be there, locked together, steadfast as a mountain. Was this what people meant by unconditional love?

Georges-Minh had fallen in love with Dong because of the wheeze in her lungs, her hallowed beauty, her viper tongue. Or was it because she could have been anyone, but it was she who walked through the clinic door that night to supplant the guilt and shame he felt over having caused the mermaid's death?

This mountain feeling of I-shall-not-be-moved, the weight and heat of it, that he felt for the baby he was sure would remain forever. He wiped his eyes with his handkerchief and put it back in his pocket, jostling the boy, who giggled.

Dong looked up from her salad roll. "Are you still crying? Don't worry, I think it's sweet. Men *should* cry when they hold their children."

After her meal she said to Georges-Minh, "Your pupils look funny. They're really big. Are you feeling okay? Why are you so sweaty?"

He managed to slip some more opium under his tongue without Dong seeing. He'd only brought a small supply. He wondered how many days it would last.

The meal had revived her, but not in the way he might have liked. Georges-Minh worried about the rabid energy with which Dong began to twist her hair into coils and replace her hat on top of them, point out the scenery, remove her hat, brush her hair, restyle it, replace her hat, remove her hat again. At least she was breastfeeding the baby, but he was glad he'd brought her with them so he could keep an eye on her, and the boy.

"Take a rest," he said.

"I don't *feel* tired."

It wasn't like her to act so frenzied. Still, what had been ordinary in the last twenty-four hours?

"Once upon a time a man collected tiny sea-swallow nests," Dong said. "He collected them from cave roofs with candles on his hat."

The train's clacking overpowered her words.

"I can't hear you." He smiled at her and wrung his hands.

The train rumbled and the ocean, when it appeared, was as blue as glass. Boats flecked the mouth of the bay.

"He had a bamboo ladder that he built with his own hands," she shouted. "He climbed up and down it every day. But one day his ladder broke. His work to find the swallows was already dangerous, you see, but without a ladder he couldn't make soup at all. So where do we go after Hue?"

"Soup?" Chang said.

A haze rose from the water, obscuring the horizon. The shadows of faraway islands were painted in shades of grey. At times the train hugged a coastline with such a sheer drop from the cliffs to the beach below the train seemed to be flying, the tracks poised on the edge, a cutaway beneath. Dong leaned her head on the window. She opened her mouth to say something and then closed it again.

They went through a tunnel. Georges-Minh spoke loudly to control his tremors, to project confidence, and to compete with the unbearable screeching of the train. "We'll go north to be safe. There are nationalist sympathizers there. We'll hide in the jungles of the Central Highlands, in Dak Lak, until things cool down." If they could make it to the Srepok River, an arm of the Mekong, it would flex through Dak Lak province to Stung Treng town. There were few roads in the diminished area, but the Lao traded with the Khmer upstream. He'd heard that the area's tribal leaders had birthed a strong resistance movement. Then, who knew? Maybe Thailand? Switzerland?

How to wrench someone from their life, then reveal they'd never get it back? He could feel the cracking in his own heart, a piece of himself drifting away like a peninsula cast adrift from the mainland.

40

Squatting on the forest floor, Thu shuddered with cold, though the night air was not that cold at all. The spiderworts along the ground tickled her thighs. In Cam Ranh, their first stop along the coast, all the hotels had been booked for the holidays and so, afraid to sleep on the beach, where they were open targets for muggers and pickpockets and rapists, Thu and Mai hiked toward the bamboo forest to spend the night where they'd heard the Cham villagers lived, because it was said the people of the bush were friendly.

After setting up camp, Thu skirted the bigger river creek with large, smooth granite rocks and sandstones, and went into the bushes, saying she needed to urinate. She removed the writing paper she'd stuffed down her bodice.

We had to leave in a hurry, she wrote Birago, balancing the paper on her knee. *Remember I told you Cong was sick? Mai went to a fortune teller, and now we are looking for her husband. I'll tell you more when I get back, but for now all I can say is there are things between me and Mai that I regret ever having happened. I'm sorry I had to leave and I hope you'll forgive me for not saying goodbye. If I could explain to you why I need to look after Mai it might make more sense but my mind has been clouded of late, except for there's the one sure thing on which I can count as if on a hitching post in a storm, to which I can tie myself, so I don't get lost, don't drift too far, don't fall too deep, don't wander too long, and that's I love you more than anything. Even more than my own eyes. Please understand I owe her.*

She thought about crumpling up the letter before she'd even finished it. What drivel. If only the prickle of the pocks would leave her alone. Worse than lice she'd had as a child.

How could it be they'd looked all over Saigon and not found Khieu? She couldn't believe, wouldn't let herself believe for a moment, the fortune teller had been right.

She thought about Birago's strong arms around another woman and where would she be then? If she could only make him understand she hadn't wanted to leave then maybe he wouldn't be mad at her. The only reason she'd followed Mai from that room that swallowed light and sound, was acting as if she was one of two spies on a mission instead of one of two women off to find a wayward husband, was that she'd given Mai her word. The Portuguese woman had no idea where to find Khieu. She'd help Mai for a week, make the situation clear to Birago, and all would be well.

He thought her childish. Petulant. She didn't want him to think ill of her now, lest he think his consideration to quit boxing had angered her. Like the time they'd fought over some silly question of politics and she'd refused to make love to him for a week. Or was it two?

Men cheated at the drop of a hat. And this distance between them! An excuse to leave her was the last thing she wanted to give him now. And her too far away to do anything about it!

The giant bamboo and forest trees blocked the light and made it too dim to write—indeed, in places, they did not even permit light to enter, and it was said that in some of the remotest regions of the jungle, certain tribes of people lived in complete darkness, hunted by darkness, made love by darkness, were born and died without ever seeing the sun, and had done so since the beginning of time.

She heard footsteps and a branch crack. Maybe it was a *nguoi rung* forest monster. She put the letter back into her dress and saw Mai's shoes through a gap in the underbrush. Thu adjusted her breasts to better hide the piece of paper.

"Mai. What do you want?"

"I thought I heard an animal, saw some eyes in the forest. I got frightened. With the baby asleep, I finally had time for a rest, but ..."

Back at home, Mai had been spending hours in the baby's room nursing, letting him suckle even while she slept. Her exhaustion had been manifesting itself in plum-coloured circles under her eyes. Her skin looked wan. A rash had broken out on her cheeks. She had lost at least thirty pounds.

"Did he drink much?"

"Hardly a thing. He dribbled out more than he swallowed."

"I need to pee. Give me a minute."

"I'm sorry. I was trying to give you your privacy. But suddenly I'm scared of the dark," she whimpered. Her lack of sleep had made her jumpy, and since her emergence from the bedroom with the stiff body of her middle-born son in her arms, Thu had become increasingly worried about Mai's dwindling hold on her sanity.

Thu pushed her way through the ferns, and holding Mai's hand, led her back to the clearing where they had lit a small fire. She sat Mai down and then perched on an overturned log next to her. The bamboo thicket nestling the kapok trees gaped and grinned at them, animated by the moon.

Thu crossed her arms over her chest, concealing the letter. They sat there until Mai calmed down. If Mai discovered she was writing a letter to Birago, who knew what conclusions she might jump to.

"Still night," Mai said and stroked the baby's head absent-mindedly. "Too still, almost." Then she spotted a movement. "See that?"

"You mean the shadow?"

"Yes. Someone?"

"Cloud in front of the moon. You know what the imagination can do."

"Say, what do you know about Forest People?" Mai asked. "What the fortune teller was saying."

Thu pulled the bamboo-handled knife from her bag and began polishing its blade on her skirt. "Well, I heard a story once." She waved the knife. "But it's disgusting. You don't want to hear it."

"I do," Mai implored.

Thu wrinkled her nose. "You don't."

"I do."

"No, I'm sure you don't!"

Mai giggled like a schoolgirl. There was an ease between them that felt good.

"Well, then. The story goes that a woman, a *nguoi rung*—"

"A what?"

"A Forest Person. Forest monster. Haven't you ever heard?" Mai shook her head.

"More or less, furry, bigger than us, but they don't have the capacity of speech. Anyway, she kidnapped a man. This forest monster needed a lover and she'd found the perfect one. So she brought him to her cave and she tied him up and made him do things. And she held him there, captive and—"

"They're like us?"

"Sort of. And she forced him to, you know …"

"No."

"Have *sex* with her. She made him give her babies, and she raised a family with him. For *three* years she held him captive before he escaped."

"Ugh! That's awful."

"I know. Auntie told me." She brought the map out of the bag and opened it up against her lap, smoothing out the creases in the firelight. "And all of that happened right … right there." She stabbed the centre of the map with the blade point. "Oh! That's where we're going. Look, right here."

"You're kidding."

"This is where she lives." She dragged the map through the air like a bullfighter's cape. "Thi-i-iis is whe-e-ere the Forest Man who wants some babiee-e-s li-i-ives, and he-e-e's coming to ge-e-t you."

"Seriously!" Mai pushed the map away. "What do you really know about where we're going?"

"Seriously, that's all I know." Thu held the knife to her face. The flames danced off the silver-coloured shank and reflected in the black pools of her eyes.

"So the *nguoi rung*," Mai said. "They're not human?"

Thu lowered the blade and drew an *X* in the soil. "They're ape-like, so they say. They grunt, or have a garbled speech. Even the rebels, the Montagnards, are scared of them."

She thought of Birago then, that first day at the beach, the way she'd embarrassed herself, mentioning her silly kindergarten teacher. Birago'd put her in her place, mocking her racism, her ignorance. She flushed, shook her head. "Anyway, why are you asking me? I'm not a fucking *nguoi rung* expert." A mosquito buzzed around her head and she swatted at it.

"Do they eat people?"

"I don't think so. Maybe in fairy tales." Thu yawned. "Anyway, sleep while the baby does. How long since you slept well?"

Mai sighed. "Who knows? Maybe I haven't slept well since before I was born. Before *he* was born, I mean. I feel like I haven't slept well my whole life."

"What about dreams?"

"I've been having nightmares lately. What about you?"

"No. Never. Or I don't remember them. Now I don't dream at all. Isn't it better that way? Anyhow, I didn't know you had nightmares."

"Well, a recurring dream where nobody will take me in. I've always had a mother and father, not like you, but in this dream my parents are dead. I'm an orphan, like you."

"I never think about my parents," Thu said.

"But you think about ghosts."

"I don't pay attention to ghosts."

"I believe in many things we can't see," Mai said.

"Not me."

"Gravity? The rotation of the planet?"

"Makes no difference," Thu said. She didn't look behind her, fighting the feeling she suddenly had that someone was watching her. The wind pushed clouds across the moon's face and Mai's face was alternately glowing the way angels did and was then black as a demon. "I don't think about things I can't change."

"What about love? What about destiny?"

"What difference do they make to my life? To how I put my pants on, or how I eat my breakfast?" She shivered.

She sat there, jungle behind her, looking at the fire, fingering her chest where the fabric of her dress hid the letter that she would find a way to mail to Birago tomorrow. She wished she could take it out, feel the paper, touch the words upon it. Bi-ra-go. Bi-ra-go. Bi-ra-go. Just this moment she needed something to hold.

Thu rolled herself another cigarette. She watched the moon unfurl itself from the clouds. It was nearly full, which meant her own sleep, when it came, would be fitful. And as its light shone down on her, the more anxious she became. Alone, even though Mai had finally fallen asleep a few feet away, memories of what she had left behind began to flood her—unimportant things, Birago's always-bitten-down cuticles, the lemon scent of his cologne, the sunshine on the river's lapping water. Tasting a tear, she reprimanded herself for indulging in memories.

41

Khieu had never been so far out of Saigon, making him feel anything could happen. The next day, another river. He rented a sampan. The rain had fallen all night, and the estuary rose as the deluge continued with no let-up in sight.

Water lapped the sides of the narrow wooden boat, and dead rats floated on the brown water. In the jungle that bordered both banks of the murky waterway, Khieu saw men cleaning rifle barrels, wives busily making food over open cook fires, and children playing in the trees. He could see the spires of their woodsmoke rising over the tops of the palms. He imagined the men discussing their plans and studying maps.

Khieu's trembling fingers clutched the oars, dipped and stroked in and out of the water. Maybe for them the map was something to hold at a time when something to hold counted for everything. Some said the French were building a detention centre in the area, others said a military base. Khieu hoped it was only a rumour—Vietnam was a country where rumour built upon rumour. All that held Vietnam together was fairy tales, like coarse thread holding together a fishing net.

The sun moved in the sky and the day turned gloomier. His shoulders began to ache and his arms burned. His body throbbed everywhere. The water was full of fishing boats, tea boats, houseboats, flower boats, canoes, outriggers, junks, other rafts. A peddling barber had hung a mirror from a tree branch to shave faces and give haircuts. The barber had brought straight razors and scissors. A villager with a traditional turban wanted a short haircut. He unrolled the thin strips of cotton tied to his head. More than a few men were shearing their locks as political statements these days—in with the new, out with the old. Khieu approved wholeheartedly. Khieu had not worn his hair in such a style for a long time, though he did have a memory, as a child, of his mother, who had once upon a time favoured his long hair, who began every day by combing it. Khieu looked forward to beginning his day in this peaceful way, the feel of the comb tugging at his cowlicks, his mother's fingers on his scalp. He let the current carry him. He drifted on the river past birds and rice paddies cut out of the mountainside.

He ate lunch with a family who reminded him of his own: Khieu's family was not rich like Chang's, or cultured and influential like Georges-Minh's. His family had owned a shack over the river, with a rowboat out of which they sold food, like the family he'd offered five baht to for some fried fish. Their beautiful daughter had a paralytic arm and she burned his fish while swaying her hips, winking at him when he smiled. They brought out a bottle of whisky, and the grandma emerged from the depths of their floating house with little cups and a toothless toddler on her hip.

"Time is a fleeting white colt," said the old man.

"You're right," said Khieu. "There it is, galloping past my window."

The old man, who was drunk, laughed. He had as few teeth as the toddler.

"If I wait, I'll see it run. If you're lucky, you'll see it crack." The old man couldn't stop laughing. He slapped his wizened leg, his eyes watering.

Khieu left twenty baht behind, where they'd find it after he left, and returned to his sampan.

By evening, refreshed by the encounter, he was travelling overland. He snuck through French-owned banana plantations, rubber, coconut, pineapple farms, hot and humid. Wary of being captured as a spy, or killed by the Bataillons d'Afrique, he plastered his face with mud. If someone saw him ducking through the field, would they think he was a political friend? Or the enemy?

42

Birago couldn't believe they'd shot him.

"Bad luck." The cigarette peddler offered him a smoke from his pack, bent at the tip. When the man exhaled, the smoke came out of the hole in his chest where he'd been stabbed to death.

"Are you dead, too?" Birago asked.

"We all are. Look around."

Birago began to notice the deafening, pervading noise all around him, barking dogs and shouting men, women hawking wares as they'd done in life, even children hollering, "You're it, you're it!" and throwing stones at each other while they played. A whole world of the dead that existed in tandem with the world of the living, like a world of shadows, one on top of the other.

"You came a bit early for lunch," the peddler said.

"Lunch?"

"Minh over there?" The man pointed. "She makes soup."

"I got to go." When Birago stood up, his ear fell off. He picked it up off the ground and held it in his palm.

"Here, let me," the man said, coming over to him, but Birago didn't give him a chance to help, or touch him or bite him or whatever he planned to do. Birago couldn't be dead. He must be hallucinating. That was it. He was in hospital somewhere hallucinating. He'd had too much to drink with Colonel Janvier and this was all a bad dream he would wake from.

43

They found a hotel with a view of the Perfume River on Le Loi Street in the ancient city of Hue, surrounded by pagodas and imperial tombs.

Chang stood in the doorway of the family's room while Dong went to sit on the bed with the baby. "Well, here we are." He grinned. "We made it."

"I think you'd best get a room down the hall."

"What did you think I was going to do," Chang said, "stay with you?"

Chang, who was still carrying the family's suitcases like a porter, and had been since the train station, let them drop to the floor. "Unbelievable," he said.

Georges-Minh had to admit he was. He didn't know what had gotten into Chang. He went to call after Chang, but the man was already halfway down the hall, his oiled hair black and gleaming.

"What was all that about?" Dong asked.

"Nothing. Forget it. Want something to eat? I'm starving."

Georges-Minh brought some turtle soup and tea back to the room and looked at Dong and the child, starting with their eyelashes. Like feelers. The way the sun shifted onto the bed, the sheets. Onto her body. Bodies. Two of them in his life now. Arms. Fingers. Hands. The way their fingertips touched. Their chests. They rose up and down in sleep: the loveliness of breath. The sunlight glinted on her hair, which slithered black against white on the pillow.

The baby's lips were parted slightly, allowing just enough room for a sigh. His legs were bent at the knee, forming a circle with his legs. His light seemed to radiate outward from within, lighting the room and casting a warm glow different from the sun's, more vivid, redder somehow, on the furniture, Dong's face, the floor.

From their window he could see the walls of the Imperial City. Every schoolboy knew it had taken more than twenty thousand workmen to build those walls, and enough land for eight villages lay within them. Inside, the Emperor Duy Tan, a child in king's clothes, ruled—Georges-Minh had seen postcards—"*L'empereur Duy Tan, en costume de cour*"—from his 1907 coronation: the poor little puppet, the folded hands, the tiny shoes, the serious brow. The lost eyes looking not into the camera but at a point beyond the photographer's shoulder, at a presence in the corner of the room as if at a wild animal, a sorcerer who held back a tiger on a chain saying, "You know what will happen if I let go!" Poor Duy Tan. Pawn of the French, whose father had gone insane because of the spies that followed him even in his own castle. But who knew if the story was true? The only fact not open for debate was the sad little eyes in the postcard.

He'd bought a newspaper, which he sat down to read, but instead held his head in his hands, suddenly exhausted. Though he'd been noiseless, Dong stirred. Her hair cascaded over her face and her body turned toward him, eyes closed. The baby shifted and began to snore. Then the baby shifted again, and the shifting turned to fussing and then the baby awoke, swinging his head to the left and right searching for a nipple. Georges-Minh tried to wake up his wife, first by kissing her cheek, then by gently jostling her shoulder.

"Dong, wake up, wake up. The baby's hungry."

It became clear this wasn't just sleep.

"Dong? Dong?"

The infant mewled with hunger.

Her eyes flickered open for a moment, her gaze locked with his, and he could see that she recognized his face. Then the eyelids fluttered closed again.

He clutched her limp, warm body, rocking her to his chest, urged her to fight back, to push against the thing that was pushing her. "Wake," he said, "wake up, do you hear me?" But the hand smothering her was stronger than the both of them.

"Chang! Chang!"

44

With the water lapping the sides of their narrow wooden boat, to Thu and Mai the day seems almost peaceful. *Seems* instead of *is*, because in the jungle on each side of the murky brown waterway, nationalists are cleaning rifle barrels and packing the food provisions that wives are busily making over open cook fires whose spires can be seen rising over the tops of the palm trees.

In circles, fighters discuss plans and go over maps gone over a thousand times already but once more never hurts and besides it gives the restless mind something to focus on, nervous fingers something to hold.

In one hut a man packs away into his knapsack, heavy with ammunition and rice pancakes, a stone given to him by his daughter. Who knows why a stone? But the daughter, only four years old, handed it to him on one of their many walks along the shores of this same river, where two women and a baby boy now paddle, after first polishing it against her skirt, gave it to him as an offer of love and gratitude, and, smiling, he took the stone from her hand for what it was, a stone, no more, no less.

Now he places it in his pack next to the rice pancakes and he wonders briefly if he should have wrapped it in cloth first before it got lost among the metal shell casings and other accessories of war, but it's too late. He lets the stone drop and he closes up his pack and leaves by the door of his hut and goes to join the men, ready and waiting, in the circle with the map.

Thu imagined the impermeable darkness of the jungle as she had seen it the other night, and the activities of the people within it, and this line of reasoning caused her to contemplate for a moment that other impermeable darkness that awaits us all, and she quickly cast a look at Cong, as if afraid that while she was daydreaming of a man with a map and a stone he might have disappeared, but Cong was still there, lying peacefully at the bottom of the sampan on a blanket, or so she told herself, because it was easier than thinking of any alternative, such as he'd fallen into a coma from which he would never awake. She wondered how the nationalist struggle was going in general, how it fed people's hearts, and she dipped her hand into the warm, murky waters that lapped the boat's sides and her movement shifted the prow slightly—the boat and its passengers yawed in the water, something slipping, then regained—and Mai looked up from her own languid daydream, glanced away from the water skimmers and the hovering mosquitoes whose presence added to the brown liquid apathy of the day, and contemplated Thu as if for the first time.

"Khieu," Mai said, as if continuing some earlier conversation, "whatever else his faults, at least he had some ideals. In his way he is a brave man." Like many other words Mai had spoken in her relatively short lifetime, they simply fell out without rhyme or reason.

"You mean because of his art?"

239

"Well, he chases a dream."

"Like us now."

Mai dipped her finger into the water. "Maybe bravery is a trait easier to discover in others than to see in oneself."

"Or maybe bravery is just easily confused with stupidity. Bravery and stupidity often walk hand in hand. Are the same trait, really. Bravery *is* stupidity, just seen through a favourable lens." Thu looked away from Mai, out over the water. "Some might say I'm stupid for following you through the jungle."

After all her time in Mai's service, Mai still cared nothing about her, would plunge her into the heart of danger, for all she knew, to make her find some good-for-nothing man. Had Thu married Khieu, he wouldn't have left in the first place— not that she would have married him—that oily-haired man, that gap-toothed smiling man—get that straight, she had never been attracted to him! Oh, he'd been hot for her. White teeth and all. Dared to put his hand on her knee more than once while his wife was in the other room.

Thu figured Khieu had hooked up with the wrong girl and her husband had gotten wind—that's why, if the fortune teller was right, he'd been forced on the run, because some cuckold was on the warpath. Rotten luck for Thu: what did she ever have to do with any of it, except to try and be a good surrogate mother to Mai's children?

It wasn't that she was jealous of Mai, of her having a husband, a son. She'd get married someday. And just why couldn't a Senegalese man and a Vietnamese woman get married? Just because one was black and one was not? Just because it wasn't often done didn't mean it couldn't be done.

In addition to the letter, over the past three days, Thu had secretly sent Birago two postcards: one with a haiku about the landscape, another with a little free-verse erotic poem, dirty-talking him as if whispering into his ear.

"That again. Will you ever be done with him?" Mai's face grew red.

Thu wanted to say, *As long as there is still a man waiting for me in Saigon.* Every fresh mile between her and Birago unlocked a different ache in her heart. "This fight is ongoing in more ways than you can know," she said finally, thinking of the postcard in her dress ready to mail. Then, with a note of resignation and a faraway look in her eyes, she added, "And it won't end soon."

They had been rowing along the water's edge using the hanging overgrowth for protection: the branches grew out over the water and they could use them for shade from the sun, and to hide, if needed.

From out of the mangroves a man grabbed Thu's tow rope. A little girl stepped into the boat and took Thu's hand and bade her rise and began pulling her into the forest of cinnamon and black varnish trees. Thu panicked, reached for Mai who had scooped Cong from the bottom of the boat and was clutching him to her chest.

45

Khieu shuddered against the cold of the mountains, the fog and the mist, trying to find some warmth in his thin shirt by clutching the sleeves and trying to pull them more tightly around his body while the Montagnards inhaled from the pipe and tilted their faces to the falling rain. Smoke stung his eyes when the breeze blew it toward him. He coughed, though the villagers didn't. Even the children seemed unaffected.

The villagers were epic storytellers, and even though the language was foreign to him, their talk sounded holy, as if they'd connived a direct line to the spirits.

So far his life's talk had been bluster, meant to sound like something meaningful. And fool people it had—he'd even believed what he'd said himself at times.

He missed his wife, his children.

He didn't speak Cham and only one villager spoke broken Vietnamese. The villager talked of an armed uprising, a revolt against the French.

In the following days Khieu watched the daily habit of children sprinkling water on the ground to draw tactics onto the dust with sticks. In the land of lychees, loquats, and longans, the villagers shaved bamboo spears and sharpened wood into halberds and swords. They built crossbows and taught younger boys and girls how to shoot. Children trained and ate hibiscus seeds on breaks.

The gum-lac like small black ears in the branches of trees waited to be gathered as salve while boys macheted paths through the woods. Elders ordered maps, though who needed them, Chams understood the forest like their own callused feet. Their water buffalo trained for battle. The village perfected the art of patrol, the advance and retreat. Let the French think they were unorganized and untrained. They travelled to other villages. Discussed, palavered, composed attack cries and war songs.

Even the youngest helped, cleaning rifles and boxing bullets. They laughed as they readied for battle, and their casualness in preparing for death drew Khieu into himself.

He imagined the French soldiers. "Tran Khieu, you're under arrest for the Saigon Poisoning Plot." They'd drag him to a wagon, transport him to a city's market square and a guillotine.

He took a deep drag of marijuana mixed with tobacco from the pipe passed hand to hand. A lame grandfather with cloudy pupils stared at him across the fire. Khieu turned away and looked at the watercress-covered fish ponds cloaked in darkness, thinking how they were kind to take him in, but maybe he'd search for somewhere safer to hide, at least until the battle was over.

46

Georges-Minh rocked her, clutching the boy in the crook of his arm, while Chang tried to balance the turtle soup. Wobbling on the mattress, Chang almost lost his balance. "God, Georges, what did you do to her?"

"What did *I* do to her?"

"She's totally out of it. Did you drug her? She's good like this. Pretty. Quiet. I didn't know you liked them so inanimate. Had I been the one to think of it I'd be congratulating myself right now."

"I'm not playing. Really, I can't wake her."

"Obviously. Hello, sweetheart. Hello, Sleeping Beauty."

"Don't give him that."

The shock made Chang spill some of the soup, barely missing the baby's head.

"Don't you know he's too young for anything but breast milk?" Dong held the boy to her breast, her upper lip sweating. "Why are you two fussing over me? And why are you trying to feed my baby turtle soup? Get your hand away from my forehead. What's wrong with you, Georges?" She pushed his hand away.

The baby made sucking sounds at her breast and a bead of milk dripped from his lip to his chin.

"You wouldn't wake up."

"Don't be ridiculous. I thought you were getting food. I'm starving."

"I did get food. It's right here."

When Dong got upset her nose curved like a parrot's and she raised her lip enough for her incisors to show. "Careful what you eat," she said. "They may be trying to poison us."

Georges-Minh wanted to rejoice at her return from the dead, but narrowed his eyes. "Who?"

"Who's trying to poison us?" Chang said.

"The soup. The poison's in the soup."

They hadn't misheard.

She pushed herself upright. "God, I have to piss."

"Come on, I'll help you to the bathroom."

"Help," she said, reaching for an empty vase on the top of the table, "by passing me that."

"She's mad," Chang said.

"It's on the floor, too."

"There's nothing on the floor."

She strained in the direction of the porcelain vessel, tangling her toes in the white sheets until Georges-Minh had no choice but to help her balance over the vase or she would have soiled the bed.

Chang slipped out of the room while she relieved herself.

Georges-Minh helped her back onto the bed and under the covers.

"I think the floor has poison on it. I think my shoes do, too. I want you to make me some new ones."

"Some shoes?"

"Yes. Shhh. Quietly. The walls hear you. You can make them out of napkins."

"What's wrong with yours?"

"I told you already. I can't be sure they don't have poison in them."

"Oh. I could check them."

He had never negotiated this kind of territory before. Khieu had his days, but in a different way: his craziness was based on needing a distraction from the politics and so he pulled rickshaws or studied the stars. Georges-Minh didn't know what to do or say to ease her mind. Part of him thought playing along with her would comfort her. The other part believed that corroborating her fantasies would prove that indeed something did lie on the floor waiting to harm her.

"Look," he said, deciding on the latter. "I'm walking on the floor and I feel fine. If there was poison I think I'd be feeling sick by now. Maybe you're mistaken. Maybe it's okay. Why don't you try."

She said, "So perhaps it's me they want. Not you."

"What poison is so selective? Think about it. Have you ever heard of a drug that metabolizes in one person but not another? I haven't. It's not possible, Dong. I'm a doctor, I should know."

The irony didn't escape him: that he had poisoned Birago and Janvier, and now his wife was seeing poison everywhere she looked. "Now look. Look at me. I'm going to remove my shoes, and even my socks."

He glanced up. Her eyes widened. He went back to peeling off his socks now that he'd gotten her attention. Vindicated. He walked a circle around the bed, then back again the same way he had come. His feet left prints on the tiles. "See? I'm fine."

She swung her hair back and tucked it behind both ears; the motion made the baby bounce on the mattress.

"All that proves is my point. Exclusive poisons do exist. A poison made for me or maybe me and the baby. But I'd never put him down to crawl around on the floor anyway—what kind of mother would do that?"

"Who would go after the baby?"

"Oh, you know, people."

"What people?"

"Bad people."

"Monsters."

"Monsters?" She giggled. But it was neither friendly nor flirty. It patronized, and accused Georges-Minh of wasting her time. "Who would be trying to stop us? Think about it."

His head hurt. He needed to eat. To eat and to think. He massaged his temples, circling his fingers around and around.

"Soldiers. Who else? After all you've done to us. How could you forget? How could you ruin our lives?"

On their wedding night Georges-Minh had caressed her body. Her lung fever had made her so thin that he could fit his finger in the spaces between her ribs. He'd started kissing her neck, her breasts, amazed her body could be so loosened with trust. Loose as Birago and Janvier had been when they'd brought the cognac glasses to their lips.

They used to be the kind of couple that made people stare, good-looking, confident. Her full lips, so much like Chang's, were always smiling, even when her eyes were worried or sad. He liked how forgiving she was; how he could do the most insensitive things and she would carry on as if she hadn't noticed until receiving his apology, always acting surprised when he said sorry, as if she appreciated it but it was unnecessary for him to beg her pardon because she loved him that much.

"We should think of a name for the baby," Georges-Minh said. "Don't you think?"

She picked him up. "Look at you. Big boy. I grant you peace, luck, longevity."

"We could, I suppose," he said, "name the boy after my father. Do you like the name Tan?"

She furled her brow.

"Or we could choose another family name. What do you think your father would like?"

She raised her eyebrows, shrugged. "I choose *freedom*." Laughed.

"What do you think of Long?" he said. It meant "dragon," and he didn't think she knew it was Khieu's middle name.

He poured them both some tea in silence, the amber liquid burbling into the cups, steam rising from the surface. The baby burped and spit up a little. She wiped the milk that dribbled from his mouth with a corner of the bedsheet, and a smile crept across her face at the novelty of performing this motherly duty. Maybe she was getting better. Maybe everything would be fine, after all.

Georges-Minh suddenly wished Chang would knock on the door, but Chang never did. He thought about going down the hall and fetching him.

Georges-Minh hadn't really the liberty to leave, though, for Dong took every absence as an insult, a conspiracy. She'd become far too skittish to be left alone, even momentarily.

So he took a sip of his tea. He swallowed the wrong way, coughed and set down the cup.

Dong left her cup untouched, gave Georges-Minh the baby, grabbed his newspaper from the bureau, and began making paper hats from the pages.

Or were they sailboats? He remembered crafting them, too, when he was a boy and sailing them down the Saigon River behind the house where he'd grown up, where his mother and father-in-law lived now, from which he would remain in exile how long, he didn't know.

Her eyes continued to focus on her paper-folding task. Her tongue lolled out of her mouth the way children's sometimes did when the activity at hand absorbed their attention.

"Are you making hats or boats?"

She stopped folding. "The difference is what you decide to do with it in the end." Unfolded the paper. Brought it close to her nose as if she was going to smell it. Was she switching to flowers? Maybe an origami lily. She held the small print to her eye, as if looking for something, until the article in question was nearly under her nose. She read quietly at first, to herself. When she looked up, her face was pink. "What's this? What is this?" She shook the paper toward Georges-Minh as if in accusation. Then she read out loud. "In Hai Phong twenty elephants were killed by two tigers in a wondrous display put on for French officials." Her shoulders shook and she looked as though she was going to cry. "How did they do it? Get so few tigers to kill so many elephants?"

"Starved them, I guess. Over a period of weeks, maybe even months." He wasn't sure why she was so upset.

"How?"

"Make them angry. Then let them loose."

"Time past, elephants always won."

He doubted this.

"The royal family had declared them symbols of eminence."

"Maybe they took out the tigers' claws."

"Elephants are beautiful. They should never lose. There's something I never told you. What I dreamed. When I was pregnant."

"Thing is. If you starve them. Beat them down, first—fight or be trampled, then—"

"Yes," she said. "But there's something I wanted to tell you. I dreamed about elephants."

"Don't tell me. White elephants."

"As a matter of fact."

Every child in Vietnam knew the story of white elephants. Sacred ones. The mother of the Buddha, when she was pregnant, dreamed of an elephant, white, giving her a lotus flower, white, which represented wisdom. To see a white elephant, it was said, brought the seer eternal luck. White elephants, it was said, cradled the souls of the dead. All a lord needed, so people said, was land, a harem, and an elephant. Preferably white.

Dong folded the paper in half. She held her breath. Then she folded the paper again with the effort of anyone doing origami. She ran her finger over the fold until her finger bled. The paper turned red. Georges-Minh took the paper away.

She reached for the baby, coddled it, spoke into his long, silky hair. "I dreamed of white elephants when I was pregnant with you. I dreamed of them not once or twice but many times. I dreamed of a white elephant the very night before your birth. And more than that, I know what this means. For us, and for this country."

Georges-Minh's gut knotted. She really had gone mad.

And moreover, Khieu had foreseen this sleepwalk. Sleepy elephants among an incursion of tigers. She sounded like the priests at the temple, like the Buddhist monks who recited blessings for alms, or even like the soothsayers who chanted over sick bodies to cure them. If his own wife collaborated in her weakness, how could his people rise up? They were a nation of sleepwalkers.

"My elephant baby," she sang. "My baby elephant." Dong continued to sing to the baby. Her song turned into a prayer. He closed his eyes and flopped onto the bed next to her. Of course, look what rebellion had got *him*. He'd fought back, and where was he now? He leaned onto his elbow and peered into Dong's lap, at the boy's face, and the boy gazed back at him. The boy. His flesh and blood. His blood and flesh. The nameless one. Like their group. He picked up the boy's hand and the boy grasped his finger and squeezed. He burbled. Georges-Minh found himself making cooing noises at the boy.

"You know, the last Dalai Lama is said to have been born with fair skin," Dong said. "And as an infant his head was shaped like a parasol. The last lama was born by a bitterly cold lake in southern Tibet near a tree that flowered out of season. They say he also was born with a headful of glossy black hair, just like our baby. Though my mother said that he had a single white strand, growing right out of the centre."

"Doesn't the Dalai Lama need to be dead before another one is born?"

She looked out the window and shrugged.

47

Earlier, from the southern tributary of the river, Thu and Mai had heard thunderous claps that shook the palm trees down the marsh edge for miles. They'd paddled on, listening to the claps until they grew in volume.

Thu shipped her oar. Cong put down the marionette he'd been playing with all morning and Mai hid it under the slats and covered it with an ox blanket next to the bag that contained, besides their supplies, a creased map with an *X* in the centre and the bamboo-handled knife. Thu had gotten into the habit of toying with the knife at night, fantasizing that one day she may yet plunge it into someone. After a while, when they felt safe again, Thu slipped the oar back into the water and Mai pulled the marionette back out from under the slats.

"What's that sound?" Mai said now, hearing the thunder clap once more.

"You should keep that toy packed away. I keep telling you only city boys have puppets. We can't travel undercover if you keep pulling that thing out."

"Could that be guns? Or is it fireworks?"

Thu pointed at a man with a weapon on shore and held her breath. Then she saw the shack behind the man and another man with a rifle, and she fumbled with her Montagnard disguise, jerking the ragged cloak more securely around her.

Thu had decided they should wear disguises and row along the shoreline, hoping the mangroves would shadow their journey, so they could duck into the thick growth, if needed, and run for protection. From whom? To whom? Were those fireworks or fire-fight noises? The rebels were doing battle against the French—would they be caught in the crossfire? The intermittent smoke and blasts from shore disoriented them; in the smoke and fog everything was ablaze with confusion and the women hadn't slept well in days. They had wanted to believe it was fireworks; the task of believing chased sleep away.

"Keep Cong quiet, and don't say a word."

Yet a hand grabbed their tow rope and they found themselves being pulled landward, toward a path Thu hadn't seen until now. Her fear diminished when she saw it was only a little girl with her ragged father, as dishevelled as she was dirty.

"I have meat for sale," the girl said, dragging Thu by the hand. "Buy some, support the cause."

Both women were tired, too tired to argue, though Thu had the presence of mind to reach for the bamboo-handled knife.

"She's poor, I guess," Thu said.

"You'd better go," Mai said. "She looks desperate. Maybe you could ask if they've seen anyone from Saigon in these parts."

Thu looked up the river and scanned the southern tributary beyond the veil of heat and steam and dust and fixed her eye on the sheets of grey metal and knew it was a French gunboat making those noises, firing at the shore, and she guided the sampan to a makeshift dock where the girl was now leading her.

By then they were not alone. The girl and her father were joined by a man and then another flanked by two teenage boys, and they were moving toward a shack. The girl held tight to her hand and pulled her up the slope. Her hand was like hot gunmetal.

"We have thighs and legs, breast meat, too. Pay only for the cut you want. Follow me."

And if I don't want a cut, thought Thu, but she didn't say these words.

By the time they had clambered up the path and reached the door, a few others had joined them, a handful of ragged others minding the outer flanks of the resistance with their tarnished rifles. More men in hats, maybe Cambodians. Thu was sure something about the situation felt wrong.

A man with a packsack entered the shack first, followed by the little girl. Thu went in next. All the other men joined after.

The little girl looked at Thu and giggled, holding her hand over her lips. A prisoner gibbeted like a marionette from the rafters, hanging by his wrists. Faraway rifle fire rolled through the door, and the sounds of a distant gunboat come to quell the uprising. The hanging man—could he be called a man with his toes missing, his ears, his nose, one eye gone, the muscles of one thigh carved away to the bone?—swung from the rope. His feet hung lazily in mid-air, drifting through the brown dirt-smoke, pointing east toward the open door, west toward the wall, then east again. His chin rested on his bloodied chest. She startled when she heard a whistling sound coming from the hole where his nose had been. One of the soldiers levelled his gun at her. Thu glanced at the door. She could never make it back to the sampan, much less row away to safety.

The girl giggled nervously again. "We have breast meat or you can have a leg or a thigh. What do you want?"

The soldier across the room thrust a butcher knife toward Thu.

"You get to choose," the girl said. "Pick your cut."

She understood at once that the prisoner had collaborated with the French, and if she and Mai wanted to get out of Central Highland territory, continue down the Srepok River, she'd have to prove her loyalty to the nationalists, cut a piece of meat off the man, who was not really a man, she could see now, but a boy, a child of no more than sixteen or seventeen, hanging from the ceiling.

"We kill traitors," the girl said. "Are you a traitor?"

"Of course not," Thu answered. "I have my own knife."

Thu's head spun. *Was* she a traitor? Of course not. She loved Birago. She could do anything. She could be anyone. On a day like today she could start screaming and never stop. She was sure of it. Knew this nightmare would follow her long into her years. For this boy's sake she must be willing to become someone else. A monster.

She approached him. Poked him with the point of her knife. The boy opened his eye.

"Do you want me to help you?"

"I want to go home," he said.

He didn't look away. He pierced her gaze with the same intensity the bird in the market had right before feral cats tore it apart. Neither one broke the stare until his head flopped forward.

"I'll help you," she said.

"No talking," a soldier warned.

"The heart," she said, "is my favourite piece of meat."

"Cut, cut," the girl said.

Thu held up the knife. Ran it across his chest, the knife she and Mai had been given in the dusty room with paintings of the royal family on the wall. Velvet ones, weren't they? Lavish, she remembered, because they didn't match the poverty of the shack, the gaps in the wooden floorboards through which she could see half-eaten mangoes gnawed by rats. Dust everywhere. She plunged the knife in where she hoped his heart might be. He gasped once, then exhaled. His nose stopped whistling.

She leaned into him. He was kicking and she wished he would stop.

They could hear the fighting approach.

"Quickly, we have to go," the little girl said.

A white-faced dog with its bowels spilling out shivered into the thatch-roofed shack and snapped at her before dying in the corner.

When they stepped outside the laughter had turned to screaming and she heard a man shout they're shooting while he ran, another stumbled, men on the ground with their guns disassembled trying to fit loaded cylinders where they belonged. She ran back to the sampan and saw the oxen loose on the hill. They trampled down the fallen and she saw children shot and silenced mid-cry. Among the wounded some seemed dumb and without understanding and some were red through the hoods of dust and some had fouled themselves or tottered brokenly into the jungles of Dak Lak.

48

Khieu cooked, half-crouched. Waited out the daylight hours, reciting poetry. Smoked, in a pipe carved by a Cham craftsman, the marijuana given to him by elders who had wrinkled their brow over his departure. With the villagers as the only link he'd had to the outside world, the real world, he'd set up camp in a cave in a patch of woods that was so dense he doubted even the locals knew about it; even if they knew about it, they would probably lose themselves in it. *Just until the Chams have had their battle. Then I'll go back.*

Khieu enlarged the cave, essentially just a mouth in a mountain about five kilometres from the Cham village, digging it deeper, ten feet underground, with a bone shovel of his own making. He wanted a hiding place unknown to everyone. He wanted to go farther away.

He dug it narrow as a coffin. He had to wiggle backward on his stomach over the bleak ground to reach the back. In the very rear, he'd hollowed out a space wide enough to huddle. And this is where he lived.

The mouth of the cave was barely visible above ground. The surrounding bamboo created an optical illusion, making the cave opening seem solid, even from a few feet away: trees, shadows, darkness, light.

A bitter wind blew from the back of the cave to the front, encircled him, took him in hand like a ghost's arms.

He surfaced for provisions only when necessary. He always waited for the sun to set in case spies watched his location. The tunnel drew air from outside like a pipe and blew it back out, whistling. The fresh breeze lobbed about, and the movement was like a phantom, making him think about death. If he died in here, no one would find his bones. Or maybe he'd sink into the earth: that would be more appropriate, he thought, given his current situation. Feet then hands, head, until he was swallowed up, run over by bugs, millipedes and beetles, thrush and babblers laughing about his demise.

"Did you hear what happened to Tran Khieu? Let me tell you about this crazy son of a bitch from Saigon. Built himself a coffin of earth and died in it. Let the ground swallow him up, kee-kee-kee."

For some reason no boars or bulls or wild cats had visited, but from one end of Vietnam to the other the babblers and thrush would talk. No animals of any kind, no tracks by the cave mouth, which he'd hidden with brush, not even to sniff around, no droppings, nothing, which was unusual. Maybe it had formerly been the home of a forest monster, a *nguoi rung*, and its scent had scared off every other kind of animal.

At first, afraid boars would attack him while he slept, he'd kept a fire going. Then, worried about soldiers, he'd put it out. Now, he wondered if the constant howling, eerie as a banshee, scared the predators for the same reason it scared him. He slept in a tomb, already a dead man. Maybe the wind wasn't the wind but a spectre just like he'd thought in the first place. Maybe the place was haunted.

Hunted. He feared thinking about what decision had prompted him to seek shelter in the forest in the first place. Hadn't he been better off with the Chams? Even if it meant going to war? What had all that talk been in Saigon if not about standing up for one's beliefs? Rebellion? Revolution? What had any of it meant? He was too much the Maybe Man. The Why-Me Man. Maybe-Better-to-Stand-with-the-Montagnards-and-Fight Man. And why was he in this cave? He couldn't remember. Was it his wife? His children? Some strange Stomach Ache and Feeling he had to Preserve Himself instead of Getting Shot for Some Ideal? Well, then, why hadn't he stayed with her and been the husband he was supposed to be in the first place?

Sleeping was the hardest. Curled in a ball, no room to stretch his cramped legs. The earth writhed beneath his feet. Millipedes, beetles, ants, viewing him now as a rock and inanimate for his lack of movement, scurried over his bare toes. His shoes, shredded after all this time in the woods, the leather rotten from the damp of the highlands, offered no protection.

And not only that, he reeked. A yeasty combination of deteriorating clothes, falling-apart shoes, and unwashed hair. He flicked one foot and then the other, trying to get the bugs off. Half clung on tenaciously. The ants began to sting. The constant damp in the highlands had made his clothes cling to his body, and this accounted for the stench. Everything this high in the hills was always wet, slippery, coated with moss or a kind of algae. He ached with the fear that his oxygen would run out. What scared Khieu the most, worse yet, was that a French soldier would discover his hiding spot and trap him by pushing a boulder over the mouth of the cave. If there was any way he was most afraid to die it was that a French soldier would bury him alive and the last sound he'd hear was laughter.

He crouched behind a thicket of bamboo, knees shaking. The cave mouth breathed and yawned and sighed cool air.

Khieu, ready to flee at a moment's notice, dared not move. Nothing but drafts emerged from the cave. Still, he waited, biding his time. Motionless. Minutes passed. He crouched, still watching. The sun moved in the sky. Laughing thrush and babblers sang *kee-kee-kee*.

Between the insects, the stench, and the fear combusting, Khieu could idle in this purgatory no longer. Raising his fists like a boxer in front of his face, he rushed the cave entrance.

But sometimes, upon his return after a night of gathering food, the sun would roll back layers of fog in the sky the way his mother would roll back his blankets as a boy when waking him for school, and the cave did not seem dank. His feet hurt, and he was tired, and he looked forward to its soothing darkness, to the coolness and the whistle.

He welcomed rest, craved sleep. He should have feared the pull of the earth. Did it mean part of him was readying for death?

He wiggled into his tunnel, pushed himself against the soft earth on the palms of his hands. The whistle surrounded him. A high-pitched sound, similar to a baby crying alone in a room. The voice drifted down to him, as down a long hallway, saying *leave*, a final warning, as if foretelling danger, but in his bones he felt no fear. Something had shifted, and though he couldn't see, there was a clarity, finally, in his mind's eye. Yes. He wasn't going blind, he could see. He would make new tools, and dig an even deeper section. Eventually, he would never have to leave.

From a distance he heard his mother's voice: "Get up."

"No," he responded. "Leave me alone."

Another voice chimed in, maybe Georges-Minh's, telling him things he'd heard in French school, that it was better to live on his feet than die on his knees, and he tried to ignore it. He looked around. No trace of animals, just ancient bones. He swung a femur across his knee. Began thumping a tribal rhythm into his palm. He needed a plan.

At the back of the tunnel-like cave he began to dig. At first with the leg-bone shovel to test the earth. Then with his hands, when he saw how giving the earth had become. Digging was no problem now. In no time at all, he'd hollowed out a body shape. Then two. Then three. He lay down in the hole and dozed.

49

Flies settled in the empty bowl of turtle soup on the bureau in the hotel room on Le Loi Street. Dong, burning up with fever, refused to get out of bed, refused to let Georges-Minh out of her sight, or to take any of the medicine Chang brought back for her. Day turned to night and back to day again. They'd been in the hotel thirty-six hours now. Georges-Minh stroked her hair and considered what to do next. He told her stories by Victor Hugo, making up the parts he couldn't remember. Chang said they should keep moving, try to cross the border into Laos. As she dozed, Georges-Minh looked out the window at families strolling, holding hands.

Well-behaved children charmed their parents into buying candy or small cheap toys not meant to last more than a week. He could see the pride of their fathers, men with big-chested embraces. Their virile sense of ownership bestowed a level of care upon the owned. Mothers who knew how to be demure, knew how to let themselves be protected. Outside, lives were lived; inside, shadows flashed indigo.

He went down the hallway to tell Chang that he'd decided he was right, they should move on, but first they should drop Dong off at a hospital. He'd carry her there if he had to.

"Everything's ending," Georges-Minh said, sitting down on Chang's bed.

"No, it's not. This is just a beginning."

How could he still be optimistic. At a time like this? "So why does it feel like the walls are closing in?" He wanted to tell Chang he'd just come to the realization that he loved something, for the first time in his life.

"Georges, you've been stuck in a ten-by-ten cell with a crazy person for almost two days. You're not thinking straight."

"I have a bad feeling."

Chang punched his shoulder. "You don't believe in omens."

Georges-Minh started to sob.

"What's this now?"

"I do."

"What now?"

"That night at the den."

"The boy."

"And then the mermaid, the one I killed. She was fourteen. It's all related."

"You didn't kill anyone. The difference between killing someone and not saving their life? It's significant."

"You made me violate the kid."

Chang wrinkled his brow. Sat down and smoked a whole cigarette before he spoke. "Because I asked you to go, you blame me."

"I'm sorry," Georges-Minh said quietly. "I never would have gone there if it wasn't for you."

"Why won't you just admit the real reason you can't love me back? You love Khieu. It's not a *crime*."

"Shut up. Khieu was a bastard who left his wife and kids." He couldn't say he loved Khieu because doing so would break his own heart in two. "Khieu betrayed us."

Hell was not a person waiting for his revenge. Hell was learning other people existed. Instead of being a man he could respect, the kind who protected what was his, he'd put at stake a pair of small hands, a smile, and hair the colour of night.

"We voted," Georges-Minh said. "It was a sacred trust." He hadn't rescued himself from cowardice. In fact, the colonel haunted him. He saw him everywhere. At the head of the bed when he went to sleep. Following him when he went to buy food. When he shut his eyes at night. The colonel never spoke or tried to touch him. But there he was. Just staring.

"Two men or two hundred," Chang said, "they'd have had our heads either way. Makes no difference. Except to the struggle."

Georges-Minh felt nauseated hearing the same poetic drivel Khieu had fuelled his speeches with come from Chang's mouth.

"I thought we'd win," Georges-Minh said.

"He never forced us to believe," Chang said. "Hey, you feeling okay? You're shaking."

"Do you think those we hurt are waiting for us when we die?"

"Who?"

"He's waiting for me, so he can get even. The colonel, who else?"

Chang followed Georges-Minh back into the room, blabbering that this was for the best. They should go into Laos, then Thailand, and then?

"And then what?" Dong said, waking at the sound of their footsteps rushing around her bed. "Where are we going?"

"On a vacation," Georges-Minh told her. "You like vacations, right?"

"What if people try to chase us? The people who are trying to poison me, for instance? Don't you care?" Her high-pitched voice pierced the room's aqueous humidity. She tried to get up but collapsed back onto the mattress. "I'm not leaving here. I know they have this place surrounded. I can see through walls. You can't. I know there are soldiers out there. Right now, waiting for us."

Because she was struggling so much, they decided to leave the luggage behind.

Georges-Minh held her up by the waist. Chang took her hand. Georges-Minh, with the baby in the crook of his arm, led the way down the stairs.

50

Forest eyes watched Khieu collect vines and bulbs and trap rodents. On a good day he killed a large rat or a small pig. The eyes never blinked. They belonged not to the Chams, not to the Moys, which were what he thought the tribesmen in the next village were called.

The beastlike eyes carried with them the musk of apes. They stared from the bushes while he collected food. Tonight they watched him pick mushrooms. So long as their eyes stayed where they were, he had other things to worry about. Like his wife, his children, his own death, and when the French were going to find the Chams and when their battle was going to start.

He untucked his shirt and made a pouch to collect the long-stemmed brown ones. He'd collect enough so he wouldn't have to leave his cave for weeks: let the bullets fly over his head. The moonless night made telling tan from brown from black impossible. He devoured them as he picked, too hungry to wait, the dirt mixing with their flavour though everything tasted bad without salt.

He usually foraged away from the Chams because he didn't want to run into any of the villagers by accident. Mime, How go the battle preparations?

Then what? An awkward shrug? He felt the coward, ate more slowly, thinking about a woman who had sponged the sweat from his brow when he'd once been poisoned; he began to sweat as he picked some more mushrooms, his hands shaking. He could still remember the curve of her hip barely covered by the brightly coloured shawl that she wore wrapped around her waist, and how she'd giggled, and the way her tongue had clicked in her native language every time he'd slipped his index finger between the fabric and her flesh trying to move the fabric aside, teasing her. As he returned to the cave his hands kept trembling. Last time he'd eaten undercooked rat and gotten sick for two days. Had he poisoned himself yet again?

Now he was sick and it wasn't like the ordinary bouts of diarrhea he'd contended with before, and as he began throwing up he considered walking to the Cham village, but his legs were trembling so, and he began seeing more eyes in the trees, and when he tried to stand he collapsed again and all he could do was retch blood and crawl back into his cave. He was dying for sure. He knew it.

The Moy village was closer than the Cham village but he'd had no contact with the people who lived there. They wore caps decorated with metallic coins. Men, women, and children wore bracelets on their arms and legs, from their wrists to their elbows, from their ankles to their knees. Wherever they walked, in the jungle and in their village, a boy clutching a handful of red weeds, a girl feeding the red weeds to a duck in the pond water, they made a tinkling sound. For all he knew they were at war with the Chams, had hunted each other for generations. Maybe they'd seen him with the Chams and considered him the enemy. Too weak in any case, Khieu put his head down on the soil.

Voices spoke to him all night long. The cave walls came alive, spoke like the hooting of a night bird in the trees. The bird seemed to be telling him time was not on his side and the eyes knew it. He covered his ears. He refused to open his mouth. Eyes stared at him all night. The eyes blinked— brown or black, tinged with green, encircled by a hazel ring, long-lashed, thick-lashed, short and straight-lashed, crying, or red-eyed and dry. He tried to make them melt but they wouldn't go away, no matter how often he blinked. Dammit, his eyes burned, he was coming unglued. He tried to make them go away. Still, the eyes blinked and batted and flickered and forced him to remember Mai's eyes gazing deep into his trying to share the love she felt the night they were married. The eyes that haunted him with their blinking were not show-ing any kind of feeling; they blinked for lack of anything else to do.

It took Khieu days to recover. He didn't want to be poisoned again. What was left? Not foraging.

He'd steal it. Not from the village, where they knew him. He'd steal food from the Moys.

One step, two, toward the closest village. He'd watched the men bring home their catch from the lake in the evening. The night followed him and allowed him to steal some vegetables from the sill of the first house and half a rat snake in a basket from the entrance of a second.

The next night and the next he snuck through wooden houses with roofs of dwarf palm leaves and wondered if he would hang according to highland codes if he were caught.

So it went until the fourth night. Pulling himself along on his stomach where early Tagalogs from Manila, who had been part of the Spanish expeditionary corps, would have also pulled themselves through mimosas, creepers, and long-tailed lizards. There was a snap, a jolt, and suddenly Khieu was ten feet in the air hanging from a net of vines in an elephant apple tree.

Below him a group of men pointed spears. Some of them looked African, which could only mean one thing: soldiers. Even in the moonlight Khieu could be sure of one man's kinky hair. He heard three distinct languages: French, Vietnamese, hill tribe. Children too, now. Underfoot. Laughing.

He landed with a thump and the voices stopped as the hill tribe cut him down. Now that the moonlight shafted the right way he discerned their uniforms. He could neither speak nor run. After everything, this was it. He wet himself as the children poked him. Now the men laughed. White eyes in the moonlight. Women came too, to look, to stare.

They didn't pull their children away. Some of the children sat, as did some of the adults, in a circle around him. An old man yanked Khieu's ear through the netting in which he was still trapped.

Khieu whimpered.

A French soldier said, "They thought you were *nguoi rung*."

A few of the men helped him out of the net. The villagers told him someone had been stealing their food for the past four days. "We were only protecting ourselves, and caught you instead."

The soldier explained he and the other soldier were deserters from the Bataillons d'Afrique originally from Morocco and now fighting with the Vietnamese independence movement.

Too stunned to comprehend his luck, Khieu shook the leaves from his hair. "They thought I was a forest monster?"

"And before that another *nguoi rung* kidnapped a villager. Held him for years in captivity, forced him to give her children."

"I was hungry, that's all," Khieu said.

"You mean it was you?"

The elder of the village came forward and offered Khieu some tea and boiled peanuts. He spoke Vietnamese very well. "That's why all the children wear bracelets on their wrists and ankles. So that if the *nguoi rung* grab them, they can slip out of the bangles and run. Ever since our villager was kidnapped we have done so. There is an old woman, she is a seer, she lives on the outskirts of our town, and she lets us know when evil *nguoi rung* is coming. The reason she did not alert us to your presence is now clear."

Khieu laughed. He told them he'd been on the run from the French. He put on an ape's face for the children, clawed the air and roared.

An elder shrugged, making the crazy sign.

51

Thu placed the fifth postcard into the postmaster's hands and paid for the new one she was buying. She'd left Mai in the forest suffering from some kind of diarrhea.

Hunted was how Thu felt, as if everyone suspected her of something. Haunted. And maybe she was. By the death of the boy. Could that be it? Guilt? Was his ghost following them, waiting for her to slip up? She told Mai she was going to buy some fruit for breakfast, something to settle her stomach. So Thu did her rounds, buying a few provisions with the pitiful little money they had, what few coins remained that wouldn't last much longer, the proceeds of Mai's wedding ring and some other odds and ends still of value.

In the market, close to the train station, while Mai leaned with her head against a makeshift pillow in the forest nursing a sick baby, knees to her chest, agonizing over her own stomach cramps, Thu found a shady spot on the patio of the courthouse, and with her meagre groceries beside her, began to compose a new postcard to her lover. She repeated the oft-recited syllables to herself as she withdrew a pencil nub from her inner clothing. She could keep the precious tool free from harm close to her breast. Bi-ra-go, her Senegalese soldier.

Next to the post office, a line of French deserters was escorted by a soldier from the police station. The deserters had been shackled by their necks to one another. Their captor led them through the street as another group of soldiers emerged from the station and waited for them to assemble in the courtyard. Thu could see it all from her perch: the street parade, the patrons looking up from their coffee, a window shutting its blinds, a bread-seller lowering her head, the station courtyard, the fence line and deserters being led back to it. The waiting soldiers pulled out their pistols. The deserters, up against the fence, were killed one after the other. Each bullet still ringing in the ears of one before the prisoner shackled to his neck was shot down.

Mai picked at the shale stones as if she hadn't heard what Thu said. One on side of them, thick forest; on the other, granite outcroppings. Everything was the colour of mud puddles.

"I know you're alive," Mai said to the sky, pale and weakened from her cramps. "I'm sure of it, Khieu, I can hear what you are about to say. Around this fire you always open your mouth. You're about to say the name of the village, the jungle hamlet ..."

If Mai mentioned the fortune teller one more time, Thu was going to hit her. "I told you what I saw in town."

Mai turned to her. "But before he tells me where he is, the conjured image disappears."

"The Montagnards are at war with the French. We're playing for keeps now, Mai. This isn't a joke. We could get caught in the crossfire, confused for spies, we could *die*, do you get it?"

"I know he's alive. I'm sure of it. But when I try to conjure his image, sitting around a fire with men who speak a language foreign to us, it fades."

"Mai, you said that already. Damn." She squinted her eyes shut. "Have you ever considered how much trouble he's put you in? If you honestly think he's here, what do you think made him come up to this godforsaken place? What do you think he's doing up here? Really?" Still no answer. "He might be involved with politics. You've got Cong to think about, you know," she said, grabbing her hand.

"Okay. If he's not here, we'll turn back," Mai said, almost inaudibly.

"Seriously?"

"Yes. I have faith. Not like you. I can say it because I know he's here. I know we'll find him today."

Thu shook her head. "That's it."

"We've come all this way." Mai burst into tears. "Let me complete the ritual."

"It's been five days."

Pillars of stone the colour of ashen skin pushed up from the ground between old foot trails in skeleton shapes, like embedded fossils, holding up the weight of ages. There were so many ways for a road to end. Thu could see herself wearing out, like flesh grown papery and thin over time trying to find the right path to follow. The wind in the carved channels and rain-sculpted grooves of the ashen cairns echoed like bells and was filled with the loneliness that always inhabited such vast spaces. Bats flew from their hiding places, disturbed out of sleep. She missed her bed, even if it was in a closet. She knew she shouldn't be leaving a trail, sending Birago postcards. But the thought stole her breath. She knew that without the lead of a pencil nub, without the paper itself, she would waste away.

Thu, tucking Cong under her arm like a chicken from the market, dug in her bag and found the bamboo-handled knife wrapped in cloth. She handed it to Mai, who unwrapped it and put the cloth in her pocket. She rubbed it against her chest until it shone. She lifted the blade to her lips, blew on it, steaming each side, then kissed it. She held it up to the sun, what light emitted through the clouds that lidded the sky.

Thu felt trapped by the heavens, oppressed by the gods, their cruelty and absurd rituals that humans were compelled to call life. Perhaps she and Mai and Khieu and Birago, the lot of them, the whole human race, were nothing but insects in a jar, humanity and the earth upon which it spun nothing but a god child's elaborate experiment, a science project watched over this very moment by its teachers, their current undertaking being graded.

A wind kicked up, blowing Thu's hair about.

"Feel that?" blurted Mai. "It's a sign."

Thu vaguely remembered the soothsayer's words. To throw the knife into the wind. Mai must have remembered the same thing because just then she did. And called his name. "Khieu." But the knife misfired, rambled into the hood of grey. It meandered over the two women like a reluctant drunkard, wavering at its peak, unsure which way to fall, and landed in a crooked position near a rockslide of shale.

"Now, we dig."

"I'm not digging. Do what you want." Thu began to walk away.

In spite of how ill Mai was, anger made her strong. She ran over to Thu and pushed her down from behind. "You owe me." Thu tried to get up on all fours but Mai toppled her over with her foot. The postcard fell from her bodice.

Mai picked it up from the mud. *To my Senegalese Soldier, My anger is as strong as the ocean, as steady and patient, too. It will wipe out everything, leaving behind only a clean slate.*

Mai looked down at her. "You betrayed me. How could you?" Thu spat.

"That's why we haven't found him."

Thu hoped she never did.

"Your bad luck sabotaged us."

274

Mai dug. All afternoon, Mai dug. Sick and sometimes retching, she dug.

Thu watched her struggle with the shale, her ivory hands scrabbling. Mai deserved to struggle. Because if Khieu had married Thu instead of Mai, he never would have left the Paper Flower Inn. Khieu was not Birago, uncompromising, complicated, hard to please. Khieu was malleable, easy.

And yet. She pushed Mai out of the way. Cong lay asleep on a pile of rags near malevolent creepers and strangling figs. "Tend to your baby," she said. Because of a jade comb. Because of a kind doctor. Because the consequence of her presumption had been the sin of pride.

Sweeping her hair off her face, Thu began to dig.

She imagined returning to the inn. Birago, waiting to meet her. Would Birago be happy, or would there be a bitterness in his voice as he welcomed her home, a stiffness in his embrace? Would he blame her for leaving so abruptly? The bougainvillea in their pots, blooming for the second time. Crazy Auntie in her usual place, the children running about the yard. For a moment would it feel as if she'd not been gone at all? She missed kissing Birago's knuckles, his bruises. She missed the salt-sweat taste on his skin. She would tell him so.

Thu was sure she had heard a bird hooting in the trees. Some would have called it an omen. And there was something, too, about the old woman's sunken mouth.

The old woman, holding a basket, wearing a banana-leaf scarf, had said to Mai, "I know where your husband is."

The old woman saw it, and Mai saw it too: the distance in Khieu's eyes, the faraway look that meant they would not be going home soon, not to Saigon, not south.

Bad luck, this reunion, at least for Thu.

Khieu said, "If it wasn't for her, we never would have known about you two. She lives on the outskirts. Talks to spirits."

Mai held her hands in the air. She fished for words to fill the gap. "I don't know what to say. I wish you'd never left me."

"I missed you," Khieu answered.

How could it still be he had a wandering gaze?

Awkwardness filled the space between them.

They weren't like Thu and Birago. They reminded Thu of the stones placed around a campfire. Meant to contain the flames they held, certain stones with cracks exploded. They protected nothing, but damaged all those around them with shards. Such stones, split down the middle, could never be whole.

52

A migration, leaving the north, with Phuc headed against the flow. The road as wide as an ox cart was full of families, bone-thin donkeys, clanging cookware. No forwarding addresses. No ex-wife anywhere. Though why should Phuc look? Dao Ly had left him.

They headed south with their oil lamps, bedding, pots and pans. Grandmothers switched at flies while the healthier children played in the road. Amid all this Phuc spotted a melon, lying to the side of the road. Wrapped in brown paper. Why would someone leave food behind? Unless it was poisoned, or a trap. Yet there it was. Sitting by the ditch, covered with road dust.

He looked over his shoulder, then above himself and behind. He approached slowly. He couldn't remember how many days it had been since he'd tasted a melon. Sweet, a hint of citrus, setting the teeth on edge.

People walked away from Phuc, people who in spite of having no leads hoped for a better life in Saigon.

Phuc drew near to the fruit. Nudged it with his toe. Flipped off the brown covering and smelled something sour.

It wasn't a melon.

"Jesus." He rewrapped the infant's swaddling. Everyone around him looked tired.

The infant, about four weeks old, opened its eyes, closed them again. "Jesus," he repeated.

No going back now. He'd picked it up. He knew enough. That you didn't leave a baby abandoned, for dogs to maul, birds to peck out its eyes. Wrapped in paper, disguised as fruit. He glared at every passerby.

Phuc, who knew nothing about babies, tucked the infant under his arm the way he carried his pipa case on his way to a show. Would the infant die before morning? Probably. In a way, the thought reassured him.

He waxed poetic to his friends about the north. But in truth, he'd spent every passing year trying to burn away every vestige of it from himself. The country bumpkin.

A rough voice with shale around its edges snapped him out of his thoughts. "Hundred baht for your lute."

Phuc bah'ed him away.

"Hey, buddy. Buddy." A hand gripped him.

A voice like a rice mill said, "Friend. Wait up. You a musician?"

They were two teenaged boys. Their flat cheeks, sunburned noses, and half-empty shoulder baskets marked them as farmers. Broad hands that could have knocked Phuc out with one blow. Their feet, stinking of earth, were muddy and bare.

"Hundred baht," said the taller one.

Phuc doubted they'd ever seen a hundred baht.

"Hungry? Trade you for a bag of rice."

The core of the Confucian canon exhorted in the Book of Rites, A gentleman does not part with his pipa without good reason. Phuc looked down at the infant in his arms.

"The baby looks hungry. How about two?"

They corralled him, one on either side. "Where you headed?"

Phuc pointed north and began walking again. They joined him.

"Who you going to visit?"

"Van," said Phuc, making up a name. He had to admit, they were scaring him a little.

"We know Van."

"Yeah, we do, and he's an *asshole*."

"Yeah, that's right. An asshole. Why you going to see him?"

Phuc sped up. The rhythm of their words fell upon his ears like a cleaver chopping vegetables. What the fellows had said of his own accent, teasing him, so many times. He could hear it, now that he'd been gone so long.

"Come on, give us a try." They reached for his pipa. "You come from the land of so much. Look at your shoes."

Only Phuc's life was more important to him.

He began to run. He didn't even stop when something hit the back of his head.

Only later, when he'd gotten off the road, found somewhere he'd be safe from bandits, did he raise his hand to feel the bump. Coin-round and swelling. On this pine-covered hill, a mountain goat clung to a ledge. He would build a fire, spend the night, and head northward again in the morning.

His instrument's history went back to Confucius. Even further. To the Yellow Emperor, founding father of China who, legend said, had invented it.

Phuc could play floating sounds or crisp. Notes clear as the full moon. He could play a mountain wind moving through pines, a hundred hills without a footprint, a thousand rice fields and no bird; red-river silt, an old woman fishing, the stir of heat in an iron stove.

On visits to the city, instead of immersing himself in his father's activities, tools for the farm, the trade of rice, Phuc would marvel at the Citadel of Ho, ancient, rivalling China's finest buildings.

His father, a man of great ingenuity, had perfected the husker and the mill. His mind, every villager agreed, where they lived on the Dragon's Belly by the Hong River, was beautiful. He could blend shape, colour, and function. Make poetry from golden rice. And Phuc hated it all.

Country life depended on one thing. A most important thing, which could be neither substituted nor controlled. Rain.

The word for "water" and "country" was the same, a fact that puzzled Phuc as a child. During a drought all the plains became one. Boats dredging the riverbeds for gold pitched uselessly on their sides. Flood and famine. Drought and famine. Hailstones. Fire, storms, wind. Corrupt officials. Abusive politicians seizing the land. Rumours abounding of the French destroying crops.

Though iron oxen were placed in rivers to ward them off, rivers, streams, and tributaries joined to become one during a flood: plain soil joined plain soil. A stone moved from one river to another. A tree branch broke and resurfaced somewhere else. Everything looked the same when the flood waters ebbed, but it wasn't.

Water, like blood, flowed downhill. Aggression, like anger, flowed downhill. From the north, from the highlands, they flowed downhill. Shifting as they flowed. The country could shift shape. Had always been forced to shift shape, from the Chinese onward, for the last thousand years. Perhaps that's why, concluded Phuc, the word for "water" and "country" matched.

He'd left the north wanting to control his life. Left a father who'd moved water like a god.

He awoke to growling. Stiff and curled in a semi-fetal position, the infant was sheltered in the curve of his chest.

Slowly, he opened his eyes. The growls grew louder. He clenched his jaw.

Could he play dead? Ridiculous. Soon the dogs would pounce, dead or not.

He reached into the embers. Grabbed the only branch still burning. Jumped up with his tiny torch. Held it aloft like a spear. Pipa under his other arm, he left the baby where it lay and vaulted into the darkness.

Counted the eyes thin as slender knives. Two small dogs, one medium. Skeletal bodies. He could beat them back with the stick.

One of the dogs leaped and when he swatted it on the nose, the other two drew back. But then they jumped too, snapped at the stick, springing toward the flame, unafraid. Ashes flew like butterflies into the moonlit darkness. He cast, thrust. Barks punctuated the growling. The stick broke.

Phuc threw down the stick. The dogs circled. One nipped at his calves.

All he had left was his pipa case, which he swung like a boulder, smashing, pounding. His sudden viciousness scared them. Phuc got one down, kicked it. The other two ran.

Phuc lay his pipa case on the ground. In the moonlight, and what was left of the burning embers, part of him already knew.

The baby was crying.

Had the crying preceded the growling?

He imagined his pipa like a thousand puzzle pieces in the seconds it took him to force his fingers to unlatch the three rusty locks and open the battered black box.

He picked up the baby.

The beaten dog was taking shallow breaths. Phuc returned to the dying fire and thought for a while. Having made up his mind, he killed the dog. When the dog had stopped breathing, Phuc stopped shaking.

"Not bad for a city boy," he said, still wishing he was.

He gathered more wood and rebuilt the fire. He pulled some meat off the dog with his bare hands and cooked it. If he could keep the fire going, stay awake ...

Morning would come soon. He chewed the meat to a pulp and laid his lips on the infant's. Let the food dribble in.

Eyes gritty with sleeplessness, he began walking again the next morning. In Saigon he'd wondered about his mother and his father many times. His father had once taken him to the Jaw Bridge, a beach full of tiny crabs. At Porte d'Annam the two of them had ceremoniously read a poem inscribed on a rock by a long-ago emperor near a Ming dynasty gate.

Now, so close to home, as if pulled by a beacon, he dared not ask about his village, his family, not a single question of the people he'd passed on the road.

He'd lost weight, gone a little grey. As he walked, he imagined his parents meeting him at the gate. "Stranger, where are you from?" He felt homesick. But for here? Did he have a right to feel homesick for here?

Every day as a child he'd visited the Hong River. Rivers materialized as dragons at night. Slithered from mountains two hundred feet long. Every village had its own shrine to the river goddess. He loved her, but not for the same reason as the rest.

The goddess from which all flowed, the goddess of knowledge, the goddess of poetry, was also the goddess of music. So when the sun had risen and serpents came to warm on stones near her statue, he prayed to her.

To play in the Royal Theatre of the Imperial City for the Son of Heaven. Done with bamboo thickets and grey and red dust. To play for mandarins, scholars, and poets. Courtiers, bodyguards, and princesses. How could he survive any longer in the narrow valley of the Hong River? When in another universe the Son of Heaven's wives and his errand boys revelled in his music. His one hundred concubines and one thousand eunuchs, all listening. Done with silt-burdened streams. His sisters nagging him to collect snails in the water. Others were already enraptured by his notes resounding off red-painted ironwood columns with golden dragons.

And he'd given everything he had—the black hairs on his head, the food from his belly. Music thieved his nights, made them sleepless. Never mind. He was happy to pay the river goddess, his muse. He gave her joy and peace. His heart, his dreams. Typical appointments, accolades, quiet moments, such as can be had. Children he'd forfeited. Dao Ly. Or was she stolen? No matter. Music would soothe him and attack on his behalf. He gave, she stole, a matter of semantics. Because you gave yourself away for art.

Art swallowed you whole. Like a river into whose mouth you must gladly throw yourself. This was the price the true artist must pay.

"You *still* here?"

The boys from yesterday's high foreheads and flat faces reminded him of his own. Whose hair smelled like soil, clothes like chicken shit. He realized he'd been walking in the opposite direction, toward their shack. On the dust road, dumb. Dumb as a farmer.

The shorter one said, "I think you hit him too hard."

"Cat got his tongue."

"You want breakfast?"

He couldn't answer. The boys from yesterday. The baby seemed a flimsy shield.

Any words he spoke would come out stupid. Would come out a story about the dogs. About how the shaking one looked before he killed it. How he couldn't get the whimpers out of his head all night. Did they want the infant? They would laugh at him.

The brothers slung their arms through his.

"I'll take that." The shorter one grabbed his pipa case.

Phuc followed.

Sitting in their shack, he looked out at a hillside dotted with apiaries. Terraces sculpted from the mountainside, like ladders to the gods. His father's land. The earth where his mother was born. *Que cha. Dat me.* An old saying.

He'd never noticed how beautiful it was. As a child all he knew was dunces had shacks in the country. *Nha que* was what he heard whenever he went to the city in his rice paper hat, his bare feet. Farm boy.

The mother prepared rice gruel, a traditional northern dish, and his stomach growled.

He'd come north to save his head from the chopping block. But why had he really come? To find his ex-wife Dao Ly? Or?

As the smoke from her cookstove rose he remembered last night's sun setting on the valley, fireflies filling it.

The taller boy set down a bowl of gruel in front of him.

"So where do you go from here?"

"*Que cha. Dat me.*"

"I thought you were from here. I heard your accent."

"Play something?" the shorter one asked.

"*Nha que!*" The mother swatted him on the head. "He's eating."

Phuc opened the case, displayed the damage.

The brothers looked at each other.

"I don't care."

"Give me a turn."

"Me."

Taking away his empty dish, she smiled kindly. "You have a lucky name."

His songs were the colour of the tree and the sky. Something in his throat was not meant to be there. He wanted to thank her for her hospitality. He had to hold back and simply nodded. He wondered how long it would take them to notice his pipa on their dirt floor after he left.

53

Birago's ghost had been trailing Thu and Mai for days. He'd felt especially heartbroken when the gunboat was shooting and he'd discovered there was nothing a spirit could do.

He'd made a decision. If he searched deep down, he knew the answer had always been there. The difference between the man he should be and the one he'd turned into. Or maybe in essence had been all along, the way a swan will hold an ugly duckling forever at its core. The kind of man who left a doll on a street or could never really love a woman because he loved himself more. A ghost. He'd suspected himself of these things and flashed on the truth in the Dien Bien Phu highlands, watching colourfully dressed tribespeople descend the hills to look for marriage partners in a field where flowers decked the earth like gowns. He'd admitted it in a plain surrounded by mountains, in an ancient pagoda where one room held a clear still pool, the other a shrine with poetry carved on the walls. The pool mirrored his sorry reflection, sorry in that he was forced to accept that he had never been the man Thu thought he was—not a spiritual man, not a political man, just a shallow materialist, no more, no less. His head ached. This truth, compounded by the new transparency of his joints, forced him to confront another, much harder situation: to transcend this life, Birago would have to learn to give up shallow pursuits and shallow pleasures.

Transparency was something new to him. It ached in a different way than the pain of battle, pain he could deal with. Truth was new. He could feel himself on the verge of losing it. Passing out, the way he might feel in the last round, his legs wobbling. He took roost in a banyan tree with other souls of the dead, among them the broken doll.

The boy's shoes hung ridiculously off his feet, like buckets hanging from fence posts, the leather uppers stitched back to the soles with fishing line.

Certain memories came to him clear as the bottom of a holy water font; others appeared then escaped, guppylike, distorted as if moving at the bottom of a fast stream. He'd gained extracurricular knowledge since his death, but it was selective and he was still trying to decipher the logic of what he remembered.

"I know you," said the boy. "I think. From the sidewalk, but I don't remember exactly how I got there beside you. It was after I heard the cannon. Maybe I slipped, maybe it was these shoes. There was a light. Then I saw us both. Then I was in this tree with a big headache. Did you get hit by a rickshaw, too?" He looked at the blood on Birago's uniform. "Does your head still hurt?"

"You don't remember?"

Birago stroked the hair away from the boy's eyes and held him. "My head hurts."

"I'm sorry."

While continuing to rock the boy, Birago began to work at his shiniest shirt button, pulling at the threads. The thread was good quality and held fast. Birago used his thumbnail, sawing across the fibres. The hollow at the back of the doll's head was like crushed ice and fit as perfectly as a puzzle piece against Birago's forearm.

"I miss my mother."

Birago did, too. He missed his whole family. Aunts, uncles, cousins. Nephews, nieces.

Free from the shirt, the button looked like a gold coin. He gave it to the boy.

The boy looked at him, puzzled.

Birago shrugged. "Maybe you can pay the ferry man."

Birago, who'd always been a man of shallow pursuits and shallow pleasures, felt himself drawn to the Perfume River, its call, his hunger for vengeance.

The French wanted the coal mines of Hon Gai. The miners paraded the head of the corporation on a stake. The French brought in tanks. More leaders went missing. The miners weren't giving up their tunnels: the caves filled with ghouls and ghosts. From Lao Cai to Hanoi to Hon Gai, every rock had a spirit. Towns joined by the death of twenty-five thousand conscripted railway workers. Bound by wood and iron railway ties. The ghosts took up residence at the foot of mountains, inside Shan Tuyet tea leaves, crops of cinnamon. Wagons of tin shuttled from the earth's bowels at the foot of the hill, beneath two vessels of gold and silver, like ceremonial rice plants, ensuring a prosperous harvest.

The River of the Dead, which trickled celestial green on its way from the Realm of the Jade Mountain down to the Infernal Region, was known by three names: River of the Dead, River of Forgetting, or the Perfume River. Birago gazed upon the Perfume River now, where hungry ghosts ebbed and flowed.

It was said that men had seven souls. Maybe souls were split open at death, half occupying the Infernal Region, half waiting.

No one lit incense at an altar for Emperor Hiep Hoa's troops killed when French fleets opened fire here. How could they? So many ghosts. Look around. In the last weeks he'd circled the country.

He flew like a white bird and saw chemists, tailors, boot makers, ironworkers, trunk makers, candy makers, seed vendors, women with tiny bound feet on which they could barely move, Chinese shopkeepers with imported goods from France, and little Min Huong Chinese half-breeds running around everywhere. Vietnamese men wore their hair in a chignon covered by a turban like the Malay, while Chinese men had long pigtails that hung freely down the back like a whip. Those from Hainan in the south had skin the colour of rice, while those from Canton had skin the colour of a European tea biscuit.

He saw time fold and expand like an accordion. He saw a few stone houses with red tile roofs. A woman emerged from a house on bound feet like cloven hooves. The path from her house was neatly swept. She tottered on her cloven child's feet down the path lined with cabbage palms to meet a man, a vegetable seller from Fukien. Birago suddenly knew all sorts of things he didn't before. His skin the colour of soy sauce. A basket of dragon fruit in hand.

He circled a needle woman he'd once donated a few pennies to, who sat on a street corner opposite a man fixing eyeglass frames. She wore a paper nose to hide a face ravaged by syphilis. She was mending someone's buttonhole, a basket of rags at her feet. He saw grocers, fortune tellers, and cyclo drivers. He saw women just like Thu waiting on merchants and officers. Girls with waist-length hair walking on men's backs in rooms fragrant with coconut oil. Babies wailing next to breadfruit in the market and girls with bread baskets on their heads singing the lullaby, "Sleep, ghost, sleep. Come afternoon, I stand in the backyard, looking toward my mother's land."

He saw coal mine ghosts, railroad ghosts, vengeful ghosts. Birago had seen them all on his way here. Some small as cats. Spirits made of teeth. Spirits who wore clothing made of wind. The living left rice porridge and wine sweetened with honey to settle their bitterness, but still the Perfume River ebbed and flowed.

So far he'd made black rain fall on his shooter. Made red rain fall on the officer who'd signed his death warrant. Struck down with cholera the families of those who'd bound his hands with rope.

He knew that to move on he'd have to abandon such desires, move beyond the pleasure of harming those who'd harmed him. But he couldn't. Not yet.

54

Outside the hotel in Hue where Georges-Minh, Chang, and Dong had been holed up for thirty-six hours, the Perfume River flowed and the Marble Mountain stood watch. The light blinded them.

A group of French soldiers was drinking on the corner on the patio of a French restaurant called La Rotonde, not far from a man fixing eyeglass frames and a scorpion vendor's table littered with bottles of elixir. Beyond the soldiers, another French restaurant, and a letter writer's booth, as well as a bath house, a cane liquor stall and one selling stir-fried crocodile, as well as two rows of palms corseted with tree guards. Dong rested her hand on Georges-Minh's arm and they proceeded down the street.

The soldiers stood up and began singing "Le Bon Roi Dagobert," clinking glasses, swaying arm in arm.

"We need to find a rickshaw," Georges-Minh whispered over Dong's head. He tried to communicate to Chang with his eyes what he couldn't say. The soldiers mustn't see their faces.

Their wanted posters would have been put up all over Vietnam by now. Where was a rickshaw? They needed to tell the driver to take Dong to a hospital, before the soldiers spotted them.

Dong's arms trembled. "I can't go on."

Chang's eyes scanned the street.

"I have to sit," Dong said.

Georges-Minh tried to stop the baby from slipping as he held Dong upright. "Not here. A little further."

Dong salvaged her balance and leaned against a lamppost. One soldier in particular had mean eyes, red and watery, the kind that belong to the sort of person who takes pleasure in torturing others. He seemed to focus then lose focus on the group, squint as if they'd grown invisible before his eyes.

"Hurry," Georges-Minh whispered.

Dong had grown pale and she'd barely made it fifty feet. Part of Georges-Minh wondered if he'd get out of this alive, if he deserved it after what he'd done, to her, to his son, to unlucky Sing Sing, probably in the penitentiary by now.

If he had to choose, better to turn himself in this moment than watch his wife succumb on this corner. She could barely stand and was too weak to speak. Her hair fell across her dirty cheek as her eyes locked onto a white bird in the sky.

At last Chang found a rickshaw and Georges-Minh pushed Dong toward it, releasing her from his grasp as he should have long ago. But Dong stumbled, and he with the baby. A woman selling roasted scorpions emitted a "Woop!" The soldiers stared as she said, "Don't drop that package," and the ensuing commotion as the baby flew up in the air instead of down made a few pedestrians suck in their breath, dart out of the path of the falling woman and the baby.

The soldiers abandoned their table.

Perhaps because the soldiers were drunk, they pulled out their revolvers sooner than they ordinarily would have.

The drunkest began shooting and the group ducked behind a shoe repair shop.

Dong threw her body over the baby, draping herself over him like a blanket, her blouse already reddening at the shoulder.

Chang and Georges-Minh crouched over her. "Take him," they heard her whisper. "Take the baby."

To run with both her and the child would be suicide. Georges-Minh pictured himself running with them both under his arms before the soldiers rounded the corner of the shoe repair shop; they couldn't see him, not yet, but he saw the next years of his life, the running, the hiding, stealing backward glances. This is what he'd brought his family.

Bullets whizzed, pinged when they hit the ground. Chang wanted nothing more than to leave the baby and what he represented where he lay on the dirty ground. Better yet, let him die. Why not?

Then he could run with his lover to the Marble Mountain near Hue. Chang would finally have Georges-Minh to himself. They could read Verlaine.

Leave him under his mother's body. Why not?

A human's venom is ten times stronger than a snake's. *Drawing a snake, adding legs.* An old proverb for making things more complicated than needed. *Dog dies, story's over.*

It took all he had not to grasp Georges-Minh's hand and say, Run. Rather, push his body and yell, "Go!"

Thinking not of Dong, nor of the baby, but of Georges-Minh telling him love couldn't be captured like a songbird in a cage, he lifted the baby away from Dong. Standing up with the infant in his outstretched arms, he walked as slowly as he could toward the soldiers, holding out the baby like a talisman, and surrendered.

"Yes!" he said with his every action. "You were wrong. See, love can be captured." He wanted to shout to Georges-Minh, *You only had to believe that it could.*

Georges-Minh bent toward Dong, shaded by the shoe repair shop's white clay wall.

"I'm sorry," he told her, imagining picking her up and how he could have run, somehow gathering up her weight, somehow carrying her to Laos and a reality different from this. Then he ran. Not seeing the soldiers who glanced at the flesh wound and lifted Dong and took her to their headquarters for questioning. Who, later, took her to the hospital where she rejoined her infant son.

He didn't think that she would be better off without him, even though it was the truth. Not now that his son would never know him.

He'd never imagined kissing her for the last time. Not once. He'd never imagined last times for anything.

He simply ran. Ran until he felt as thin as wind and until his teeth grew cold, past doorways empty and full, two monks in orange robes, a circle of children playing with pot-bellied pigs, a field covered in fallen coconut trees. He ran until he could no longer feel his legs. He ran until he couldn't remember whether he'd told Dong he was sorry or if the thought had only risen like a plume of smoke and then disappeared.

55

Georges-Minh waited on an abandoned rowboat platform upriver from a Cham village for a transport train to take him to Atouat, in Laos. He was setting out to cross the mountainous humpback ridge of Vietnam and Laos and into the green basin of Siam. From Siam he could travel westward through Burma and Bengal. He felt a breeze, and Birago appeared next to him.

His ear had been shot off. The ghost silently stared out at the valley and lake below. Georges-Minh shuddered, and to avoid looking at the bleeding wound, gazed at the mountain above.

When the train came, rebels filled the boxcar, as well as Montagnard men, women, and children, goats and pigs.

"Khieu was planning to go to Atouat, too," Georges-Minh said. "At one point, he'd tracked Nguyen Du's verses to the top of the mountain."

"No kidding."

"Something to do with the polarity between a concubine from an anthology and people from another planet." Georges-Minh looked out the open door. Even from the corner of his eye he could still see Birago's bleeding bullet hole.

"These hills are rich in spacecraft sightings," Georges-Minh said. "Healers speak with them. Ask the new gods for blessings."

Below, the ground sloped into a valley. A plowed field, a thatch-roof hut, cows, a river. Next to the river, an *ao dai* was drying on a bamboo fence. On the other side of the fence was a field with pigs, and over the water, a wall of flowering grass.

"That what Khieu told you?"

A temple stood beyond a hill on a road that bumped into a village, past a fork that led out of town to cities Georges-Minh had never seen but knew existed all the same. At the fork in the road, the ground was tamped down; donkeys had stopped here, their riders weighing which way to go. Ox carts groaned as their drivers deliberated.

"I got shot," Birago said.

"They thought you did it?"

"If I had, why would I go back?"

"But I wrote a note."

Birago snorted.

"Why didn't you go home?" Georges-Minh asked.

"That's what my woman would have said."

The transport ground to a halt. Sunlight the colour of egg whites shone on rebels more haggard than the ones in the transport. At riflepoint, the rebels ordered everyone off—soldiers waited up the line. They would go no farther today.

"She came to you," Birago said.

Georges-Minh and Birago stepped off the train.

People constructed makeshift lean-tos.

"I can see many things. It's like having more eyes than I used to."

"Your woman?"

"Her name's Thu. Little shoes. Flowers on them."

Georges-Minh nodded, staring down.

"Let's climb," Birago said.

The mountain upon which spacecraft landed and healers worshipped wasn't far. The landscape changed the higher they went. Lowland fruit and waterfalls gave way to the authority of highland areca nut trees.

"The only part I don't get," Birago said, "is were you sleeping with her?"

"I'm married."

Birago laughed. "So are a lot of men."

"I, also. I prefer men."

It took them just over an hour to reach the peak.

A patchwork of plowed fields spread out beneath Georges-Minh. High above him flew a white seagull. Not a sound but the wind in his teeth, the rushing of his own blood in his ears. Up close, the view morphed: a square foot of pebbles, a snake's view, every blade of grass unique, both more imperfect and more beautiful for its imperfections.

Birago was standing over him now.

The hungry ghost dealt not in justice but bitterness that biled the heart. Feasted on it, gnawing from the inside out until all that remained of what he was or had been was hunger.

Georges-Minh pulled his hell money from his sock, unfolded it, and took out the opium. Ate the whole thing. Shortly the bitterness under his tongue paved the way for his floating. *First the sharpness, then the sweetness.* What his mother had said of bitter melon. He was a phoenix, riding the thermals. He licked clean the centre of the large paper rectangle.

There were different types of hell money for different purposes. Some money was made of rice, some of bamboo. Some had gold-cut overlays, some silver, some copper squares elaborately designed to appease the spirits. If one didn't use the right kind of offering, the spirits became angry. An army official ghost might punish you; a close relative might cry in frustration.

Georges-Minh did not light the hell money. Rather than set it on fire and let the wind carry the smoke to Son Tinh, the God of the Mountain, he lifted the money to the breeze. Made his wish over the paper as it swayed in the air.

"You sure you got the right kind of ghost money?" Birago said.

"Want to check it?"

"What are you praying for?"

"A gold sedan chair."

"Not a spacecraft?"

"Just a chair."

Birago laughed. "Is it coming? Do you see it?"

What did Birago care? "Yeah, I see it. Don't you?"

"Know what I see?"

"A homosexual?"

"A coward."

"Maybe you just need to open your eyes."

"Maybe *you* have a little help," Birago said.

Let him mock Georges-Minh. He no longer felt any need to argue with anyone. "So when are you going to kill me?"

"Are you ready?"

He stood up.

Georges-Minh had heard of the mountain god making water fall. The great limestone cliffs would open for a river to ferry away souls who'd earned it. Tin workers, coal miners, men who'd died building the railway. A friend of his father's had even claimed to see the cliffs close on a cascade, leaving not a drop behind.

"Is your chair coming to take you away?" Birago asked.

Georges-Minh gave the sky his full attention. The gathering clouds, the claps of thunder, the rain pattering the areca palms.

"There's no chair there, Georges-Minh. No chair."

"It's okay." Georges-Minh tossed the hell money into the air. Stepped off the cliff.

Between when he jumped and when he hit the ground, the mountain god would receive the hell money he'd released. Then he could mount the clouds, rise into the sky. As he fell, the paper fell with him, fluttering with its square inlay of gold.

ACKNOWLEDGMENTS

Thank you to Grant Buday, Laurie D. Graham, Mary Kimak, Shaun Oakey, and Jim Wong-Chu. I'm indebted to Frank Proschan for his paper "Syphilis, Opiomania, and Pederasty: Colonial Constructions of Vietnamese (and French) Social Diseases," as well as to Barley Norton for the book *Songs for the Spirit: Music and Mediums in Modern Vietnam,* and to Nguyen Khac Vien's epic work *Vietnam Une Longue Histoire.*

Thank you Denise Bukowski for sticking by me, Nicole Winstanley for seeing my vision and taking a chance, Jet for your cooking, my parents, Paul and Hanna Thanh, Maisie for eating your supper and being good, and Hank for your soundtrack to our crazy lives.

I'd also like to thank the Writers' Trust of Canada for their generosity and for providing me with a Woodcock Fund grant in the nick of time.